AWAKENED

BY WOLVES AND BLACK COCKATOOS

ALFONSO J CAPITO

Contents

INTRODUCTION

Introduction and Thanks

A violent, gruesome murder takes place in an idyllic Italian country town (Assisi), and an unsuspecting Australian (Alex Campbell) finds himself embroiled not just in its resolution, but also in an assassination plot to kill the Pope. The crime story is, however, a potent backdrop to Alex's personal journey to becoming Awakened.

Alex is an Australian crime journalist who is totally unaware of the real nature of the world he lives in. In 'Awakened', life conjures up a series of personalities and events to enlighten and awaken him.

In the story, the author explores fundamental concepts such as Karma, Past Life Reincarnation, and the importance of Repentance, Compassion, Forgiveness and even Prayer, to finding Meaning in Life. He also tackles the rare and evasive "synthesis" of various religious beliefs, including Australian Indigenous traditions.

In the process, the book traverses several sensitive topics such as, child abuse by church clergy, domestic conflict, racism including indigenous atrocities, an atheistic verses dualist morality, anti-vaccine themes, hidden church secrets, the concept of an illusory world, sexual addiction, suicidal themes, the world of miracles and demonic possession, including exorcism.

This story is not for the feint hearted.

ABOUT THE AUTHOR

Whilst the author has Degree and Master's qualifications in Law, Economics and Business, he is self-taught in Theology and Philosophy and, like many of us, also in life's ecstatic as well as brutal learning experiences.

He has previously published a book entitled "Life's Purpose, Write it, I will Guide you" (2017), being a reasoned non-fiction account of some of the themes mentioned above.

Thanks, from the Author.

A special thank you is owed to my wife, Giselle Cooke, for assisting me with this work. She has not only helped me with its publication, but has, over the many years of our relationship, walked the journey with me leading to the development of the thoughts and sentiments reflected in this book. It would not have been possible without her.

CHAPTER 1

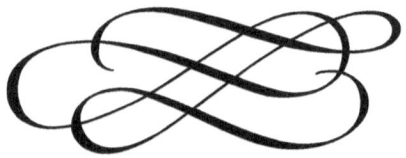

Degno

The little Catholic church was nestled in amongst the beautiful hillside forest of Assisi, Italy. In it, the local Bishop of Assisi, bishop Degno, was preaching the homily at the regular Sunday morning service.

Degno:

"And we must remember that the Lord watches over us all constantly, and can see everything we do; those things we do to impress others, as well as the things we do in secret. In the end, we will be held accountable for our actions that are based on pride; as well as for our inactions based on a lack of compassion for others."

As he spoke to the small, devoted audience, comprising mainly of elderly Assisi residents, they listened with intent, but also with a clear realisation that their church community was slowly dwindling as residents gradually passed away, and with no one replacing them, in the small local township.

The only young person in the service was the twelve-year-old altar boy assisting the bishop during the service.

to commence a twenty-minute walk through the majestic local Assisi Forest.

He was on his way to have lunch at the home of Signora Donatella, one of his widowed parishioners who regularly invited him over for lunch on Sundays. Her husband had died a year ago and Degno had since been a regular visitor to her home on the pretence of providing her with communal support for her bereavement.

However, some parishioners suspected that there was an unusual level of interaction between the bishop and Signora Donatella. But of course, it would have been almost sacrilegious for anyone to even suggest there was any impropriety taking place.

The local parish community could not countenance the idea that there might be any impropriety in its local bishop, regardless of it seems, no matter how obvious it appeared. Of course, this only meant that the bishop had grown accustomed to never being questioned over anything and so his arrogance in being able to get away with iniquities was palpable.

CHAPTER 2

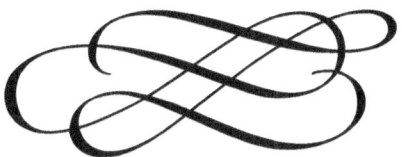

Karma

On his way to Signora Donatella's, Degno meandered his way through the picturesque forest of the Assisi hillside. Passing along a pathway shaped by majestic trees and the colours of the autumn foliage. He was reflecting on how he had done well in his priestly career and what a wonderful life he had managed to create for himself.

Suddenly, he heard the rustling of footsteps coming sideways out of the forest. As he turned to see who it was and faced his surprise attacker, he felt an almighty blow to his head that rendered him unconscious. His attacker then dragged Degno's unconscious body into the forest, some fifty meters away from the picturesque pathway.

After some twenty minutes or so had elapsed, muffled screaming could be heard from the location where Degno's body had been dragged to, along with the regular pounding of what seemed like a sledgehammer on wood. There was no one nearby to hear Degno's stifled echoes of excruciating pain. This went on for some time.

A few days later, the putrid odour of rotting bodily fluids alerted a passerby along the pathway. Dengo's body was discovered by an elderly man who had to be treated for shock from the traumatic find.

Degno was found in a rotting pool of blood and bodily fluids. His hands tied behind his back. His feet bound together. No clothes below his waist. His mouth stuffed with parts of his underclothes and taped tightly around his head to prevent him screaming.

A large, thick long wooden pile was wedged up his back side. It had been pounded in by a sledgehammer up his arse, through his body and the pointed end had penetrated out through his front abdomen. He had undergone a slow, excruciatingly painful death. His body and remaining clothing were soaked deep in a pool of putrid foul looking mud, created out of his own blood and body fluids.

The circumstances of his death made world news headlines and sparked a man hunt for his killer or killers, which has so far proved fruitless.

CHAPTER 3

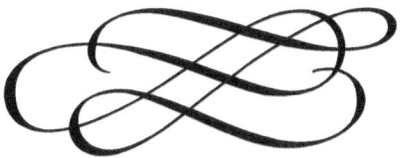

Alex and Angela

Alex Campbell is a Sydney based journalist who works for an Australian news group called World Observer. He specialises in crime cases but lately his boss Bruce Evans, who is a larger-than-life character, has had him doing a variety of stories which Alex is not happy about.

Alex is married to Angela. Alex and Angela have been trying to have children now for a couple of years without success. This is causing anxiety in their relationship given that Angela is approaching 38 years of age and Alex desperately wants to have children.

Alex has slowly come to the realization that all the work accolades he has achieved over the years, and all the travel he has done, and all the "niceties" of a comfortable life, do not really give him a great sense of satisfaction in life.

Whilst he has more than enough wealth for a comfortable life, he feels that having children will give him someone he can use his wealth to benefit, as well as be a focus for his love. And hopefully, a source from which to also ultimately be loved by someone other than Angela.

This particular Monday morning, Alex is getting ready to head off to work having just scoffed down some breakfast. He mentions to Angela that he thinks his diverticulitis is playing up as he feels some pain in his abdomen.

Angela responds, "Start taking some turmeric tablets for a few days and see if that makes a difference."

Somewhat dismissively, and tempting fate, Alex replies, "Darling, I'm only a journalist, but my understanding is that there's no scientific proof that supplements cure anything."

Since Angela is an avid natural medicine advocate, which Alex knew, this was enough to rile Angela, whereupon she bleats out, "I don't need fucking scientific proof. What my body tells me is proof enough!"

And she went on, "You're like all these natural medicine deniers who keep banging on about the lack of scientific proof. The fact is, there is scientific proof of many natural medicine cures, but the mainstream medical complex refuses to acknowledge it. And why is that the case? Because it fucking suits them not to acknowledge it, otherwise, who is going make piles of money selling pharmaceuticals if people realise that inexpensive naturally available cures exist that actually fix their problems rather than just address the symptoms, and without a bucket load of adverse side effects! It's the same fucking logic behind the Climate

Change naysayers! The evidence is there, but it just doesn't suit the big multinationals and their crony governments to acknowledge the issue because it means they can't do whatever they want to do!"

And she kept on going, "Plus you don't have to take my word for it. Why have generations upon generations of people from all parts of the world been swearing by ancient herbal remedies and other healing practices for centuries? Are they all stupid imbeciles who can't tell the difference between feeling better or not! Fuck you! and the whole medical complex. It's all fake news, generated by an agenda of making money. And so they criticise and kill off possible threats. And they do it in a surreptitious way, so no one has any idea its going on. Who do you think funds all the research studies that say herbal medicines and ancient cures are worthless!

"They constantly bang on about the need to have fucking double blind random testing in order to prove things scientifically. The fact is, that ancient people were smarter than that, and they didn't hang around waiting for science to prove things before trying them. Because they'd be dead otherwise. Science is constantly behind the eight ball. Even today's science can't explain how gravity works, or what the mind or consciousness is, or how to create life from scratch. It freely admits that it knows only 4% of the known universe, and calls the rest Dark Matter or Dark Energy, meaning it doesn't know what 96% of the fucking universe comprises of! No wonder it can't explain miracles or anything that appear to be unusual. On top of that, you've then got people and multinationals with hidden money agendas also gaming the system. You're supposedly a smart journalist, why don't you do your own research into that!"

Alex knew he had touched a raw nerve, but not even he thought he'd get that full on reaction. And then without thinking too much about the consequences, he went on to say, "Well, I know from my own research that IVF scientifically works, and I still can't understand why you're not prepared to go down that path since that is clearly a proven concept."

This comment, naturally, also hit a raw nerve with Angela, as Alex knew that Angela had an objection to using IVF, and given his keen desire to have children, he has not been able to accept Angela's reasons for not trialling it.

Angela retorted, "You know damn well why I don't like IVF!"

"For a start, I'm the one who has to go through it all, not you, you insensitive prick! Do you have any idea what IVF, and its often-failed attempts, can do to a woman's body, let alone her mental state?"

"IVF wasn't invented so that money hungry people like you and I, focussed on careers to fund travel and luxuries, and who leave childbirth until it's far too late in their lives, can turn around and have kids whenever they want. There's plenty of good reasons why nature expects you to rear children before the age of thirty-eight, and you and I have chosen to leave it too late! Now you want me to go against nature and produce the unnatural while you sit back and watch! You are so selfish! I only want children if they come from nature, which is how God intended it to be, and with plenty of good reasons for it. If you want unnatural children, find yourself someone else, and do me a favour and Fuck Off!"

The phone then rings, and Alex walks into another room to take the call.

It's a call from Alex's boss Bruce to tell him that he needs to get to the office as soon as possible, to get briefed on a story his boss wants him to do on Aboriginal sacred sites that are starting to generate large tourist dollars.

Alex tells Bruce that he is a crime reporter and knows nothing of religious matters or sacred sites. He, in fact, loathes religiosity and says its "All Bullshit." He tells Bruce that even his wife uses religion to avoid going on the IVF program.

Bruce responds, "Look mate, I'm not a doctor or a clergyman, so I can't help you with that, but right now I'm short on staff because people have gone on holidays left, right and centre. So, get your arse down here ASAP! Alternatively, if you don't like this job, you can Fuck Off!" whereupon Bruce slams down the phone.

Alex thinks to himself, that's the second time in ten minutes that two people have given him the same advice, namely, to Fuck Off!

CHAPTER 4

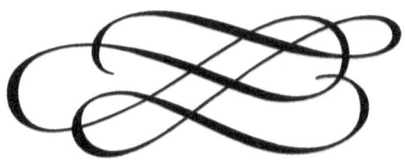

Moree

Alex reluctantly took the brief on the Aboriginal sacred sites story. The next day he arrived in the northern New South Wales outback town of Moree, close to the Queensland/NSW border.

Bruce had told him to stay at the lodgings at the Moree town pub and to speak to the town publican Harry Burns, who had agreed to brief him on the local story, and along with the local traditional owner Michael Monk, to advise on the key sites Alex should visit.

Alex caught up with Harry and Michael at the local pub for an interview and briefing. The first thing that struck Alex was how dusty and rugged Harry looked. He seemed like a dusty farmhand rather than a clean skinned publican. But it turns out that Harry was a local officer in the town's fire brigade and had, that same morning, been out in the bush with his team conducting back burning operations. It was bushfire season and the town was particularly vigilant on bushfire prevention, given a terrible bushfire a few years back when many farms were lost, including three lives, to a major blaze not far from the town.

Michael, on the other hand, even though dressed in simple shorts and T shirt, had an air of grace about him. His long but tidy black and white beard, and his well-set eyes and large forehead, gave him the semblance of Aboriginal aristocracy; especially appropriate for someone who had been initiated in traditional Aboriginal ways. Alex could immediately relate to why he was the respected local Traditional Owner, colloquially referred to as the "TO".

Alex:

"So where are these sacred sites everyone is apparently interested in seeing?"

Harry:

"Mate, they're not just interested in sacred sites, they're interested in seeing the spirits dancing around some of these sites."

Alex, on hearing the notion of dancing spirits, immediately put his hand to his eyes and rubbed them then squeezed his nose, in a way which evidenced his internal anguish. He knew he was about to hear some bullshit aboriginal story about ancestors and ghosts; and if he had little time for western religious mumbo jumbo, he had even less interest in Aboriginal religious nonsense. But he knew he had a job to do, so he continued without belittling the topic.

Alex:

"What do you mean 'dancing spirits'?"

Michael:

"Ancestor spirits bro. They live on the sacred sites and white fellas sometimes see them on their photo cameras."

Alex:

"What are these ancestor spirits?"

Harry knew enough to answer this one before Michael could get in.

Harry:

"Not WHAT, WHO are they? you should ask.

"The local aborigines believe that when their ancestors die, their spirits survive and live around certain sacred sites. They then return in another body in another lifetime. In the meantime, they congregate around certain land or water sites, along with kindred spirits from the same totem clan."

Alex:

"Are you telling me that Aborigines believe in reincarnation, like Hindus and Buddhists?"

Harry:

"Mate, they've believed in all this stuff for over 60,000 years, well before the other mobs you just mentioned. It's just that they keep this secret stuff to themselves. That's why no white fella knows much about it. People think the aborigines make up sacred sites out of nothing, but most of these sites are places where their ancestors live on the land, or in the trees, or in the water. That's why young pregnant women are often banned from visiting these places or else a spirit will steal its way into her baby."

Alex rubs his head as a sign of disbelief on hearing what sounds to him as total cockahoot. He then looks at Michael and directly asks him, "so what clan or totem do you belong to?"

Michael:

"My totem is the cockatoo bro. And my ancestors live up on Mount Kaputar."

Alex:

"Is that one of the sites that people have seen these spirits on?"

Harry:

"Sure, thing mate. A group camped up there a few weeks back and caught them on camera."

Alex:

"How far is that place from here?"

Harry:

"About a 90-minute drive."

Alex:

"Ok, well looks like that's the place I need to visit. I will pick up some camping supplies and make my way there tonight with my camera."

Harry:

"A couple staying at the pub are going up there tonight to shoot the sunset. They can give you a lift there if you like. You'll find them having a drink in the lounge."

Alex:

"Great. Thanks guys. Anything else I need to know for now?"

"I will let my mob on the mountain know who they can expect," said Michael, meaning his own spirit clan.

Alex, knowing exactly what Michael meant, looks at Michael with a sneaky smile and nodded, saying, "You do that brother. Most appreciated." He then headed off to find the couple Harry had mentioned to ask for a lift.

Alex was a long-time camper and actually enjoyed camping. In his younger days before he met Angela, he would often go camping alone and held no fear of spiders or snakes, nor isolation, and certainly no fear of ghosts or spirits as he knew they were nonsense.

He would always carry a machete and had a collection of machetes at home. In his younger days he would love hacking his way through bush trails with them. Even now he carried a machete with him, even though there was hardly any need for it on this trip, given the sparse nature of the bush in this part of the country.

CHAPTER 5

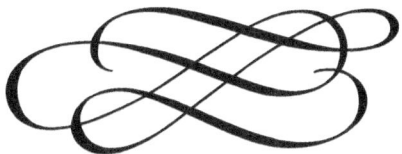

Mount Kaputar

The couple staying at Harry's hotel drove Alex up to Mount Kaputar. They had heard it was a great place to watch the sunset. They knew something about it being a special site for aborigines but not much more than that.

The park rangers had constructed a purpose built look out at the top of the mountain. A small plaque was erected at the foot of the lookout. It read as follows:

   "Ancient Aboriginal Proverb
   'We are all visitors to this time, this place. We are just passing through. Our purpose here is to observe, to learn, to grow, to love ...and then we return home'."

This meant nothing to Alex at the time, but little did he know that he would later come to understand the real meaning of this proverb.

About fifty meters below the lookout there was some flat cleared ground that people could camp on, if they wanted to stay the night.

Alex set up his tent in the clearing and then joined the couple just in time to take photos of the sunset. And what a magnificent sunset it was. A red blood orange sky spanned the horizon, as the sunlight lit up the haze that had been lingering in the area from the recent bushfire clearings.

Alex saw no evidence of spirits or ghosts, either with the naked eye or on his camera shots. That's pretty much what he expected to find, namely, nothing.

The couple staying at Harry's pub commenced their drive back into town and wished Alex all the best for the night sky viewing, as there were some scattered clouds which could impede a magnificent vista of the night star scape, once all the sunlight disappeared.

Alex retreated to his tent and had some cold tin dinner. Lighting fires on the mountain was prohibited this time of year.

From Alex's radio he could hear that the local forecast for the evening was for hot and humid conditions with a thunderstorm warning. But little or no showers were expected from the storms. That is the type of forecast that Harry Burns and every experienced firefighter would dread, since a storm with no rain is a recipe for spot fires starting up.

After dinner Alex enjoyed immensely the solitude and the view of the Milky Way through breaks in the cloud mass. He had seen plenty of night skies in his time, having camped in many places, but here the night sky vista was extraordinary, with every piece of the sky dotted with endless stars, only interrupted by the odd cloud grouping.

Alex was looking forward to a good night's sleep on his trusty swag bed that he swore was as comfortable as any home mattress he had ever slept on. He hadn't been sleeping well at home for a few days, especially after the recent confrontation with Angela, but the mountain air, a full stomach and the endless entertaining vista, provided the perfect combination for a restful night's sleep. Alex fell asleep as soon as his head hit the swag.

What he did not know was that the surrounding bushland hadn't experienced a bushfire for years, and was blanketed with dry undergrowth. The approaching dry thunderstorms eventually arrived when Alex was in a deep sleep. The sporadic thunder and lightning did not wake Alex, as he was a heavy sleeper and after some sleepless nights during the past few days, his body craved a long deep sleep that night.

Unbeknownst to him, the lightning set off a spot fire at the base of the mountain. This, coupled with the storm winds which blew straight up the mountain from where the fire had started, a bushfire of growing intensity was hurrying up the mountain towards him.

The fire's billowing smoke preceded it, and soon Alex's tent was surrounded by smoke and haze. The smoke only served to stupefy Alex even more so, as anyone ever caught sleeping in a smoke-filled house knows only too well, assuming they survived to tell the story.

As the fire raced up the windy side of the mountain, roaring through the dry trees and scrub, with Alex in a state of slumber, the outcome appeared obvious. Alex would soon be engulfed by a burning force that would annihilate him before he could wake up to appreciate his horrific destiny.

But just as all this seemed tragically destined to occur, Alex was woken up by the constant screeching of two black cockatoos prancing around outside his tent. Alex was still in a smoke induced slumber, but he quickly realised there was imminent danger. He slowly dragged himself out of the tent entrance, which thankfully, he had left partially open. The cockatoos kept prancing around the tent, still screeching incessantly. But Alex could now at least hear the roar of the fire howling up the mountain side behind him and felt its heat beating down on his head and back as he stumbled his way to the opposite side of the clearing.

Despite his awareness of the danger at hand, the sheer oppression of heat and smoke, coupled with his still dazed mind, made him disoriented, and he had no idea of how to navigate himself away from the fire front racing up the windswept side of the mountain.

Just then he saw, or at least he imagined he saw, Michael, the TO, draped and painted in full Aboriginal ceremonial colours, in the scrub some thirty meters in front of him, and motioning calmly to him to come his way.

Alex half stumbled, half ran, towards him and the TO, keeping his distance from Alex, began calmly walking down a mountainside pathway, on the opposite side of the mountain to the fire. He slowly led Alex away from the fireside of the mountain. Alex followed him from a distance, as the TO, although moving calmly, was making good ground. After thirty minutes or so, he lost sight of the TO altogether. By then Alex was well away from the fire danger. At this point he realised how exhausted he was, and he just collapsed to the ground unconscious and fell asleep.

When Alex awoke it was mid-morning the next day. He had slept a good six hours straight. His neck and back were aching from the uncomfortable position he had slept on the forest floor. But the exhaustion of the previous night was more than enough to outweigh the hardness of the forest floor.

He made his way to the base of the mountain where the main road leading up the mountain was. It did not take long for a fire truck to drive by, as the local fire service was attending to any spot fires that may still be around after the main fire burnt itself out after reaching the top of the mountain where Alex's tent had been pitched.

Alex waved them down and they pulled up. There were two firefighters in the truck and they were surprised to see a thirsty and dishevelled camper, with no gear, so far down the mountain.

They drove Alex to a nearby camping ground at the base of the mountain that had become a rendezvous point for firefighters in the area. From there, Alex got a ride with one of the Moree based local units back into Moree, where he got dropped off at the local pub he had been staying at.

As he walked through the main pub doors, Harry saw him and ran to him and embraced him warmly.

"Strewth Mate, I thought you'd be a burnt vegemite sandwich by now!" said Harry. "What happened to yah?"

Alex responded,

"One minute I was in my tent peacefully nodding off to sleep. Next minute, I wake up to two screeching cockatoos, with all hell fire heading my way. If it wasn't for those bloody cockatoos waking me up and Michael, don't asked me how he got up that mountain, showing me the way down the mountain side, I'd be completely toasted now."

Harry retorted immediately,

"Michael!? You must be dreaming mate. Michael's been here in town all day yesterday and evening. He's been at the local hospital. I bumped into him in the main street as he left the hospital last night."

Alex replied,

"Well, if it wasn't him mate, he must have a twin brother because I've got a memory for faces, and I swear it was him. And he was all decked out in face paint and Aboriginal colours. He kept walking and motioning to me to follow him down that mountain on the safe side. Up there I had no idea where I was going with all that heat and smoke and my head all fucked up from it."

"Michael wouldn't be painted up unless he was in ceremonial mode or," Harry paused.

"Or what?" asked Alex.

"Astral Travel," said Harry tentatively.

"Astral Travel? That's bullshit," retorted Alex.

"Mate," said Harry, motioning to Alex to sit down at a nearby table and almost starting to whisper to him, "there's a few stories of these black fella elders who can apparently do this stuff. Fly around the place. You know what I mean?"

Alex looked at Harry incredulously, but Harry kept going,

"Look, one time both Michael and I had to get to a local aboriginal mission a few miles out of town because of some commotion going on there amongst the locals. I was driving there and as soon as I got out of Moree, I see Michael on his way there walking on foot. So, I pulled over and offered him a lift. He tells me he'd prefer to walk because he was thinking things over in his head along the way. I told him he'd take ages to get there as the mission was a good fifteen-minute drive out of town. He told me not to worry and that he'd meet me there.

"So, I take off knowing he is going be way late. When I get to the mission, bugger me, what do I find? Bloody Michael, standing on the main street chatting with some of the locals! By the time I got there, he'd sorted things out! Mate, I can't recall any car overtaking me and there's only one road from Moree to that mission. So tell me what the fuck is that all about then!" as if asking Alex to explain.

Alex shook his head thinking he doesn't really need to work out how all these stories should make sense, since he thinks they're all nonsense anyway.

Reflecting on Harry's comment about Michael being in hospital all day yesterday, Alex said, "Well what's wrong with Michael? Why was he at the hospital?"

"Oh, it wasn't for himself," says Harry. "Michael's son is autistic and often has to spend time at the local hospital when his medication gets out of whack."

"Sorry to hear that," responded Alex.

"Yeah," continued Harry. "Michael's had some bad luck. He and his missus swear their son was right as rain when he was about eighteen months old; laughing, playing, and looking just fine. Then they took him in for one of those regular vaccinations for measles and whatnot. And ever since that injection the nurse gave him, he's been a different person. Doctors later diagnosed him as autistic, but they all refuse to acknowledge that the injection he got, had anything to do with it. They reckon it's just not possible. But Michael and his missus, both who would never tell a lie, swear it was that bloody injection they gave him."

As if on cue, Michael walks into the pub and comes over and puts his hand over Alex's shoulders and says, "Good to see you Bro. My mob on the mountain told me you were in a spot of bother last night."

Alex says to him, pointedly, "Were you on that mountain with me last night?"

Michael says, "Maybe I was in spirit bro," giving Harry a smile and a wink as if Harry would understand.

Alex says, "I swear you were there mate, although I admit I was half whacked with all that smoke and all.

And a couple of screaming black cockatoos woke me up to get me out of that incoming inferno."

"I told you bro, my clan's the cockatoo clan," said Michael. "They want to look after you. They reckon you helped some of them get away in that Myles Creek massacre years ago," said Michael with a smile on his face.

Alex had heard about the Myles Creek massacre but before he could ask any questions, Harry saw the uncertainty in his face and blurts out, "Bloody Myles Creek! What a shocker! That was a hatchet job by seven white fellas of an Aboriginal camp in the 1830's. Most of the adult men were out hunting, and seven white fellas on horseback rode into the camp and shot and butchered the locals. A couple of the locals managed to get away to tell the story. All seven were eventually hanged for it. But they reckon that one of them was a reluctant participant and that he may have refused to kill the ones that got away. They hanged him anyways."

"Are you telling me that I'm a reincarnation of one of the seven hanged for that bloody massacre?" said Alex disapprovingly looking at Michael.

"Hey bro, all I'm telling you is what I'm getting from my mob," replied Michael. "Whatever good you done in the past, they still remember it now."

"Fuck off out of here you city wankers!" one of the patrons sitting at the bar yells out at this point, as three climate change protesters walk into the pub, all wearing "Stop Mining NOW" tee shirts.

"We just want a drink mate," one of them replies.

"Go tell your greenie mates to fuck off back to your inner city digs and suck on a few more weeds!" retorts another patron.

Harry says to Alex, "They're up here to protest against the coal mining. Problem is that it's coal mining that provides a good number of jobs around here."

Alex is curious what Michael thinks of the protests and asks him, "Hey Michael, what do you think of all these greenies?"

Michael shrugs his shoulders and says, "They don't understand the needs of the local people. And the local people don't understand the needs of the planet. All this mining, even if it provides some local jobs, is still hurting the planet and she's alive man. And when she starts to hurt, she's gunna retaliate. And these droughts and fires we've been having ain't the half of it. If she really gets mad, we're all done for!"

At this point Alex's phone starts ringing. Fortunately, he still had his phone as he kept it in his jacket pocket. Last night he had kept his jacket on when he went to sleep given how cold it was on the mountain. It was Bruce his boss calling him.

"Hello," says Alex knowing its Bruce calling.

"Morning," replies Bruce. "I need you to drop what you're doing and get back to Sydney ASAP to be briefed on a new assignment in Italy."

"Italy!" says Alex. "What's up in Italy?"

"I need you to get to Assisi ASAP!" replied Bruce, "to cover a story involving the macabre murder of a catholic bishop along with the imminent visit of the Pope to the town."

"Are the two connected?" asks Alex.

"No-one knows yet," said Bruce. "That's part of your brief. There's been talk of death threats against senior church leaders recently but there's so many groups out there that hate the Catholic Church, any number of crazies could be gunning for them."

"Not that I don't like Italy boss, but I need a few more days here before I have anything worthwhile to write up," says Alex.

"The bishop's murder is white hot," says Bruce. "Every crime reporter worth his salt is heading over to cover it. I need you on a plane over there in forty-eight hours. Got it!"

"Boss, I've been here just one night. I nearly got my arse toasted in a bushfire last night and I've got half a story but need another day or so to flesh it out," replies Alex.

Bruce is wound up by now and bleats out, in a manner even audible to Harry and Michael, "Get your arse on a plane back here tonight mate, otherwise your arse will definitely be toasted! I've got management breathing down my neck to get this Italian story covered and if you're not up to it you can pack up your desk and Fuck Off out of here!" The phone hangs up.

"Fuck! I hate that bastard and the whole fucking lot of them!" exclaims Alex to Harry and Michael. "Everything is on a 24-hour cycle. Everything is urgent. There's no time for considered writing anymore. Fuck! The whole world's gone to reading 24-

hour real-time trash. People no longer have time for anything."

"That's not a problem for us bro," says Michael with a wry smile on his face and teeth gleaming. "We got time for everything. We don't even have a word for 'Time' in my language, because we are always living in the present."

Alex looks at Michael puzzled and intuitively knew there are things he could learn from Michael if he could spend more time with him. Alex says, "I would have liked to spend more time with you guys out here, but as you no doubt just heard, I don't have any fucking time to myself."

As he put his phone down, Alex remembered that in addition to taking photos of the Kaputar sunset on his camera which got destroyed in the fire last night, he had also taken some sunset shots on his iPhone. So, he opened up his phone photos to show Michael and Harry.

"Here look, I actually managed to keep some photos from my time on the mountain," said Alex as he flicked through showing the photos to the guys. "As you can see there are no ghosts or spirits in any of these shots, nor in any of the camera shots I took which got lost in the fire last night."

Michael took Alex's phone, and with his eyes squinting, started to look intently at the shots. Then he points out one photo to Alex and says, "Hey bro, what do you reckon those lights are?" pointing to a couple of small, tiny light flashes in one of Alex's sunset shots.

One was a green colour and the other a light blue colour.

Alex, looking somewhat puzzled, says, "I think they're just camera lens reflections mate."

"I don't reckon so," replies Michael, "To me, looks like thems some of the spirits living in the dust on that mountain."

"Spirts, living in the dust?" repeats Alex somewhat disbelieving, but not wishing to get into a discussion on the topic since he thought it was all bullshit.

Alex then thanked the guys for their help and friendship over the last two days and headed up to his room to collect what few belongings he had left. He then took the next flight home to Sydney.

CHAPTER 6

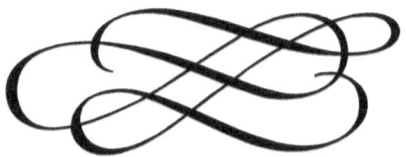

Back Home

"Hi Darling!" exclaims Angela when Alex walks in the front door and runs over to him and gives him a hug. "I literally just heard about the fires in and around Moree."

"Nothing to be worried about Darling," responds Alex casually, "there's nothing much to burn up those parts since constant droughts have killed off most of the bush already."

Alex was not going to share with Angela the close shave he had with death on the mountain. He rarely shared with her any dangerous moments of his career, as he knew it would just make her more nervous whenever he went on assignment.

"I would have loved to stay a few more days there to finish my story but bloody Bruce calls me and gets me to drop everything to head back to Sydney for an urgent assignment. God, I hate those fuckers in the office. They treat you like a mechanical tool. Just a part of a machine aimed at making money. They have no regard for any human aspect. No empathy or compassion," said Alex.

"Then why stay in the company? Go somewhere else," replies Angela.

"Ahh! They're all the same. I've got mates in other companies and their bosses and administrations are just as fucked," replies Alex.

"Then why keep doing what you're doing? Why don't you try something different?" Angela asks.

"Because I love journalism Darling. I believe in it. I believe it's critical to a free and transparent society. It's what drove me to be a Jurno in the first place. I felt I could make a difference. And I'm not going to let a crappy bunch of media administrators in the industry try put me off doing what I still passionately believe in," said Alex.

"Ok Darling. I haven't heard you be that passionate and committed to your work for a long time. I'm glad you feel that way. So, what's this urgent assignment you had to drop everything for?" asks Angela.

"Bruce wants me to get on a plane asap to Assisi in Italy to cover a recent murder of a bishop there," responds Alex.

"Assisi! Wow! That's a very holy place. It's where Saint Francis and Saint Clare come from," noted Angela, reflecting her catholic knowledge and saying it with an air of disappointment that she won't be accompanying him.

"Well, some bishop has just been murdered in a bizarre manner and Bruce wants me to see if it's an isolated incident or part of some anti-church reaction, especially since the pope is due there soon to celebrate the 800-year anniversary of Francis's death," said Alex.

Angela nodded and replied, "You know I've been following Pope Francis for years and he must have plenty of detractors because he is trying to clean up and rebuild the Catholic Church. He's trying to oust all the paedophiles, open the church hierarchy up to women, reform church dogma on gays and divorcees, improve interfaith relations, and of course, clean up the sordid Vatican finances! No wonder he has people within the church gunning for him. It's not outsiders that hate him. He's their champion. It's the insiders who are threatened by his reforms that hate him!" noted Angela emphatically.

At the time Alex didn't realise it, but later he would come to recognise just how accurate Angela was on the topic.

"Well, right now I need to focus on this bishop murder. But you've just summarised all the things wrong with the Catholic Church and I'm still buggered why you, and people in general, bother paying any credence to it. It's an absolute shambles," noted Alex, knowing that Angela is in that camp.

Angela retorted in no time, "Because spiritual people would never let incompetent church administrators get in the way of true faith. You just finished telling me you wouldn't let your dickhead bosses sway you from the importance of a free press because you believe in the ideal, not its administrators. Well Church people believe in the Faith, and no amount of dickhead corrupt bishops and priests are going to sway them from what they know to be true and good. So don't be a fucking hypocrite and pretend that what's okay for you in pursuing your ideal, despite your dickhead bosses, is not equally applicable for me!"

Alex had no comeback on that one. She clearly had a point, and a big one.

Angela went on, "And anyway, you should know that you need turmoil and disruption in an organisation for there to be meaningful change. If everything goes along nicely and no one upsets anybody, then nothing meaningful ever changes. Surely, you've heard of the principle of 'creative destruction'?

"You need to pull down the old before you can build the new. And that's what Pope Francis is trying to do. He's rebuilding the church by destroying all that is wrong with it; all the bad stuff that has become ingrained in its system over centuries.

"He's the first Pope to ever take on the name of Saint Francis! Which tells you a lot about prior Popes who clearly didn't want to live a life of poverty like anything approaching that of Saint Francis.

"And just like Saint Francis, a Saint who Christ himself asked to rebuild the Church back in the Middle Ages, Pope Francis is a builder. But he needs to demolish and level out the old place first. That's why all the fuckers who stand to lose from all the change he's bringing in, can't handle it!"

Just then Alex's phone rings. It's Harry from Moree.

"Hey mate," says Harry. "You the left the place so quickly I forgot to tell you that Michael brought around a bag of herbs to give you for your sore stomach. I got it here, but was wondering what's the best way to get it to you?"

"How did Michael know i had a sore stomach? I didn't tell him," said Alex.

"I asked him that myself," said Harry. "He said he saw it in your eyes and in your aura."

"My eyes and my aura?" said Alex in disbelief. He was taken a back, as he had no idea how Michael could have known about his diverticulitis.

"What's in the bag?" asked Alex.

"It looks like turmeric roots," said Harry.

"What the," said Alex exasperatingly. "That's what my wife's been trying to give me for the same thing, but I've never bothered with it."

"Well, what do you want me to do with the bag?" asked Harry.

"You keep it, Harry. I've got plenty of turmeric supplements here," replied Alex.

And with that, he again thanked Harry for his assistance during his time in Moree and hung up.

Alex was due to fly out to Rome and then Assisi tomorrow, so it would be at least a couple of weeks before Alex and Angela would be together. Since they were trying to have a baby, they both knew that tonight would be the last chance for a while to make love.

Alex helped Angela prepare the evening meal and, after watching some light-hearted shows on TV, they retired to the bedroom.

Angela put on some lacy underwear and turned down the bedroom lighting. Alex showered and joined Angela in bed, and they embraced and started their love making routine. Angela was always a great bedroom performer. Alex had also been good in bed in the early years of their relationship, but once they decided they wanted to have a baby, he felt the pressure to perform in bed and this somehow got to him, and from time to time he would struggle to ejaculate.

Tonight, should not have been ones of those times, especially since he would not see Angela for a few weeks. But this added pressure made things worse, and Alex just could not bring himself to complete the love making. At a certain point after trying for some time, he withdrew and apologised to Angela.

"Sorry Darling, I just can't tonight," he said.

Angela, obviously disappointed, replied, "You can't get it off and yet you are always having a go at me for not wanting to go through IVF.

"So, because you can't perform your manly duties, I am then the one who has to go through all the IVF pain and trauma they put you through, while you sit back and say, 'Sorry Darling, I can't tonight!'

"Well, Fuck You! You either start performing pal or go without kids from me!"

Alex was already feeling disillusioned with work. He didn't need to be smashed around by Angela about his lack of manliness and apparent selfishness the day before he was due to head overseas. But that's exactly what he got.

CHAPTER 7

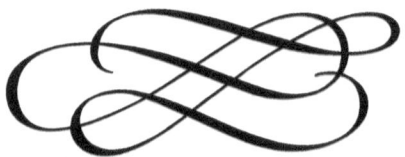

Assisi

Alex arrived in Assisi early morning by taking the train from Rome, having flown into Rome on a flight from Sydney. The whole trip took over thirty hours and he was naturally tired, not having slept well on the long flight.

Even so, as he alighted from the train in Assisi and looked up at the picturesque hillside that showcased the picture card icon of the Basilica of Saint Francis, he experienced an immediate sense of calmness and tranquillity. It was as if time momentarily stood still so that he could take in the view and feel present in the world. It was a rare moment of experience for Alex. He already sensed that there was something special about this place.

"Hey, you must be Alex," said a young-faced man with an Aussie accent waiving at Alex as he approached. "I'm Tommy, but they call me Junior. Bruce sent me your travel details, so I knew where to find you this morning."

"How long have you been in Italy?" asked Alex.

"Three years, I'm based in Rome but I'm here in Assisi for a while to cover the 800-year Franciscan anniversary. The boss told me I couldn't cover the bishop's murder because he needed an experienced crime writer to do that. So, I guess that's you, eh?" Junior said half asking.

"I guess so," replied Alex with a shrug of the shoulders.

Junior helped Alex put his bags in Junior's car and asked, "So what do you want to do now?"

"Well, i understand you have a contact in the local police. We need to find out as much as we can about the details on Degno's murder," said Alex.

"I can do that," replied Junior. "I know a detective working on the case, Ludovico Nero. I'll see what i can find out.

"What else?" said Junior.

"You need to background me on this town and what's happening locally," replied Alex, "and show me around this place."

"Best way to brief you mate is to start there," said Junior, pointing up the picturesque hillside to St Francis's Basilica. "That place has the history of this town plastered all over its walls."

Junior drove Alex up to the Basilica and took him inside and walked him around pointing out all the key painted scenes and their meaning. As he did so, he relayed to Alex the history of Assisi and it's two heralded saints, Saint Francis and Saint Clare.

Alex had some knowledge of Saint Francis but had never heard of Saint Clare before Angela mentioned her the day before he left Sydney.

"How come you know so much about this place and all this artwork?" said Alex with a clear sense of respect for Junior's level of knowledge.

"I have an Arts Degree," said Junior. "I also studied Religious History and did a major in Renaissance Art. All the artwork in this place not only preceded Renaissance Art, but some say it actually led to the movement that caused the explosion of genius we saw during the Renaissance."

"What's that scene all about," asked Alex pointing to a fresco that had Saint Francis gazing at what appeared to be a tame wolf.

"That's Francis befriending the wolf of Gubbio," replied Junior. "The story goes that this wolf had attacked and killed a number of people in the nearby town of Gubbio just up the road. Francis apparently cut a deal with the wolf that if the town's folk fed and looked after it, it would behave itself and not attack anyone."

"That's gotta be bullshit," refrained Alex, shaking his head in disbelief that such nonsense could possibly be believed by people, let alone be depicted on a Church wall.

"Yeah, it certainly sounds weird doesn't it," said Junior. "But believe it or not, in the 19th century they dug beneath a Church that was built in Gubbio to commemorate the so called 'deal with the wolf', and *they found the buried remains of a wolf that actually dates back to the time of Francis."*

"Probably bullshit evidence planted to make the story even more attractive to tourists," replied Alex. "Who can possibly cut a deal with a wolf, for fucksake!"

"Mate, I know what you mean, but these Saints, I tell yah, are meant to be able to do the impossible," said Junior motioning with his hand at all the paintings in the Basilica, many depicting miracles.

"Ok Junior," said Alex somewhat dismissive of his last point, "I really appreciate the history lesson. Most helpful. However, I should head off to my hotel now. Although I could do with a walk in the fresh air to help with my jet lag."

"Sure mate. Why don't I take your bags to the hotel, and you can walk to the hotel through this beautiful landscape," offered Junior as he motioned up towards the Assisi hillside.

"It's only about a half hour walk and I will show you how to get there. It's easy."

Alex thought that was a great idea and Junior then left him instructions on how to get to the hotel.

What Junior neglected to tell Alex, is that the pathway to the hotel included the section where the bishop's body had been found. Moreover, although the pathway was well fashioned and easy to walk through, the forest through which it meandered was dense and with the fading sunlight of the afternoon, could become somewhat dark and eerie during his walk.

Alex commenced his walk along the pathway mapped out by Junior and was in a good frame of mind. He had just been given a thorough briefing on the history of the town and its religious significance and he knew Junior would be a great help to him on this assignment, since he had a good grasp of the town's history and had developed some useful local contacts, including with the local police.

Nonetheless, Alex knew he needed to get a better feel for the social fabric of the town, especially what the locals thought of the church hierarchy here and whether animosity towards the church was widespread. Was this murder an isolated grievance, or a reaction to a broader anti-church sentiment?

He knew he had to search for the rationale behind the murder and who the range of suspects could be. A useful starting point would be for him to spend some time with the locals and understand their perspective on the murder. But he had to do this in a way that did not make people feel threatened or concerned about what he, as a journalist, was up to by asking questions about such a bizarre crime.

As he strolled along the pathway, he realised that the dense forest made the pathway dimly lit in the fading sunlight. And as the sun started to set, the temperature cooled down and a slight wind started to rustle the autumn leaves strewn across the forest floor.

After a while he regretted not having taken his coat out of his packed bag and worn it on the walk. As the light dimmed further, and the wind started to bite through his light shirt, the eerie nature of the place suddenly dawned on him.

He was not sure whether he was anywhere near where the murder had taken place, but nonetheless the hard reality that a murderer was probably living in the town and might be lurking around suddenly hit home to him.

Here he was, he thought to himself, a total stranger walking around in a dense forest pathway on a dimly lit evening, in a town where potentially a maniacal murderer is on the loose. Just as that thought crossed his mind, he heard what appeared to him to be strange rustling noises coming from the edge of the pathway behind him. His heart skipped a beat, and he found himself starting to jog nervously along the pathway, as much to warm himself as from a sense of fear. The wind and the swirling leaves on the ground created a constant rustling whirlwind noise that only heightened his anxiety.

He decided he would jog along as far as he could, and he knew he was letting out a spurt of nervous energy by doing so. As he continued to jog along, he had a sense that someone or something was watching him. The coolness in the air, the noise of the rustling wind and swirling leaves all added to his heightened sense of unease.

At that point, and out of the corner of his eye, he saw something dark move in between the forest trees on the edge of the pathway. That really frightened him and set him hurrying down the pathway. He was running now, not just jogging. He had no idea what he had seen out of the corner of his eye, but he sure as hell was too scared to stop to find out, or even look back as he ran forward, for fear of not seeing where he was going along the now poorly lit pathway.

Junior had told him the hotel was about a half hour walk and he figured he was well past halfway. So he decided to keep running for as long as he could. As he picked up his intensity by running, it seemed as if the cool wind and darkness also intensified.

By now, Alex was really running hard with fear propelling him. He had no idea whether anyone or anything was following him as the noise from the swirling wind and forest floor leaves cancelled out any possible footsteps that he might have otherwise been able to hear.

Suddenly, he heard the most chilling sound he had ever heard. It was the loud howling of a wolf. It went through his bones and raised the hairs on his neck.

He ran even harder, and he was now running at a pace that was unsustainable, even though he was very fit. Pretty soon he would have to stop as his heart was pounding. But right now, it was pure adrenaline that kept him going.

As he approached a turn in the pathway, he found himself doing something he thought he would never do. Even though he was running fast, he found himself not just hoping, but actually praying, that at the end of the turn he would come to the forest end. He had no idea to whom he was praying, but praying he was.

"Please! Please!" he heard himself saying, as he kept running.

And as luck, or perhaps providence, would have it, as he turned the corner, he saw the edge of the town and could see the lit-up sign of his hotel entrance.

He ran a further thirty meters or so past the end of the forest and collapsed on the ground not far from the hotel entrance, under a nearby streetlight. There was no one around but he knew he was now in a safe place, and he lay there panting and going through the phases of delayed shock.

"Thank you. Thank you," he said as he lay there panting, not really knowing who he was offering thanks to.

As he sat up and looked back towards the forest, he knew there was someone or something out there, and he was grateful to the Universe for having avoided it.

CHAPTER 8

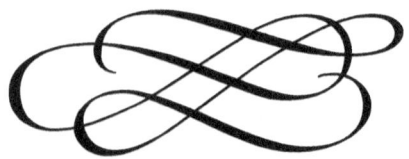

The Locals

Alex set out the following morning to visit an area of Assisi where the poorer town's folk lived. He wanted to get a feel from the town's 'coal face' what they thought of the Church and, without being too obvious about it, what they thought of the murdered Degno.

Alex had studied Italian at school and maintained some fluency in the language over the years on his many visits to Italy. So he was quite comfortable with being able to interact with the locals.

He made his way to a poorer part of the town that Junior had told him was the "Bible Belt" of the township.

As he wandered through the streets of this area, he came across an old man sitting on a stool on the street pavement outside the rundown facade of an apartment, where he presumably lived.

Speaking always in Italian, Alex said, "Good morning," to the old man, who in turn nodded and acknowledged him.

"I'm a journalist and have come to Assisi to cover the coming Franciscan anniversary," said Alex. "I was

hoping to ask some of the people in the town what this anniversary means to them, and what they think of the church and the current Pope?"

"Oh," replied the old man, always speaking in Italian and waiving his right hand as he temporarily looked away, "if it wasn't for this blessed Pope Francis we have now, the Church would be a disaster. A complete disaster. The people respect him because they can see he is a holy man who wants to change things. But it's very hard, even for a Pope, to rebuild a broken Church."

"Why do you think the church is broken?" asks Alex knowing full well all the ailments of the present Catholic Church.

"Ahh," says the old man, again waiving his hand and looking away from Alex, as if Alex should know the obvious. "The churches are full of old and dying people. Hardly any young people come. No one wants to be a priest today. Look at all the problems with priests and what they have done to children; then there's always talk of money problems at the Vatican and of mafia involvement; look even at how the church treats women. Our Holy Lady Mary was a woman! How can you suppress women when the most holy person we pray to, the Saint of all Saints, is a woman!" again gesturing with his hand in the air.

Somewhat hesitantly, and not sure what the reaction of the old man would be, Alex asks, "Do all these problems mean that you have lost your faith?"

At this point, the old man straightened up and with gleaming narrow green eyes looked at Alex directly, and pointing his finger sternly at Alex said, "I never lose my faith! I never lose my faith! I always have faith in God and the Saints."

Then looking away and again with a wave of his hand, "Yes, I have little hope that the Church will soon be fixed. But that is the Church! It is not the faith! The faith is always pure. Always true. It's the priests, bishops and even cardinals that are the problem!"

Pausing momentarily, and then continuing, but always talking with his hand waving from side to side, or up and down, depending on the intonation he was using, "Yes, yes, it's true that in earlier times the church had even bigger problems. Many Popes have been corrupt. They even started wars. Crusades! Ahh! But this is a problem of the Church. Not the faith!"

"You sound exactly like my wife," said Alex.

"Then your wife has understood things well," replied the old man.

"But what of all the suffering the Church has caused? How can people still respect something that causes so much suffering?" said Alex reflecting his own view of the hopeless state of the current Catholic Church.

The old man looked at him with a steely stare which, after a pause, then melted as he again looked away and began speaking, still motioning with his right hand, "Suffering. Yes. There has been much suffering. But the world is full of suffering, not just the fault of the Church.

"Without suffering there is no need to change things; no lessons to learn; no need for compassion or *forgiveness. Suffering is the way of the world. It is the reason why we are here. It will always be like this. How else can you teach people to improve, or that there is a better world to aim for, without it?"*

Then pausing and looking again at Alex, and pointing at him with his finger, "What matters is how you respond to suffering."

Alex, not content with his response and wanting to entice a view about the local's perception of the town's church clergy, goes on, "Surely people should not just stand by and simply watch all the suffering created by the Church and do nothing? Surely justice requires that those who do harm to others be punished for their actions. Why are people not demanding that Church injustice be punished?"

"Those who have done wrong WILL be punished!" retorted the old man, still looking sternly at Alex. "They WILL be punished!" as if he felt it necessary to emphasise the point. "Either in this life or the next. The Universe records everything. Nothing unjust goes unpunished!"

And then, as he looks away and with a wave of his hand he adds, "unless, of course, God forgives you."

"Do you really believe a god exists that would forgive, for instance, a priest who molests a child?" implored Alex.

Turning back to look at Alex and speaking emphatically, the old man exclaims, "I could never forgive this! Never!"

Then turning away again, and again motioning with his hand in the air, "But God knows better than me what to do," responded the old man.

"Surely, no one could forgive such a heinous act; not a just God, surely?" Alex again implored.

"Forgiveness is a difficult thing to understand," replies the old man, speaking with the seeming air of a great philosopher. Then looking away into the distance he adds, "We are all guilty of something. No one is perfect. Are you?" then a pause, not expecting Alex to answer, and continuing, "If we were already perfect, we would already be with God! Everyone needs to be forgiven to truly understand what it means. And also, everybody needs learn to forgive. People forget this. Compassion and Forgiveness is what Jesus came to teach us. To move away from the Jewish law of an 'eye for an eye'."

Then pausing, he again looks at Alex and says, "Could i forgive a priest who abuses a child? No! I could not do it. Instead, I would like to kill him with these hands!" lifting his hands up to Alex. "But I'm not perfect, and maybe not ready to be with a merciful God," he continued, as he lowered his hands.

Alex pushing his luck asks, "What did you think of Bishop Degno and his bizarre murder? Was that revenge by someone for what the Church is doing, or did someone want to kill the bishop for some other reason?"

The old man was smart enough to realise that Alex was a journalist who could write something in the local press, and so guardedly replied, "Degno was the town bishop," raising his right hand well above his head, "this is a small town, and he did things he could get away with in this town," this time extending his hand sideways and motioning towards the street. "The police will eventually find who did it," he added.

"Do you think whoever killed him did so because they hated the Church? Or hated him?" Alex said, effectively repeating the same question.

"I don't know. I don't know," said the old man shrugging his shoulders and looking away, clearly not wanting to engage in that discussion.

Alex knew there was little to gain in pushing the conversation further, and so he graciously thanked the old man for the time spent in discussion and moved on.

He continued his walk down the street. After a short walk down from where the old man was, he came across a young woman sitting on a wooden packing box and leaning with her back against the street wall, next to an eatery. She was smoking a cigarette and dressed as a waitress. She was on a break from her work duties.

She wore black clothes, and her arms were somewhat elegantly tattooed with various designs. She wore earrings, not only on her ears, but also a small pretty one through her nose. Despite her plain clothes and tattoos, she was quite attractive. Dark eyes, large lips and a well-proportioned body with shapely protruding breasts, despite being fully covered by her loose clothing.

She was staring out across the street as Alex walked by and glimpsed at him as he approached acknowledging his presence, just as she blew out a vector of cigarette smoke with her head slightly tilted to avoid blowing it onto Alex.

Alex stopped in front of her, and using his standard line of engagement for the day, although this time in English, given that he thought she was young enough to speak English fluently, said "Sorry to bother you. My name is Alex and I'm a journalist and have come to Assisi to cover the coming Franciscan anniversary. I was hoping to ask some of the people in the town what this anniversary means to them, and what they think of the Church and the current Pope?"

She looked at him up and down, and then took another drag from her cigarette and again blew out smoke to the side, away from Alex. She responded in English, albeit with a strong accent, "I'm Lilliana. I do not think I can help you as I do not know much about the Church or the Pope."

"I'm surprised," replied Alex, "I was told Assisi was a very holy town and just assumed everyone, even young people, would have a view on Church matters."

"When I was a child, my mother would take me to church all the time, but after I realised it was all nonsense. I stopped going and am not interested in such bullshit," she replied.

Alex, realising she immediately reflected his own views on the subject, was interested in how she came to such a realisation.

"What made you realise it was all bullshit?" he asked.

She immediately replied in a typically Italian expressive manner, bringing her hand up to her chest with fingers coming together, cigarette still in hand, and her head coming slightly forward to almost meet her hand, "Hey, do you believe that if you want to enjoy yourself as a young person, it is a sin and that you will go to hell! This is what my mother and the priests told me, from when I was a child."

Then pausing momentarily, and continuing, "Especially, when the same priests that tell you this, do whatever they want behind everyone's back? And that you should be happy to be living poor, and to just pray for a miracle that you will be okay one day!"

"No, i agree with you. I too don't believe this," replied Alex, using a language style that he thought would better resonate with her, given her accent.

Then pausing, "What does your mother think of you now?" Alex ventured to ask.

"My mother believes i am lost and will go to hell," Lilliana said very casually. "She prays for me every day, which i tell her is a waste of time. For me, I believe you have to do whatever it takes to improve your life. I believe in business not religion. I work two jobs. A day one," she said motioning with her head towards the eatery, "and a night one," using a typical Italian expressive action raising her hands and shrugging her shoulders, but with an arresting look as she mentioned her night job.

Alex gathered what she meant from the way she looked and motioned at him regarding her night job. She was a hooker, as well as a waitress, and by her manner of expression she was happy for Alex to know this. He could immediately see that in a hooker's outfit she would be an alluring temptation.

She went on, "And one day I will marry a rich man and his money will be security for me and any children I want to have. So, all this, and plus because I do not believe in God, for my mother means I am no good and will go to hell!" motioning with her right hand in an abrupt upward movement exclaiming the point.

"You don't need to believe in God, or fear there's a hell in order to do the right thing," said Alex. "There are many good people who have no faith."

"Of course!" affirmed Lilliana, and went on, "You always need to be good to people because you never know when you need them. It's good for business too. This is so obvious to me. You do not have to believe in God to know that being good to people is good for you."

"Is that the only reason you would be polite or friendly with someone?" asked Alex inquisitively.

"Well, why else?" she replied bringing her open hands up towards her chest, shoulders shrugged and motioning as if it was a dumb question Alex asked.

She went on, "If you know you never see someone again, or that a person will never be able to help you, why do you need to be nice or waste your time. Better to spend time with someone who can help you. No?"

Alex, wanting to protest against her thesis that only self-interest warrants courtesy and friendship, but nonetheless struck by the force of her logic, replied, "But surely, even if that person could never do *anything for you, should you not care enough to be courteous or show compassion?"*

"I'm always friendly to everybody because I told you that you never really know for sure if someone can help you in some way. If I knew for sure that someone could never help me then why waste my time with them? There's no god watching if you are good to people or not; there's no god who will put you in heaven or hell if you are good or not!" she proclaimed, again opening and lifting her hands Italian style, effectively intimating to Alex why doesn't he understand her point yet.

Alex, getting somewhat frustrated that simply because she had no faith, just like him, meant that only self-interest warranted compassion towards others, retorted, "Well you are taking the time to talk to me, and you probably will never see me again but you still are courteous and interested in me. Yes?"

Lilliana again looked him up and down, but this time with an arresting look in her dark eyes. She reached up to her head scarf with both hands and untied it and allowed her black silky hair to roll down her neck, shaking her head as she did so. She then slowly reached up to her neckline and unbuttoned the first two buttons on her black shirt revealing a titillating view of her gorgeous breasts, tanned and incredibly voluptuous. She looked irresistible.

"Yes, it's true, i am interested in you," she said with a sensuous voice. And she moved closer to Alex and then reached out with her hands and slowly unbuttoned the top two buttons on Alex's shirt, and

gently touched his birthmark that was etched across his neck, now revealed by his open shirt. And then ran her finger gently down his hairy chest to his shirt button.

And, in an even more sensual voice and with that constant alluring look in her eyes, said, "Maybe we can meet at your hotel, when I finish work?"

Alex was completely flawed. His heart rate had kicked up. He could feel his heart pounding in his chest. She had, in fact, answered his lame attempt to justify the natural good of compassion, by making it very clear that she only acted out of self-interest. But even knowing that she must be the pure embodiment of self-interest, Alex was nonetheless irresistibly drawn to her. Not just to her alluring beauty but also her rational, albeit brutal, logic for which he had no real satisfactory answer.

Taken by surprise and visibly aroused, and in two minds about how to respond, but nonetheless trying to maintain a modicum of coolness, Alex responded, "Maybe not tonight, but I know where to find you," as he stepped cautiously backwards and slowly started to walk away, his eyes still on her, and his heart still pounding.

She looked at him with a wry smile knowing that he had found her very attractive and didn't know how to handle it. She then began to curl her hair and set it back into shape to put her scarf back on.

"I'm here Monday to Thursday," replied Lilliana, as she motioned with her head towards the eatery entrance, still fixing her hair.

Alex walked on, still in shock and totally mesmerised by Lilliana's beauty and shear affront at propositioning him.

He continued his sojourn through the local area he was in, where very soon, he would meet someone who was the complete antithesis of Lilliana.

CHAPTER 9

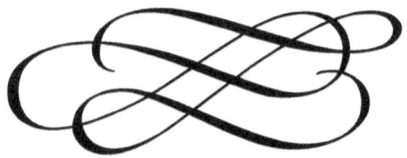

Sophia

Alex continued through the area turning now into a street where the streetscape took a turn for the worse, even poorer looking than the area he had just been through.

Here the street became narrow, with small piles of street garbage sporadically located along the way. In amongst the garbage and shanty looking entranceways to where people lived, there were some old crates and dilapidated chairs where, sporadically, people sat looking forlorn.

The odd street cat made its way slowly along the narrow street as it avoided strewn garbage and puddles of dirty water. The smell of garbage wafted across the street at times.

As he slowly walked down the street, Alex noticed a young lady, seemingly dressed as a nun or a nurse, he couldn't quite tell which. She was bending down and talking to one of the old ladies that was sitting despondently on one of the box crates along the street, with her back resting against the wall next to a shabby looking accommodation entrance.

The young lady was holding the old lady's hand and talking to her in what appeared to be a reassuring manner, although Alex was too far away to hear the conversation.

As he walked towards them, the young lady concluded her conversation and she straightened up and waved goodbye at the old lady, who in turn, raised her hand to acknowledge her.

She then walked down the street towards an old man sitting in a rusted chair some twenty meters from where the old lady was, and then crouching down to reach his eye level, she appeared to ask him how he was.

Alex assumed that she was either a nun or charitable worker checking in on the wellbeing of the street residents. He thought to approach her to get a perspective of what the local views were in respect of Church matters.

As he slowly walked towards her and the old man, he could not help noticing the contrast that existed between her young, clean clothed, sweet demeanour and the shabbily dressed pitifully sad old man she was talking to. She had what appeared to be a particular glow about her that stood out in the backdrop of a forlorn and abandoned looking street scape.

As he approached, he could hear her asking the old man about what food he had been eating, and whether he had been maintaining his consumption of fruit and vegetables. She then began asking him about his eyesight and checking whether he might have had problems with cataracts in his eyes.

Alex paused, not far from where they were speaking. He did not want to interrupt her in her work. The young lady looked up and acknowledged Alex and could see that he was patiently waiting to presumably talk to her.

She soon finished her discussions with the old man. She reached out and held both his hands and implored him to eat well, to keep up his daily prayers, and to be grateful for what he has in life, which seemed odd to Alex given that he didn't appear to have much at all. The old man thanked her by raising his hand in acknowledgment, but did not make eye contact with her, as if she was too angelic to be looked at directly by him.

The young lady then raised herself up, picked up a small straw basket she was using to carry her things, and began her slow walk along the street towards another seated person, as if she were some doctor at a hospital doing her patient rounds. Alex took the opportunity to walk towards her and engage with her at this point.

"Excuse me, gentle lady," Alex found himself addressing her, already taken by her piercing blue eyes and peaceful beauty. He spoke in English as he thought she was young enough to understand English, but he nonetheless used an Italian style phrase, 'gentle lady,' that, without thinking, he felt would be most suited to this seemingly kind young woman.

"Are you a nurse?" said Alex.

She looked at him, smiled and said sweetly with an accent, "I am a sort of a nurse, but actually a nun, or I should say, a noviciate. Let us say, a person studying to be a nun."

"My name is Alex and I'm a news journalist from Australia," Alex replied, this time not using his full standard introduction for the day.

"Australia!" she said, "You have come from such a long way away!" using the inflection in her voice to emphasise the phrase, rather than using her hands, which were wrapped around the handle of her basket, as she held it against her upstanding body.

"Well, I've come to write about the Pope's upcoming visit to Assisi to celebrate the Franciscan anniversary," said Alex, feeling immediately guilty about not also having shared with her that he was covering bishop Degno's murder.

"Yes, it is going to be such a special occasion the anniversary, and to also have the Pope visit us here in Assisi. Are people in Australia interested in such things?" she asked.

"Yes," said Alex unconvincingly, now digging even a deeper hole for himself by still not mentioning his coverage of a murder.

"May I ask what your name is? or should I call you sister?" said Alex nervously.

She laughed and said, "Oh no. I am not a sister yet. And even if I was, we can still be called by our name. My name is Sophia."

"Un bel nome!" said Alex wanting to show her that he could speak some Italian, "And what are you doing here today?"

"I live and study in the Convent of Santa Chiara of the Poor and this," motioning with her hand towards the people in the street, "is part of our compassionate service where we check on the wellbeing of the residents of the poorer areas of the town," said Sophia.

"I've heard of the Sisters of Saint Clare," said Alex, recalling what his wife Angela had told him, "But I hadn't realised they were referred to as the order of Saint Clare of the Poor. Is the reference to the 'Poor' because you look after only poor people?"

Sophia, laughing briefly again with the sweetness of an angel, replied shaking her head, "Oh no, we do not just look after the poor. But of course, they need looking after the most. We minister to anyone who the Lord sends our way, and who will accept our help."

Alex looked a little perplexed by her answer and sensing this, Sophia, whilst rearranging the way in which she held her basket, added "The reference to 'the poor' in our name is a reference to the Donation of Poverty given by the then Pope to the Order just before the death of Santa Chiara. It means that the nuns of the order, and order itself, must remain poor in the service of their duties."

Still looking perplexed, Alex asked, "But why would the nuns, or the Order I should say, wish to remain poor if they could avoid it? Would it not be easier to help people if the order had property or other sources of wealth?"

Sophia, smiling and nodding in a confident manner, replied, "Yes, people often ask this question.

It can be a difficult idea to understand if you do not truly comprehend God's message given to us through our Lord Jesus Christ, and also the examples of the blessed Saints like San Francesco and Santa Chiara."

Alex was expecting her to continue and attempt to explain this conundrum for him, but she finished her explanation at that point. As a result, he asked tentatively, "Do you think you could explain it to me in a way I could understand?"

She again smiled and said, "That would take some time, and I am afraid I have to start walking back to the convent soon if I am to be there in time for afternoon prayers."

Alex, keen to pick her brain on not just this issue but particularly regarding the attitude of the locals towards the Church and Bishop Degno, hesitantly asked her, "Would you mind if I walk with you a little as I am certainly now interested in this question, but I also wish to learn from you much more about the Franciscans and the Order of Saint Clare?"

Sophia replied, "Yes, but first I would like to see some identification that you are a reporter and who you say you are, before I feel comfortable walking with you."

Alex replied, "Of course. That is very sensible of you," and then pulled out his wallet and shared with her his official reporter ID and he also gave her his business card and drivers licence ID.

She carefully reviewed ID cards with accompanying photos, glancing briefly up at him as *she did so, then looked at him, smiled and said, "thank you," as she returned the lot back to him.*

As they walked back up the narrow street and then up along the slightly wider street that led to the forest pathway along the hill towards the Convent, Alex and Sophia covered a range of religious ideas, prompted mainly by questions from Alex.

As to the question of poverty, Alex again, at one point asked, "Could you please try to explain to me, and I openly admit I am not a religious person, why Saint Clare wished for the Order to remain poor?"

Sophia began, "The day before Santa Chiara passed away, yearly 800 years ago now, the then Pope visited her and granted her a gift she had sought for a long time, which was called 'The Donation of Poverty'. It means that not only do the sisters of Santa Chiara have to take a vow to themselves remain poor, which many orders of nuns do, but also that the Order itself must remain poor and not accumulate wealth and property. The Order must live off its daily labours and humble donations alone.

"The reason for this can be difficult for many to understand, but it revolves around the idea of trusting yourself entirely to God's will and providence. It is a fundamental act of faith to say to God, 'I give myself entirely into your hands because I trust you unreservedly and wish to be your servant and to do your will here on earth.'

"It is what the Lord Jesus Christ himself did when, in the Garden of Gethsemane, he vowed to do God's will regardless of the personal consequences to him. He

made the ultimate act of faith by putting his total trust in God's plan even though he could have avoided being crucified.

"It is also an example of the Incarnation of Christ as a poor and humble child into this world. Christ, before he became Jesus, was God's only Son, and through him all things were made. Yet when he chose to become a simple human by being born as Jesus, he emptied himself of all his powers and greatness and incarnated on earth as a poor and exposed human. Yes, later on he could perform miracles, but he did so because of his deep faith, just like many of the Apostles and Saints, with the help of the Holy Spirit, continued to do after he ascended back to Heaven, but not because he was the Son of God and part of the Holy Trinity.

"And so, he gave up everything he had to undertake a mission for God, his true Father; to come and become the Saviour of mankind by teaching us forgiveness and compassion, as well as showing us how to make the ultimate act of faith by sacrificing everything, including accepting a painful tortured death, in order to do God's will."

Sophia continued.

"Likewise, San Francesco, the son of a wealthy merchant, gave up everything he had in order to devote himself to a life of poverty and sacrifice in the service of God's will, which to him, was the rebuilding of God's church. He would say something like, 'Look at how God feeds the little birds of the sky when they have nothing. Do you not think God would feed and shelter you, whom he loves even more than the birds?' And so,

to live in poverty and to have faith that God will take care of you in your service of God's plan, is the purest act of faith and love that anyone can perform for God."

Alex did actually follow her logic. If you wish to demonstrate complete faith in a deity that supposedly loves you, then giving away everything and placing yourself at their service and at their mercy, even at the risk of pain and suffering, is the ultimate act of faith. What he could not understand is why on earth such a deity would require that of anyone.

And so, he asked Sophia, "Thank you for explaining all that in a way that I actually understood it. But I am puzzled why such a God requires followers to show such extraordinary faith in him. Why doesn't he, or she, let me say 'it' to make it easier, simply make itself obviously known to everyone so there's no need for people to rely on having faith in something that is invisible and unproven. If it became obvious to everyone that God existed and was good and powerful and could give people eternal happiness, everyone would be a follower and would naturally give up everything they had anyway to follow him?"

Sophia, as if she had heard this question before and was ready for it, immediately responded, "Yes, but people's hearts would not be changed! If God unveiled himself to all, then yes, everyone would see his greatness and power and might, and they would immediately drop all their preoccupation with life's distractions in order to follow him. But it would be for the wrong reason. They would follow him because they would see that they can profit from his wealth and greatness, not because they truly loved him, or had become true lovers of everything he held precious, such as compassion, respect for all, unerring kindness and generosity. They would follow him out of self-interest. People would still be the same; think the same. They would not have converted into loving, compassionate, devoted followers of the things that God himself values. They would become believers and followers, yes, but their hearts would not have been transformed into a golden heart of pure love, like that of our Lord Jesus Christ."

Alex looked at Sophia with a puzzled frown reflecting that. Although he followed her response, he had still not quite bought into the argument.

Sophia, seeing this, continued, "Look, let us say you have a very wealthy and very beautiful lady, who has inherited much land and wealth from her father, and who lives in a beautiful palace. But she is unmarried and lonely. This lady is very loving towards all people and creatures. And despite her great wealth, she recognises the transient nature of wealth and is not really interested in simply pursuing and enjoying her riches. Instead, she would very much like to find a true, loving and respectful gentleman, a kindred spirit, to share her life with. Someone who thinks like her and has her values of kindness, compassion, gentleness, generosity and help of others. Now, what could this lady do to find her kindred spirit?"

Sophia continued, "Yes, she can invite many gentlemen to her palace to meet her, and she can ask her staff to make enquires as to who would be worthy to be a suitable partner for her. But of course, everyone who saw how beautiful she was and how wealthy she was, would of course, make a case why they are best suited to be her partner, even though very few would actually be like her at all. They would all gladly give up what they had if it meant that they could live with her and enjoy her riches, No?"

Alex shrugging his shoulders and inflecting his right hand upwards in typical Italian fashion said, "Of course."

"Esattamente!" responded Sophia with a similar gesture, as she went on. "But this lady is much more clever than the people. Because, instead of showing everyone how beautiful and wealthy she is, she conceals her real situation and looks for her future companion in a hidden way; in a way that means she can find someone who has all the virtues she loves, and is not just seduced by her beauty and riches. This makes sense, No?" said Sophia imploring a response from Alex.

"Yes, it makes a lot of sense," responds Alex, "but how can she find her lover if she remains hidden from him?"

"So, for instance," continues Sophia, "she might send her servants out, in a discreet way, to look for the people that might be worthy. Or she might even walk amongst the people herself, in a disguised manner, or use other means of discrete communication with them. The right person must be one who demonstrates that he is a true kindred spirit and who comes to love and adore her before he realises how beautiful and wealthy she really is. This person must show her that he is prepared to give up everything to be with her because he loves her character and goodness and her virtues, without being enticed by her sensual attractiveness and immense riches. He must have sufficient faith to give everything up for her even without having seen her face to face."

"Yes, i understand what you say," said Alex, "but surely that would take an immense amount of faith. How could an ordinary person achieve that?"

"Yes, you are right," replied Sophia, "it is hard for an ordinary person to achieve this. Even harder for a rich person to give up everything and do this. You remember what the Lord Jesus said about, it may be easier for a camel to pass through an eye of a needle, than for a rich man to enter God's kingdom. Because the rich man has more to give up and also is more distracted by his riches. But our Lord Jesus Christ went on to say that, with God's help, anything is possible. What is impossible for us is not impossible for God! And if someone is open to God's message and is searching for him, he will receive help from the Holy Spirit to find him. We may not find him on our own, but if we search, we will be assisted. You too, Alex, can find him if you continue your search for him."

"Continue my search for him," said Alex looking somewhat puzzled, "Why do you say I am searching for him?"

Sophia stopped walking, turned towards him and looked directly at him with those beautiful blue eyes and that angelic smile of hers, and responded, "Caro

Alex, do you really think this meeting of ours today and this long discussion we have been having while we walk is coincidental? I think the Holy Spirit is already calling you, even before you came to Assisi. Perhaps, in time, you will see this too." Smiling and turning, she again started her walk back to the Convent.

Alex, although perplexed by her comment, strangely didn't do what he normally would do and immediately dismiss the notion as bullshit. He simply responded, as he continued to walk with her, "Perhaps time will tell."

Alex and Sophia continued their discussion on religious and social fabric matters as they made their way along the picturesque Assisi countryside towards the Convent. Time seemed to stand still for Alex as he was immersed in joyful conversation with someone he felt so at ease with; someone who not only physically resembled an angel, but whose aura and character emitted an angelic presence that made Alex think that this is what walking with an angel must be like, if there were such things.

Alex clearly had developed feelings for Sophia which he could not fully describe to himself, other than to know that he enjoyed very much being in her presence; in a way unlike he had ever felt with any other woman.

In all this unceasing and almost rapturous dialogue, Alex could not bring himself to taint the conversation and change the energy by raising the topic of Bishop Degno, even though that was his original interest. Finally, however, he decided that he *would breach the topic with her, but just at that point, they rounded a bend in the pathway that revealed that they were about to reach the Convent.*

CHAPTER 10

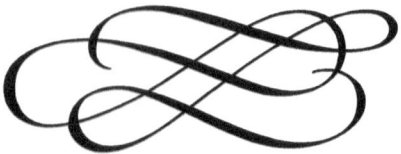

The Convent

As they approached the Convent Gate, a few local people were already walking slowly through the gate, many of them accompanied by friends or family members assisting them along the way into the Convent grounds. Alex asked Sophia why the locals were going to the convent. She responded that this evening was a healing prayer evening where everyone was welcome to come and participate in the prayer service, as well as receive a healing blessing from the Head Nun, Sister Clemenza. And that some of the people were not necessarily from the town but had come from other places.

As they walked through the gate, Alex was curious as to what was happening in the courtyard as he could see a table set up in the centre with a large crucifix at one end, and a statue of what Alex assumed was either Saint Mary or Saint Clare at the other end, and a vase of flowers in between. In front of the table was a large chair which was facing three rows of smaller chairs, upon which a few attendees and a handful of nuns where already seated, in readiness for what he assumed was to be the payer service. The rows of chairs were subdivided in two so that a corridor up the middle was kept vacant, presumably for people to walk up the middle and be greeted or blessed by the person presiding in the large chair facing the corridor.

Along the side walls of the courtyard were a series of sporadic smaller tables on which were assembled various small containers of herbs, capsules and handicrafts. These were being sold to the local public by one or two nuns presiding over each table and explaining to the attendees what each herb and capsule was for.

Alex asked Sophia what was being sold. She confirmed it was handicrafts made by the nuns' own labour, as well as herbs and compound herbal remedies, also grown and made at the convent. This Sophia said was how the nuns earned a living, along with some modest donations they received.

"Come and watch the prayer service for a while," Sophia implored Alex, "it will start soon."

"Just for a little," replied Alex, as he walked with Sophia through the Convent gate and sat with her in the back row of chairs.

As they waited for the service to start, Alex asked, "Do they sell enough herbs and handicrafts to get by?"

"They sell many herbs," replied Sophia, "they are not simple herbs, which most people can grow in their own gardens. But they are mainly unique herbs or compound herbal remedies made from ancient recipes handed down over generations. You would be very surprised what they can cure!" said Sophia with a gentle smile.

"The science world does not believe that herbal remedies have been proven to cure many illnesses, if any at all," said Alex.

Sophia replied calmly, "Well, these people do not need the world of scientists to give them proof. They see it for themselves from their own experiences, or those of their families and friends."

"That's exactly what my wife would say," said Alex smiling, "but she would say it probably a little more emphatic than the way you said it."

Sophia added, "Sometimes it is not just the herbs, but the remedy must be also accompanied by special prayers to give the remedy its healing powers."

"I've heard of healing prayers," responded Alex, "but I find that a difficult notion to believe."

Sophia looked at him a little puzzled. But before she could say anything, Alex asked somewhat tentatively, "Have the health authorities ever challenged the convent that these remedies don't perhaps really do what people pay for?"

Alex knew this was a provocative question and he expected Sophia to act defensively, but instead, she calmly replied, "Some years ago the authorities, who were themselves being paid by the drug companies, tried to stop the selling of healing herbs. Because, of course, the drug companies do not want people to be cured by buying a simple herb! Instead, they want people to buy expensive drugs."

She paused, then went on, "But then, I tell you what happened. It started with a government program to vaccinate all the recently born children against certain illnesses. Later, it was discovered that why this happened was that a big drug company had a big batch of vaccines whose use-by dates were about to expire. This company convinced the mayor of the town and the local council, probably with money, to tell everyone that a big epidemic was coming and that it was important for all babies and small children to be vaccinated. This way the drug company could sell all the vaccines before they expired. Even the mayor's grandchildren were vaccinated. After all the vaccinations were done, unfortunately, some of the children developed illnesses, including some which became permanent illnesses. And even one of the mayor's grandchildren suffered a permanent injury."

She went on, "None of the doctors would accept that the vaccinations caused the illnesses, and they said that such talk had no scientific proof. But the mayor and the parents of his grandchild were convinced that the child fell ill immediately after the vaccination that their child had. The mayor knew that Sister Clemenza was said to be a healer. In fact, he was helping the drug companies with their secret attempt, via the health authorities, to discredit the Convent and to ban the sale of healing herbs."

"Really?" said Alex, genuinely surprised.

"Yes!" continued Sophia, "but then the mayor and the child's parents came secretly to Sister Clemenza to ask if she could heal the mayor's grandchild."

"Huh!" said Alex, again surprised.

Sophia continued, "Sister Clemenza made the mayor swear on the Bible and on the life of the child, that after the healing service, if God were to heal the child, that the mayor would do everything needed to make sure that the convent could continue to sell herbs and provide healing services!"

"And that's what happened?" asked Alex, with some trepidation.

"Yes!" exclaimed quietly Sophia, "and after that no body give any more problems to the sisters to stop doing what they do. Even now that we have a new mayor, since everyone knows what really happened, no body challenges the sisters anymore."

"The child was actually healed?" Alex asked.

"Yes!" said Sophia.

"I find that so hard to believe; almost impossible to believe," said Alex.

Sophia turned to him and looked at him directly, and uncharacteristically raising her finger at him, said, "What did Jesus say? You remember from when we talk before?" then briefly pausing, she continued, "He said, 'what's impossible for man is not impossible for God' Ah!"

At that point Alex's phone buzzed and there was a text from Junior to tell him that he had lined up some people Alex could talk with tomorrow to learn more about the religious aspects of the town folk. Alex responded via text thanking him and asking him if he could now come and pick Alex up from the Convent and take him to his hotel.

Just then a nun walked out of the main convent hall and headed straight to the armchair in front of the alter table and sat down, whereupon everybody ceased talking.

"Sister Clemenza," whispered Sophia to Alex.

The nuns previously attending to the side tables along the Convent walls all took their seats and everyone in the courtyard was now seated in front of Sister Clemenza, presiding in the armchair.

Clemenza made the sign of the cross, bowed her head and in a somewhat monotonous voice, began a prayer of sorts, which the nuns, sitting in the rows of chairs in front of her along with the attendees that had come to the Convent for the event, began to follow suit.

Gradually, a few of the nuns would stand up and take one of the attendees by the hand and, still praying audibly, walk them along the middle corridor between the seats, and then individually presented them to Clemenza. They would then whisper something to Clemenza, presumably the illness that the person wanted a prayer for. Clemenza would then lay her hands on the person, and with a bowed head, give the person some form of blessing or healing prayer.

Alex did not witness any miraculous healing or anything that suggested that the prayers worked any form of remediation. Nor did he expect he would.

As the row of people lining up to experience a healing prayer gradually petered out, Sophia took Alex's hand and, standing up, she beckoned Alex to also stand up and walk with her up the isle to Clemenza. Alex was naturally stunned by this, but having this beautiful angelic lady hold his hand was itself enough to mesmerise him, and he found himself voluntarily going along with her. Moreover, he did not want to embarrass her in front of her peers by refusing her.

Sophia walked Alex up to Clemenza as the rest of the nuns continued with their droning prayers, and she then whispered to Clemenza in Italian, but loud enough to be audible for Alex to hear, "This man has been guided by the Holy Spirit to the Lord's path and seeks to know thyself."

Whereupon Clemenza nodded and lay her hands on Alex's head, bowed and prayed something inaudible. Once finished, Sophia began to lead Alex away, but not before Alex found himself saying, "Grazie," to Clemenza.

Sophia guided Alex away from the prayer group and then said to him, "Hopefully, this prayer will help you in your quest for knowledge."

Alex replied, "Thank you for your thoughts and efforts, but I think I already know who I am."

Sophia smiled in a way indicating that somehow, she knew something he didn't, and replied, "Perhaps you will learn a little more about yourself during your time in Assisi."

With that, she pulled out of her basket a small olive branch and gave it to Alex, "This has been blessed." She then looked over to the nuns in the congregation and turned back to Alex and declared, "I must go now. If you have any more questions of me, you can find me here. Goodbye."

And with that, Sophia rejoined the prayer group in earnest.

As if right on cue, Junior appeared at the Convent gate, ready to take Alex to his hotel.

CHAPTER 11

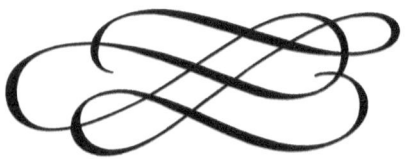

The Dream

That evening Alex returned to his hotel and after a light dinner in the hotel eatery, retired to bed.

Junior had arranged for him to meet a group of religious people from an interfaith organisation based in Assisi, to understand better the religious milieu in the town. This was organised for tomorrow at one of the local cafes.

Alex was looking forward to the meeting tomorrow but was still somewhat mesmerised by his encounter with Sophia.

He lay on his bed facing upward with the small olive branch Sophia gave him placed on his chest, reminiscing of the day's events and especially of his time with her.

He then fell asleep and experienced a profound dream, the likes of which he had never encountered before.

He was riding hard with five others on horseback across a dry dusty landscape, which instinctively, he knew was outback Australia. It was hot, sun beating down and the horses in front of him kicked up clouds of dust that he had to ride through.

The heat and dust and noise of the thundering horses' hoofs, along with the yelling of the riders as they made their way through the dry desolate landscape, made for a surreal scene. He knew not where they were headed, nor why.

He could see that the riders in front of him were armed with guns, swords or machetes. He too had a machete and knife on his belt.

As they came over a small incline, he could see some tents and bark huts and, not far from them, a group of Aborigines who looked terrified at both the sight and the thundering sound of the horsemen approaching.

As they rode towards the camp, it became obvious that the group of aborigines comprised mainly of women, children and old men. The younger men must have been away from the camp. He could see the look of terror on them as they instinctively ran towards what appeared to be the main tent in the camp, screaming and calling out to its inhabitants for help.

The closer the riders got to the group, the louder the riders yelled, as they drew their swords and machetes and waived them above their heads.

From the group of aborigines now running in terror and chaos towards the main tent, two young boys peeled away from them and ran down an incline towards what appeared to be a riverbed.

The rider next to Alex pointed to them with his machete and yelled to Alex to go after them. Alex immediately peeled his horse away from the riding group and pursued the boys down the riverbed. His horse navigated swiftly the incline down the riverbed, and he quickly reached the boys, who were desperately scurrying along the incline towards the river. Alex used his horse to cut them off their route to the river, and the boys both fell to the ground panting and terrorised at the horse and rider now towering over them and staring them down.

In the dream, Alex, as a protagonist in the dream, dismounted his horse and unsheathed his machete as he approached the boys. However, Alex as the dreamer, as observer of himself in the dream, was now physically anxious and started to sweat nervously in his bed as he watched in horror and trepidation at what he saw himself doing. Surely, he was not going to harm these boys!

Alex the rider, dismounted from his horse and walked up to the first boy. Waiving his machete he then punched the boy in the face with the handle grip, sending the boy reeling to the ground. He then advanced on him, first kicking him and then, in a motion preparing to swipe the boy's neck clean off his head with his machete, hesitated and held back at the last moment.

He paused, looked away briefly, then turned to the boy and yelled, "Fuck Off!", "Fuck Off out of here now!" as he kicked him once more.

The boy picked himself up, holding his bruised face with one hand, and scurried down the incline towards the river.

Alex then turned to the other boy. As he moved closer towards him, he realised it was a young girl not a boy. She was young enough to look like a young Aboriginal boy, even though she was topless. She was sprawled on the ground holding her hand in front of her forehead blocking the sun, as she looked up at him in horror, with her piercing blue eyes. Alex yelled at her, "You too! Fuck off out of here now!"

She had watched where the boy had run to, and still traumatised, scurried off in that direction.

Still in the dream, Alex knew he would need to lie to his comrades in arms and say that the children got away by hiding from him. Otherwise, he risked being ostracised from the group of riders to the point that they may even kill him if they thought he opted out of the agreement they had made in planning the attack and massacre.

It's possible that Alex had done some terrible things with this group in the past, and that they expected him to slaughter those two kids. But on this occasion, he could not bring himself to do it.

With that realisation still live in his head, Alex awoke from the dream in a state of panic. Sweat poured down his face. His whole body was wet with sweat. His heart still beating frantically.

This nightmarish dream would remain imprinted in Alex's memory for the rest of his life.

CHAPTER 12

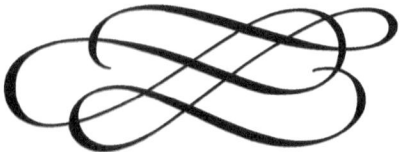

The Cafe Dialogue

Junior arranged for Alex to meet with a handful of religious believers who were in Assisi to participate in an Interfaith Conference to coincide with the upcoming Papal visit.

Junior thought it would be a good way for Alex to understand the sentiments of other faith believers towards the current Pope, and so the propensity for a possible attack on the Pope from non-Christian sources.

Alex thought it would probably be a waste of time in this regard, but he always had a personal interest in understanding how it could be possible for divergent religions to come together and find common ground in interfaith gatherings. And this was a fortuitous way for him to be able to put his long-held questions on the issue to a unique audience.

Even though he himself had no spiritual beliefs, he had done enough journalism over the years, especially in his early days before he became a specialist criminal journalist, to pick up on the nuances of the various Faiths. And so he was versed enough in the issues of the key religions to carry an intelligent conversation. Little did Alex know how helpful the meeting would ultimately prove to be in helping him with his news story.

So, the day following Alex's harrowing nightmare, and with no time in which to process that hellish dream, Junior dropped Alex off at a little cafe in the tourist part of the town and told him to wait at a reserved table, table 11. Not long afterwards, a small group entered the Cafe and, as pre-arranged with Junior, asked to be taken to table 11 to join Alex.

They all knew from Junior that Alex was a reporter from Sydney and was in Assisi to cover the upcoming Papal visit. However, Junior had not mentioned Alex's keen interest in Degno's murder, or that Alex was a specialist crime reporter.

The group had just completed a day of interfaith discussions, prayers and meditation and they were more than happy to spend a little time with a foreign reporter interested in their upcoming Interfaith audience with the Pope, before planning to head off to dinner.

The group comprised the following:
Two people of Islamic faith, Ali and Sandra
One person of Bahai faith, Farshid
Two Christians, AJ and Sanita
One person of Jewish faith, Aaron
One Hindu, Jamilla, and
One Buddhist, Bakti.

After pleasantries, and tea and coffee had been served, the discussion proceeded as follows.

Alex:

"So, tell me then, how does a group of such diverse religious backgrounds find sufficient common ground to come together and dialogue and pray together? Don't you all believe in different religious stories and deities?"

Ali:

"Yes, it's true that we have different stories and Deities, but at the core of our respective faiths we all believe that people should love and respect each other and treat one another as they themselves would like to be treated."

Alex:

"I also believe that people should love and respect each other just as you say, but I'm not religious. Do I need to have a religion to ultimately end up in heaven or reach nirvana, or is respect for humanity enough?"

Sanita:

"We believe that there is a God, or a Force for Good, that oversees us all. And that ultimately, our faith in this Deity will be our salvation. And for this you will need to have faith in a religion, being a spiritual set of beliefs, and to practice it."

Farshid:

"As a Baha'i, i certainly believe that all the key religions, Christianity, Islam, Hinduism, in fact, all the religions represented around this table, come from one original source, one God. It therefore should not matter which religion you follow as God's kingdom has many doors to it. But yes, you must have faith in a deity."

Alex:

"But if I need to believe in a God or Deity, which one should I choose? I'm not even sure if Buddhists have a God, as I recall. But regardless, can I choose anyone?

"As I understand monotheistic religions, they believe in ONE God and so to worship another God is idolatry. Yes, perhaps Jews and Muslims believe in only one and the same God, being the God of Abraham. But Christians also believe in Jesus as being God, along with the Holy Spirit, as part of a Trinity. I think Hindus believe in Brahman as the main God, but they also have Vishnu, Shiva and many other Gods. Surely, I can't just choose any of these and simultaneously do justice to monotheism?

"That's why I ask, how is it possible for a group like you to come together and pray to different Gods when you must know that the others are praying to a different, and presumably, the wrong God? Either that, or you are not truthful to yourselves when you proclaim that your faith says that there is only one God, and the others must therefore be false ones?

"So, how can you reconcile all the key religions when there is contradiction in Who is God, ie just the Father or also the Son and Holy Spirit? And how many Gods there are? Only the Abrahamic God, or also the Hindu Brahman, Vishnu, Shiva, or the Buddhist notion of God, whatever that may be?

"Moreover, as I understand it, some religions believe in reincarnation after death and others vehemently oppose it. How can these divergent positions be both true and yet come from the same source? Surely, your faiths can't demand that you abandon logic and accept obvious contradictions? Or can they?"

The group collectively pauses and is frankly intellectually affronted by Alex's logical arguments.

After a moment, AJ resumes the dialogue.

AJ:

"Alex, what you say is very true, in that, if you believe everything that the traditional religious faiths tell everyone, there are definitely contradictions. Namely, as you say, Baha'is excepted perhaps, each religion tells their followers that their deity is the True One! and so must be the only way to salvation."

Alex:

"Yes. That's my understanding of the situation."

AJ:

"And so Alex, you have very correctly pointed out a major apparent contradiction in interfaith religious matters. For example, the Christian Church tells you that Jesus is 'The Way and the Truth and the Life", and that no one can go the Father except through him. Well, then how is it possible for a Muslim, or Hindu, or Buddhist, who does not accept Jesus as God, or certainly not as the only way to salvation, to be saved?"

Alex:

"Precisely my point."

AJ:

"And yes, even the Baha'i faith has difficulties in intellectually explaining contradictions in religious beliefs such as Reincarnation in Hinduism and Buddhism, when Reincarnation is strenuously denied by other faiths; or how can they explain the Christian Trinity 'three person/one substance' God versus true Monotheism; or the Buddhist notion of 'No Self' and its aim for Nirvana as ultimate salvation, versus the concept of salvation in the form of resurrected people ultimately living in a Paradise, as espoused by other religions?

"How is it that such contradictions can intellectually be allowed to exist? Without being able to explain these contradictions in some rational way, you are correct in suggesting that, not only is the interfaith notion of religious belief potentially bankrupted, but indeed each individual religion is also undermined by the force of so many opposing Faiths.

"Today, many people see so many diametrically opposing religious beliefs, such as the ones we've touched on and they, not unreasonably, conclude that religious beliefs must therefore be totally subjective, and therefore devoid of ultimate objective truth; especially, in a world that increasingly demands scientifically explainable beliefs and has shed its reliance on superstition and incomprehensible mysteries."

Alex:

"Well said AJ. Well then how do you avoid or rationalise such contradictions, or do you?"

AJ:

"Ha! That is a complex matter and not easily explained with brevity. Moreover, I'm not sure that

93

you or my colleagues and friends would have the time now to cover this topic. Or even that we as a group would agree on things."

Alex:

"Well, AJ you certainly have my time and attention and I'm sure your friends would also like to hear your thoughts.

"Don't you all?" asked Alex turning to the other members of the group.

Collectively, the remainder of the group, by either nodding or mumbling approvingly, all indicated their willingness to hear more.

AJ:

"Very well then," said AJ as he sat forward, with elbows on the table, readying himself for what appeared to be a long story to come.

"There are two key fundamental contradictions in interfaith matters which must ultimately be rationalised. The first is, who is God? And so, do we really all worship the same ultimate supreme being?

"And the second is, what happens to us when we die?

"Indeed Alex, you have insightfully touched on both.

"Regarding who is God, my belief is that, consistent with the view of the Baha'is, even though I am a Christian, I believe there is one God, and only one, which we Christians call, 'Father' in the Abrahamic sense. Muslims call him Allah, and Jews Yahweh or Jehovah, and he is the ultimate source of all the key religions.

"But unlike Jews, Muslims and Baha'is, i also believe Jesus was the incarnation of The Christ; Christ being a mighty Angel or divine figure, (Saint Paul-Galatians 4:14, Philippians 2:6-11) who along with a similar power, called the Holy Spirit or Divine Sophia, helped to create our universe. But importantly, contrary to popular Christianity, neither of these two quasi-divine beings are, in my view, equivalent to God, as in the sense of being part of a Holy Trinitarian single-minded God.

"This Trinitarian notion, where all three, Father, Jesus/Christ and Holy Spirit, form one single-minded "God" is a dogmatic view initiated by the Roman Catholic Church, and ultimately accepted as doctrine at the Council of Nicaea in 325AD. As a result, views such as mine, even though supported by incredibly intellectually minded Church Fathers such as Origen from Alexandria and his mentor Saint Clement, both pre 325AD, were thereafter forcibly eradicated from Roman Catholic theology.

"And so, for me there is no contradiction between the monotheism of Islam or Judaism and the Christian Deity, since for me, contrary to popular Christianity, Jesus the man was not God.

"If you read the Christian Gospels carefully and in context, Jesus never refers to himself as God, and never asks anyone to worship him, despite what some Christians theologians often tell you to the contrary. In fact, he constantly draws a distinction between himself and the Father, as the 'One who sent me'.

"As for commands, he tells us only to love the Father, and to love our fellow humans, akin to all the other Faiths. And consistent with these commands, and similar to the other Faiths, to overcome and detach ourselves from the temptations of the world, and to place our total faith and hope in God by seeking to do his Will.

"Despite the fact that neither Jesus, nor the pre-incarnate Christ, are in my view God as such, Christ is nonetheless a mighty spiritual force, like a sort of mighty Angel who emanates from God. And I believe that Christ, along with the Divine Sophia, have created the world we live in; and importantly, continue to administer and maintain it.

"Because of this, then Yes, of course, for any of us to overcome the world and be ultimately saved, we need to follow the rules set by Christ, which are consistent with what we have already said; namely, first, Love the Supreme Being, whatever your Faith calls him, Father, Allah, Yahweh etc; and second, Love your Neighbour, being another way of saying, Love all of Humanity.

"And so because we all seek to follow these two rules to reach our respective faith's version of Salvation; and follow them in a world created and maintained by this High Divine Power known as The Christ, but always at the behest of his Father, the Ultimate God, then in this sense, Christ actually is, 'The Way, the Truth and the Life'.

"But we certainly do not need to worship him, or his incarnated avatar in the form of Jesus of Nazareth, or even know of him. A Muslim Bedouin, never having *heard of Jesus or Christ, can nonetheless be saved by following these rules.*

"It does not matter which religion encourages you to follow the rules, the point is that the two targets of their Love, first the Supreme Being, and second, Humanity itself, are the same. Once this is recognized, the earlier contradiction of Who should i follow or worship, evaporates. They are simply different names for the same Ultimate Supreme Power.

"In other words, remove the Church dogma that Jesus is also God the Father, and you'll find that the religions of Judaism, Islam and Christianity do, in fact, worship the same and only God."

Alex:

"Well, what about Hinduism and Buddhism. How do you rationalize those? The former appears to have multiple Gods and the later, as I understand it, none."

Jamilla:

"In Hinduism we also have one supreme being, Brahman, who is the eternal origin and cause and foundation of all existence. He is the Ultimate. And like the Christian notion of the Christ, we also have other 'Gods'. One very important one is Vishnu, who we believe, along with his consort Lakshmi and Brahma, not to be confused with the ultimate God Brahman, created the universe. Vishnu, in a similar way to the Christian Christ, continues to preserve and protect it. He incarnates himself on earth in the form of an avatar from time to time to save humanity or uplift it, and indeed, we believe that Krishna, often assimilated to Jesus, was one such avatar.

"Of course, in Hinduism we have many so-called other 'Gods'. Millions in fact. And so in this sense, we can hardly appear to be strictly monotheistic. But each god has a purpose or special following depending on your community and your heritage. From this perspective, it is therefore not unlike other religions in having a special saint you pray to depending on your specific needs, or even a saint for the town you grew up in. Christianity especially, has many saints who people pray to for all sorts of things for which that particular saint is renowned for. But in Hinduism, even though we may worship different 'Gods' we recognize the supremacy of the Ultimate God, Brahman."

AJ:

"The essence of Buddhism and Hinduism is detachment from worldly desires and devotion to a state of bodily purity, which then becomes the way to salvation. This is no different to Islam. The essence of Islam is refrain from worldly pleasures as symbolised by the fasting period of Ramadan. And in turn, one must submit not to worldly desires or concerns, but only to God's Will. Indeed, submission to God's Will is what the word Islam means, does it not, Ali? Sandra?"

Sandra:

"Yes indeed, 'submitting to the Will of God' is its meaning.

"Our faith requires us to pray regularly to Allah, five times a day in fact, so that we are never forgetful of him; to acknowledge him as the only God; to give to the poor; to visit Mecca once in our lifetime; and most importantly, symbolized by the ritual of Ramadan, to place Allah ahead of all worldly desires by submitting or surrendering our earthly existence to whatever is his Will for us.

"In this sense, it is very consistent with the Hindu and Buddhist notion of detachment from all worldly desires and fears.

"The Quran also talks about a 'Tempter', not dissimilar to the Christian notion of the Devil, or the Buddhist version of Mara, that will challenge and test us during our time here on earth, to see who will ultimately be fit to be with Allah in Paradise.

"It is by surrendering yourself totally to Allah that you can be truly free of distractions or fears that cause you suffering in pursuit of superficial and temporary earthly pleasures. This pursuit of earthly pleasures is the exact opposite of seeking the most rewarding earthly prize of all; namely, becoming a servant of Allah by doing whatever he guides you towards; that is, by doing his Will."

Alex:

"But how are you to know Allah's Will? Does he tell you what he wants you to do?"

Ali:

"Yes. If you truly seek his guidance, or genuinely yearn for meaning or purpose to your life, he will find a way of showing you your life path. Undertaking your life path involves using whatever gifts you have been given. But do not expect this to be an easy ride. You may be 'shaken' into submission, and it is only after you have achieved it, that you may realize that many of your life dramas and sufferings were aimed at you 'awakening' to his message. And I have yet to meet one such person who regrets having gone the journey, regardless of how tough that journey may have been. Of course, the journey is likely to be a life-long one, that may continue even to your death bed."

AJ:

"Jesus himself was the perfect exemplar of someone who did God's Will. For example, when he prayed on the Mount of Olives, just before his arrest and eventual crucifixion, after having long before been tempted by the Devil in the Desert to abandon his allegiance to God, he affirmed his commitment to do God's Will by saying,

'My Father, if it is possible, let this cup pass from Me; nevertheless, not as I will, but as You will.'(Matthew 26:39)

"Clearly, God had a life plan for Jesus, and it involved not only his preaching, but more importantly, in the end, also his willingness to subject himself to intense suffering and death. The incarnated Christ led from the front. He did himself what he and God are asking all of us to do, namely, to forsake the distractions and temptations of the world and surrender ourselves to God's Will. His incarnation and path to a crucified death was God's Will for him. This is why his voluntary crucifixion and death were crucial.

"If he, as Christ, the Mighty Angel, the sustainer of the universe, could not in an incarnate form as Jesus, pass the test he himself requires of all of us, then there would be no hope for Mankind. His Resurrection was therefore God's sign to all of Humanity of the success of Jesus's mission to save us all.

"This is why the Resurrection is so important. Had he succumbed to temptation and strayed from the path of doing God's Will and failed, we would have no hope. Of course, fortunately, we do not all have to face a test as tough as that involving voluntary death by torture and crucifixion, or other extreme means, although many martyrs have.

"Another incredibly relevant example for us, being here in Assisi, is naturally Saint Francis, who gave away his wealthy inheritance to pursue a humble life devoted to rebuilding God's Church, and not just in a literal sense. As also did Saint Clare."

Bakti:

"Buddha is a further example of someone who gave up his rich inheritance and his family to seek the road to perfection."

AJ:

"These essential beliefs are all capable of rationalisation once you understand the true underlying nature of each religion, and as a result realize the importance that each Faith places on the devotion and submission to one Supreme Being; even though they may, for various reasons, also pray to and worship other lesser divinities.

"There is only one ultimate consciousness or supreme power. The same one that asks us to resist temptations, desires and fears, and to trust wholly in it."

Everyone around the table nodded approvingly, even Bakti the Buddhist, somewhat to Alex's surprise.

Alex:

"Bakti, I see you nodding in agreement, but I thought Buddhism does not believe in an ultimate God?"

Bakti:

"Buddhism is not atheistic, as the term is ordinarily understood. It has certainly a God, the highest reality and truth, through which, and in which, this universe exists. However, the followers of Buddhism usually avoid the term God, for it savors so much of Christianity.

"To define more exactly the Buddhist notion of the highest being, it may be convenient to borrow the term coined by a modern German scholar, 'panentheism', according to which God is all, and one, and more than the totality of existence.

"As I mentioned, Buddhists do not make use of the term God, which characteristically belongs to Christian terminology. However, an equivalent most commonly used is 'Dharmakaya'. And when 'Dharmakaya' is most concretely conceived, it becomes the 'Buddha', or 'Tathagata'."

AJ:

"Alex, in respect of the second question, what happens to us when we die? Here again there are apparent irreconcilable contradictions. For instance,

Hindus and Buddhists believe in reincarnation whilst Jews, Christians and Muslims do not.

"Moreover, there are also differences between what the three latter Abrahamic religions believe theologically, that is, from Holy Scripture, compared to what is often believed colloquially or by the general masses. For instance, most Christians believe that when you die, you immediately are judged and are allocated to either, a permanent heaven or hell. Of course, every Christian theologian knows that the Bible does not teach this, but instead teaches that at the End of Days, on Judgement Day, all souls will be reconciled with their bodies via a general Resurrection, and the reunited resurrected body and soul will then, and only then, be judged to go to heaven or hell.

"And of course, there is also much debate about where does the person's soul reside in the meantime before Judgement Day?

"So all these differences make it difficult on the surface to come to a consistent view among the various Faiths, such that one can have any confidence that these religious groups should be respected enough to be believed on matters of life and death. Indeed, the difference between the Christian general view of immediately going to heaven or hell, or alternatively, waiting until Judgment Day for a Resurrection in order to do so, is so different to the view of the eastern religious notion of Reincarnation, that it naturally leads you to think that one view must be clearly wrong?"

Alex:

"Absolutely. Or perhaps that both views might be wrong!"

AJ:

"Correct. Because since the various religions themselves dramatically diverge on this, what possible confidence can one individual have, even if he or she were a spiritual person, that any view is correct; especially when there is no apparent scientific proof for either view?"

Alex:

"I guess that was my original point. Not only is there no scientific proof for an afterlife, but even the major Faiths can't agree on the nature of such an afterlife. So why should anyone therefore place their trust in any of your Faiths?"

AJ:

"If this were so, I would whole heartedly agree with you Alex. In such circumstances, backing one view over another is like gambling on a horse race; only actually worse, because both views could be losers!"

Alex:

"Well said AJ. But I have a feeling you're about to try to convince me otherwise. Is that so?"

AJ:

"Well, consider this. If it were possible to reconcile the apparent divergent views of the various Faiths into one coherent synthesis, then despite the lack of apparent scientific proof, and we can debate this point about proof separately, since with the progress of Quantum Physics science is starting to pay more attention to the Facts, and starting to realize that the world is much more complex and mysterious than previously thought. But leaving this aside, if it were possible to reconcile the apparent divergent views of the six various Faiths we have around this table into one coherent synthesis as to what happens to us after we die, would it not give you greater confidence that a belief in an afterlife was indeed possible?"

Alex:

"Yes, I think it would, but how can you do that given that the divergent views on this topic are poles apart?

"Some faiths say you come back reincarnated, and other faiths say you go to a permanent heaven or hell!"

AJ:

"They are only poles apart if you fail to pay true attention to the actual words of the Holy Scriptures. Take for instance the Jewish Bible, or what the Christians essentially refer to as the Old Testament. Whilst it talks about a final Judgement Day, it is silent on what happens to your soul in the intermediary period after death and before Judgement Day. The same applies to the Christian New Testament writings which also talk of a final Judgement Day, on the return of Christ to judge the living and the dead, but say nothing about where your soul resides in the interim.

"Those that follow the Judaic Kabbalah are firmly of the view that the Jewish Scripture can be interpreted as supportive of reincarnation. Reincarnation is, in fact, a key plank of the Jewish Kabbalah. Would you not agree Aaron?"

Aaron:

"Yes, what you say is true. Not all Rabbis would agree, but it is fair to say that over many centuries now, a number of very respected Rabbis believe it is the case that one life alone is not long enough for any one person to perfect himself, or herself, in the ways of all of the 600 plus commands of the Mitzvoth, not just the 10 commandments of the Torah. And so, God gives us multiple attempts, via multiple lives, to achieve this."

Sanita:

"I am an Indian Christian and being Indian, I am very familiar with the notion of reincarnation as it pervades our society. And people over many years, millennia in fact, have had a multitude of experiences to help them validate its truthfulness. We do not need to wait for such to be scientifically proven to accept it. And I am also a scientist and I like to see the proof of things too. But the long, long history of reincarnation in our society is littered with practical evidence of its proof, that people would think you are mad if you asked them for the scientific proof. The problem is that western scientists don't want to believe all the facts, but just those that meet some scientific definition of analysis such as, double blind placebo-controlled trials, for instance.

"Although I must say that thankfully, modern research undertaken at the University of Virginia in the US, under the initial direction of Professor Ian Stevenson and subsequently Dr Jim Tucker, is now showing Western society clear scientific proof of the notion of reincarnation."

Alex:

"Really?"

Sanita:

"Yes. You are a journalist. Go, please, and research this for yourself!

"The problem for me was not proof of reincarnation, as this was obvious to me. My initial problem was that the Catholic Church denies such a concept and says it is against the teaching of Jesus. But given my inquisitive mind as a scientist, I wanted to see for myself the evidence in the New Testament that they use to support this. And when I looked carefully at the Holy Scripture myself, I found no such evidence! In fact, there are passages in the Gospels that can easily be read as supporting the notion.

"And as I researched further, I discovered as Alex mentioned, that before Christianity become a state sponsored religion around the time of the Nicaean Council of 325AD; that is, in the early days of Christianity when scholars and theologians could write freely about their faith without fear of inquisition or retribution from the Church, the Alexandrian church fathers such as Origen and Clement, actually believed that reincarnation could easily be incorporated into Christian Theology. As also did the Christian Gnostics incidentally, basically for the same reason Aaron mentioned. Therefore since there is no definitive Bible reference to what happens in the interim period between death and resurrection; there is no scriptural reason why souls cannot have multiple lives in order to learn the many many lessons needed to perfect oneself in order to be saved."

AJ:

"Indeed, the Church invented the notion of 'purgatory' in the 12 th century to try to fill the void between death and the final Judgement Day resurrection, but there is no Holy Scripture reference to Purgatory whatsoever. This, and what Sanita said about the notion of reincarnation being supportable by Holy Scripture, shows that the so-called 'Administrators' of the Faiths, in this case the Church theologians, often fail to support their dogmas by reference to the actual words of the Holy Scripture.

"The Church for many years did not want people to read, and certainly not to read the Bible, for fear that people might come to a different view of Church teachings if they could consult directly the original source text. Of course, this is one of the main reasons the Protestant Church broke away from the Catholic Church. And it is no coincidence that it happened after Protestants started to use the printing press to print bibles in mass production so that people could read it for themselves.

"There have been a number of breakaway Christian groups over the years, starting with the Gnostics and much later, the Cathars, who were persecuted by the mainstream Catholic Church because, amongst other things, they firmly believed in reincarnation, and saw nothing contradictory in the words of the Christian scriptures."

Sanita:

"Yes, I can tell you for sure that there's nothing in the Bible that denies reincarnation. To the contrary,

the stories told about God loving Jacob before he was born, or about the Apostles asking Jesus about whether a blind man had sinned before birth, or about whether John the Baptist was, in fact, Elijah returned, all actually support the notion of reincarnation.

"Moreover, if Jesus thought it was a false belief like the Church tells us today, then do you not think he would have said so? Especially, as it is referred to in various conversations with him in the Gospels as I mentioned earlier. He, of course, was familiar with the teachings of eastern religions and the notion of reincarnation was well known in the Eastern parts of the Roman Empire. Moreover, the Jewish Pharisees, who challenged Jesus continuously were firm believers in reincarnation. If this was so wrong a belief and contradictory to Jesus's teachings, don't you think he would have said something about it?

"To me, it is a nonsense to deny the fact of reincarnation, especially when it is not in conflict with what Jesus has said or asked us to do."

Alex:

"Sanita i can see you feel strongly about this. But on what basis do you hold your beliefs about it? Have you had a personal experience you can share with us?"

Sanita:

"For me no, although at times I wonder why I like a particular culture other than my own so much. Or why I have such affinity with a particular country, or different nationality, when there's no apparent reason. But this for me is not convincing on its own. However, over many years I have heard stories from relatives or friends, whom I fully trust, of personal experiences they have had, or heard from other trusted sources, that validate to me everything I have researched and read myself on this topic."

Alex:

Turning to Ali, Alex says,

"Well, what about Islam then? Does it contemplate reincarnation? My understanding is that it firmly believes in Resurrection and not Reincarnation. Is this correct?"

Ali:

"The Islamic followers of Sufism, who base their Faith on the Quran, have believed in reincarnation for many centuries. Even though these followers may be a minority of Muslims, they believe the Quran supports the notion of reincarnation and they often quote some of the verses from it in support."

Alex:

"But if you tell me that the Abrahamic religions could theoretically allow for Reincarnation, and those same religions still believe in a final Judgement Day when people are resurrected to be judged, then which body is Resurrected? The last one you had? or the first one? Or which?"

Sanita:

"This seems like a difficult question, but it's not. The work being done at the University of Virginia that I mentioned before, shows that there's clear evidence that reincarnated bodies have similar traits and physical features. It means that our souls, via some form of 'soul memory' can carry through various lives a collection of similar physical traits, so that, in reality, the final body we have will be a type of aggregate body which reflects our notable bodily characteristics over many lives. Of course, this body must be a form of spiritual body, not of the same materials we are made of now, since our permanent Resurrected body cannot be subjugated to the frailties of our current bodies."

AJ:

"Perhaps examples of this would be the bodies that appeared to the Apostles during the Transfiguration of Jesus, where Jesus, Moses and Elijah appeared to them all with Spiritual type bodies. Or another example is the resurrected body of Jesus, when he appeared to the Apostles and others, after rising from the dead."

Alex:

"So, what I hear you all say is that we are given many lives in order to do what? Learn lessons on how to be good people? Reach Perfection? Then hopefully be saved? Is that it?"

AJ:

"Yes. To use the world we have been given, with all its trials and challenges, to aim at Perfection.

"As Jesus said, "Be perfect, therefore, as your heavenly Father is perfect (Matthew 5:48)."

Farshid:

"Please indulge me for one minute on this point," as he reached into his back pocket and pulled out a small Bahai book of scripture and selected a particular page, and momentarily paused and closed his eyes in reverence, before opening them again to read out the following:

" 'O SON OF BOUNTY

Out of the wastes of nothingness, with the clay of My command I made thee to appear and have ordained for thy training every atom in existence and the essence of all created things'. "

Farshid then flicked over to another selected page, as if he comprehensively knew the entire book and what page every passage was on, and with the same reverence he previously showed the text, read some more:

" 'The vitality of men's belief in God is dying out in every land; nothing short of His wholesome medicine can ever restore it. The corrosion of ungodliness is eating into the vitals of human society; what else but the Elixir of His potent Revelation can cleanse and revive it? Is it within human power, O Hakím, to effect in the constituent elements of any of the minute and indivisible particles of matter so complete a transformation as to transmute it into purest gold? Perplexing and difficult as this may appear, the still greater task of converting satanic strength into heavenly power is one that We have been empowered to accomplish. The Force capable of such a transformation transcendeth the potency of the Elixir itself. The Word of God, alone, can claim the distinction of being endowed with the capacity required for so great and far-reaching a change'."

Farshid again paused and closed his eyes as he simultaneously closed the book, and then went on to say,

"You see, the satanic forces of this world, which typically lead to much human suffering, have a dedicated purpose, to trial us and train us so that, as if being forged in a furnace, our soul essence, with the fire and brimstone of both the world and its inhabitants, can learn, grow and love, to reach a level of soul vibration worthy of joining God's Kingdom."

Strangely, what Farshid just said about souls learning, growing and loving, reminded Alex of that Australian Aboriginal proverb he had read on the plaque at the top of Mount Kaputar. But he didn't want to raise this now.

Alex went on to say,

"Well, that's quite a picture you've painted Farshid."

Unperturbed, Farshid continued.

"This world we live in is our training ground; our boot camp; Satan provides the obstacle course, and the Word of God provided by the Prophets and his Messengers, along with the Holy Spirit, the Angels and even our ancestors, are our guides.

"After we have led our life in this world, as well as lives in future existences, we either reach a level of Perfection and join the Saints and Martyrs in Paradise, Nirvana, whatever we call it, or we cease to exist."

Alex:

"But can any of us ever really be perfect? Short of a perhaps a very few, like maybe Buddha or Jesus, and some other prophets or Saints, who's ever going to be perfect?

113

"Seems to me, Paradise might be a lonely place if that's the case."

Sandra:

"But Allah is The Oft-Forgiving, The Most Merciful, The Most Compassionate, and Yes, whilst he will do as he pleases, we believe he will forgive many of our transgressions, so that many of those that fall short of Perfection, may still be able to see Paradise."

Alex:

"But who will be forgiven and who will not? Has he already decided who will be saved, as I've heard some say, and so it matters not what you do in life?"

AJ:

"God may have foresight of who will be saved, since he is not bound by the forces of Time and Space, but this does not mean he has predestined you to your fate. Your destiny is primarily governed by the Freewill he has given you. For what would it serve God to ultimately be loved and worshiped by people who have no Freewill; whom he has robotically destined to love him? He aims for the highest form of love, love given voluntarily and unconditionally, not by force or preprograming.

"And so, we believe there is Justice, a Metaphysical Justice, but wherein ultimate forgiveness is nonetheless possible. So, in addition to transforming yourself by 'Awakening' or the 'Getting of Wisdom'; that is, becoming a Believer in the 'Supreme Consciousness' or God, you must also Repent and show that you have changed your attitude towards others. Then you stand a good chance of receiving the *ultimate forgiveness, despite the fact you may not have achieved the Perfection of a Jesus, or a Buddha."*

Sandra:

"Yes. What is important, most important, is for us to reach a point of 'Surrendering to his Will' and not our selfish ego, and then of course, to follow the guidance he has provided through his Prophets, which for me, in particular, is the Prophet Muhammad and the observances we have all spoken about already.

"This is not an easy road to travel, especially having to deal with the many personal situations one is challenged by. But for those that do, then forgiveness by Allah is to come."

Alex:

"But is there not some inconsistency between the various religions on this question of Forgiveness? Since whilst you say Allah may forgive those less than perfect, my understanding is that the karmic system found in Hinduism and Buddhism does not allow for forgiveness. You must repay all your debts that you have incurred. Is that not the case? And if so, how can there be such a divergence on this important point if all these key religions herald from the same point of origin?"

Jamila:

"Yes, if I may be so bold, I agree with you that there appears to be this difference between eastern and western religions which must be rationally considered before one can truly be comforted that there is a good synergy between the key religions. This is the conflict between the notion of Karma, in both Hinduism and

Buddhism, versus the notion of Forgiveness in the other Faiths.

With Karma you will 'Reap what you Sow' in that, if you act with bad intention then you generate for yourself negative Karma and this will have to be 'repaid' by suffering or some other way, in your present life or a future life. But importantly, you have the ability to diminish your negative Karma 'balance' at any time by, for example, performing good deeds and generating positive Karma. And here Forgiveness can be a critical part of this.

"For example, if someone has hurt you somehow, you can hurt them back, and this suffering by them is then an immediate repayment of their negative Karma, that they created by hurting you to start with. But your action in hurting them will create negative Karma for you! Which must of course be 'repaid' at some point by you.

"On the other hand, if you were to instead forgive them the hurt they occasioned you initially, then for you, not only do you not create negative Karma for yourself, but instead, you create positive Karma which can reduce your own balance of negative Karma that you had from your own previous misgivings. And so, Forgiveness can be part of the Karmic system."

Alex:

"Okay, I understand that, but my point is that unlike the Christian God who can forgive your original misgivings or sins, in your Karmic example you had to 'earn' your forgiveness by doing something positive; namely forgiving the other person. So, is this not very

116

different from the Christian faith where, as I understand it, you can be forgiven without having to do anything other than repent?"

AJ:

"Is it Alex?

"Put aside what you may have heard from the generally accepted notion of Christian forgiveness, where people think you can go to a priest or minister and confess your sins, and then say a few Hail Marys and your slate of sins is all wiped clean.

"That is certainly not how it works, and certainly not what the Holy Scriptures say. Again, people fail to adhere to the scriptures; they base their beliefs on what they here others say.

"In fact, we could not have it on clearer authority than from the words of Jesus himself, and in no less than the 'Our Father Prayer' which he gave us. As the Lord's Prayer says, '...And Forgive us our trespasses as we Forgive those who trespass against us...'

"And later it is said 'For if ye forgive men their trespasses, your heavenly Father will also forgive you' (Matthew 6:14).

"In other words, to be forgiven by God you must in turn forgive those who hurt you. What Metaphysical Justice is there otherwise if you could be forgiven by God from having hurt others, but are not prepared to forgive others yourself?

"And so again, by careful reading of the Holy Scriptures, there is synergy between the Faiths on this point as well."

At this point, despite not wanting to admit it to the group, Alex finds that many, if not all, of the problems of inconsistency he thought existed in the various Faiths have been well addressed by the group. Indeed, he saw a certain power of wisdom and understanding in this group, especially in AJ, that he had rarely encountered anywhere else before in addressing religious issues.

He came to realize the power of what the group was really saying; namely, that if you had all the key religions around the table telling a consistent story about the nature of God and the afterlife, then that is a powerful validation of religious beliefs. This is especially since he, and no doubt most people, view the different religions as having massive differences between them.

As a crime journalist, he knew that if all the six religions around the table were telling essentially the same story, then it would be like having six different witnesses to a crime scene telling a consistent story of what truthfully happened. That is a powerful validation of truth compared to what he had currently thought was the case of each religion telling a contrasting story of the nature of life and death.

But for some strange reason he wasn't about to admit to the group this realization he'd come to. Instead, he asked the following final question.

Alex:

"Well okay, let's assume what you say is right, can someone explain to me Why this almighty God you all talk about would bother creating us? If he is already

Perfect, why would he need us? Most of us don't even seem to care about religion these days, and many of those that say they are religious don't really practice it or believe it with any conviction. And by the nature of the conversation we have just had, it seems we are virtually all sinners and struggle to be anywhere near Perfect.

"So why would a Perfect Almighty God need a seemingly wretched bunch of humans such as us worshipping him, praying to him and paying him homage?"

Aaron:

"Well, what's the point of being All Mighty and All Powerful if you don't have anyone to benefit, or to do good towards, especially with all your might and power, and all the resources you can command? Imagine how much good you can do? Why just sit on your hands?"

Sandra:

"Yes, and what's the point of being All Loving if you have no one to love, or in turn to be loved by? If you were rich and could have children to love and be loved by, why wouldn't you want to bring such beautiful beings into the world so that they may enjoy all your riches and providence, especially if the ultimate world you have planned for them is a Paradise lacking in suffering and pain?"

This really flawed Alex. It hit a tender part of his heart, and he could not help from showing a deep emotional reaction to what had just been said, even though he tried not to.

He, of course, dearly wanted children of his own for this exact same reason. And this point was the subject of much tension in his life and in his relationship with his wife Angela.

With his eyes somewhat reddening and almost teary, he said,

"Yes, well er, that is a good reason."

He literally couldn't say anything more, and the group could clearly sense this last discussion had touched a special place in his heart.

AJ, sensing the emotion Alex has just gone through said,

"Always remember that he made us in his own Image. What we feel about Love, it's likely he does too, and much more."

Alex then thanked the group, and they exchanged the usual pleasantries before all leaving the Cafe together.

Alex never thought about religion in the same way again after that discussion.

CHAPTER 13

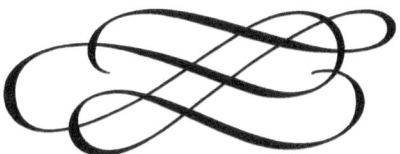

The Card Men

Alex has been filing a series of news posts from his stay in Assisi covering what is in the public domain, along with his impression of Assisi and its residents. These posts have been barley enough to placate his boss and the news editors. And Alex knows they are going to want something more interesting and uniquely newsworthy, otherwise he will no doubt get a call from Bruce telling him, in no uncertain terms, to lift his game.

Alex is expecting Junior to call him soon with the latest intel from his contacts in the police department, including whether any leads have come through from the police forensic examinations. Alex is hoping this will give the story a shot in the arm.

In the meantime, Alex decides to visit AJ and ask him about the troubling dream he has had. Alex knows AJ is somewhat of a wise sage and knows a lot about reincarnation. He is somewhat uncomfortable about approaching AJ just about his dream, so he decides to approach him and initially inquire of AJ regarding the notion of miracles, before raising the dream issue.

Alex has always had a theory that the Church concocted miracles to gain followers and create sensationalism to further its cause. So, using his interest in miracle accounts to approach AJ was not altogether deceptive, or so Alex reasoned.

Junior had told Alex that he would likely find AJ praying in, or strolling along the pathways outside of, the Church of San Damiano. So that is where Alex decided he would head to today. And it was a beautiful mild sunny day to be doing just that.

And sure enough, as Alex made his way to the Church, he found AJ sitting in a meditative cross-legged pose, next to a statue of Saint Francis in the identical pose, along the pathway up the hill towards San Damiano. Alex waited patiently by until AJ had finished meditating or praying, he wasn't sure which, before speaking to him. AJ had, even with his eyes closed in meditation, felt the presence of someone waiting close by. And so, it was not long before AJ opened his eyes, acknowledged Alex, and gradually lifted himself upright.

"Were you praying?" said Alex.

"No, actually I was meditating," responded AJ. "There is a time for prayer and there is also a time for meditation."

"Is there much of a difference?" asked Alex, giving away the fact that he probably did neither himself.

"Yes, there is," responded AJ. "In one you seek to communicate with the Lord, or someone in the heavenly world. Whereas in the other, there's no attempt at communication but rather, you try to shut out the world and transport yourself to somewhere mysterious and mystical."

The comment about transporting oneself made Alex briefly recall Harry's story regarding how Michael could astral travel. But he had not come here to talk to AJ about Aboriginal stories, and so did not mention this.

"I see that nearby here there's a statue of Saint Francis in a similar pose, like that of a Buddhist monk," said Alex. "Was he a mystic as well?"

"Of course!" responded AJ. "He was one of the best. As was Saint Clare, and in more modern times in Italy, so was Padre Pio."

"Funny that," said Alex, "I never associated anything Jesus reportedly did in the Gospels as being similar to anything a Buddhist would do."

"Well," said AJ, pausing and motioning with his hand as if there's quite a story in what he was about to say, "you know that Jesus spent many years in the East, especially Tibet, before returning to Palestine to commence his fateful ministry."

"No, I certainly didn't know that" replied Alex, surprised.

"There's been some recent scholarship on that by various authors," said AJ, "reinforcing the original 19th discovery of this by Nicolas Notovich, a Russian doctor who travelled extensively in the east, including Tibet."

Then pausing again and looking up at Alex, AJ said, "And so, we shouldn't be surprised to see meditation as part of the Christian mystical experience. Nor for that matter, as you heard yesterday at the Cafe, although stripped from Christian doctrine today, the concept of reincarnation, which is, of course, a fundamental eastern religious belief."

"Hmmm," acknowledged Alex, knowing that its precisely this subject he wanted to raise with AJ later.

However, Alex didn't want to get into that discussion now, nor entertain a discussion about mysticism, which he regarded as something best left to monks and nuns and the like. And so he decided to go straight to the topic of miracles.

"I was hoping I could pick your brain on something AJ," said Alex. "I gathered from our discussion at the Cafe that you are quite a sage on spiritual and philosophic matters, and I wondered if you could tell me a little bit about the phenomenon of Miracles, as I have an interest in the topic."

"I'd be happy to share with you my thoughts on this," responded AJ, as he walked over to Alex and put his arm over his shoulder and motioned him down the pathway.

"Perhaps we can take a short walk to my humble abode just down the road," motioning to Alex down the pathway, "and grab a coffee along the way."

"That would be great," replied Alex, as they both walked down the hill for a few kilometres towards AJ's home nearby, discussing the news and politics of the day as they went along.

A little way down the road, they came across a small piazza that was awash in tiny arts and crafts stalls and had a large makeshift sign at the entrance that translated as, "Arts Market".

AJ suggested this was a good place to grab a coffee and they walked over to the far edge of the piazza that featured a small coffee shop with a raised bar which then opened onto the piazza where people were queuing to order coffee and refreshments. The queue was long, and it meandered into the piazza proper, where people also sat at tables chatting or playing cards. AJ mentioned to Alex that although the queue was longish, the coffee would be worth the perseverance. Alex was in no rush and was happy to go by AJ's suggestion.

As they were standing in the queue, they could not avoid being captivated by an entertaining game of cards being played by a group of locals on the table alongside their queue.

Four, roughly late to middle-age men, sitting at each end of a small square table, were playing a popular Italian card game called, 'briscola'; a game which Alex recognised from his earlier experiences in Italy.

The game comprised each player being dealt three cards each at the outset, with the remaining deck being placed in the middle of the table over one solitary upturned card, which singled to the players the trump suit for the game. As each player put down a card, they would in turn pick up a new card from the middle deck to substitute for the card played.

What was particularly fascinating for AJ and Alex, was the reaction and playful antics of each player as they picked up a new card from the deck, or witnessed a card being played by their opponents. Each player was very different in this regard.

One player (Player One - Mr Theatrical) was totally dramatic in his mannerisms. As he picked up a new card from the deck, he would either vividly exhibit exuberance or, on rare occasions, tentative frustration, with accompanying facial and hand-waving features.

Sometimes, as he drew a new card, he would motion excitedly with his hand holding the card and waiving it above his head, and then he would yell out to the other players in Italian, with what sounded like a southern Italian accent, 'Ah! Now I'll fix the lot of you!' Or even more crudely, 'Ora vi fatsu u cullu tanto!' meaning something like, 'Now, I'm going to kick your arse so bad!'

Even when he appeared to draw a card that was not so exiting, he nonetheless had to exhibit some facial antic, with accompanying sound effects, suggesting that it might nonetheless be a useful card to have drawn.

Alongside him (Player Two- Mr Worry Wort) seemed to be the exact opposite. He seemed to be anguished whenever he drew a card, as well as whenever an opposing player played a card. He was constantly grimacing and frowning with every move of the game. He seemed to do so even when a good card came his way, presumably, seeing all the problems rather than the positives, that could arise with every card drawn.

The third player (Player Three - Mr Focussed) unlike the other two, exhibited little or no playing emotion, especially so for an Italian. He was totally riveted to the game, totally dispassionate and fully intent on winning. Not fearful, but neither reckless, in his attitude. It wasn't at all clear if he was really enjoying the game since he rarely smiled, or grimaced for that matter, and hardly said much at all. He appeared focussed only on winning. He seemed to have missed the fact that he was supposedly 'at play'.

Watching him, it appeared that apart from the game, there was nothing worth contemplating outside of the game itself. His world was limited to the game and to winning it; as if he'd forgotten about his real world surroundings and had become oblivious to the fact that he was amongst friends. Instead of being a sideshow, the game became his whole world.

The fourth player (Mr Easy) was again very different from the others. He quite clearly knew he was playing a game and seemed to enjoy watching the antics of the others. He was neither overexcited about drawing great cards, nor overly disappointed at losing a hand. He seemed to have an almost permanent smile on his face. He genuinely enjoyed watching the others do well, as well as laughing loudly when others despaired. Nothing much seemed to worry him. He was clearly enjoying the game and the company of the others.

As Alex and AJ watched the game and the associated antics of the players, AJ turned to Alex and said, "You know Alex, life is like playing a game of cards."

"What do mean?" replied Alex.

"Well," said AJ, "every game played is like a lifetime of experiences, with the deck representing a full range of good or bad experiences, depending on what cards you draw. Every hand or card drawn, is equivalent to a particular event or experience you encounter in your life.

"You get given a starting hand at the outset of a game, and that can be a good or bad hand, just like being born into a good or bad family. Then afterwards, although you have a greater say in how your life unfolds because you get to make choices that impact on your success or otherwise by the way you play, you are still at the mercy of the so called 'luck of the draw'. Most of the time you cannot know what event or experience will befall you. Don't you agree?"

"Well yes," responded Alex, "it is true that there will be people and circumstances that come into your life that you have little control over, and you end up having to make do as best you can with what the universe dishes out to you."

"And that's the key point isn't Alex?" AJ quickly rejoined. "You see Alex, life really is all about, as you say, 'making do as best as you can' with what the universe dishes out to you. But 'making do as best as you can', really takes a lot of skill and insight, doesn't it?"

"I guess so," replied Alex hesitantly, "but I'm not exactly sure I know what you mean."

"Well, take these four characters we are watching," responded AJ. "Just look at how each of them reacts to each card they draw, and to how the others are playing the game. The guy closest to us, let's call him Mr Theatrical, is passionate about every card he draws, and every hand played by the others. He is driven by the passions of life and is clearly self-centred. Yes, he wants to be successful in life like the others, but every twist and turn he encounters is a drama and requires a theatrical performance.

"Someone like that Alex, is likely going to be addicted to some form of passion; be it money, power, sex, alcohol, drugs, gambling. Anything to give him and keep him on a high. He will be a larger-than-life character and unless he conquers his passions, he will forever be beholden to them.

"Do you see that in him Alex?"

"Yes, I think I do" replied Alex looking intently at Mr Theatrical and nodding slowly to AJ.

AJ then started on Player Two, Mr Worrywart.

"The player next to him, looking all frowned up, now he's a real worrywart. In fact, let's call him that," said AJ as he went on.

"He is clearly driven by fear of everything that comes his way. Unlike Mr Theatrical, he will never be confident about anything in life. He will find shadows and potential demons with every circumstance that comes his way. He will likely spend his entire life worrying about everything that can go wrong and be a total energy drain for the people around him.

"You certainly would not want to have him as a friend or partner, as he would see the negative in everything, don't you think?"

"Absolutely," said Alex, "he looks like the type that would constantly look a gift horse in the mouth. You definitely would not want him as a partner as he'd drive you to depression."

"Yes," responded Alex "and without conquering his fears, he will likely wander through life in a melancholy state, joyless and bordering on paranoia.

"Moreover, his fears will generate anger in him that will consume him as he desperately tries to shun people and circumstances that frighten him.

"Whereas the person next to him, let's call him Mr Focussed, he's neither fearful nor passionate, do you see? He is clear about what he wants in life and will pursue it with maximum vigour. But unfortunately, he will not be attuned to either his or other's emotions since his focus on 'winning' in life will crowd out his emotions to the point where he too, like Mr Worrywart, will not be able to truly enjoy life, although for different reasons."

"I'm not sure I follow you AJ," said Alex, "as Mr Focussed is nothing like Mr Worrywart."

"True," said AJ, "Mr Focussed lacks the emotional fear of Worrywart, but he also lacks the emotions that would enable him to actually enjoy life, to live life to the fullest.

"You see, he is so wound up in his head, and so mentally focused on achieving his goals in life, that he has little room for feelings of any kind, including the ones that would enable him to feel truly alive. In fact, as you can see, he is so focused on the game that he's forgotten that there's another world out there; the real world involving his friends; that it's a beautiful sunny day; that he's sitting in a piazza with interesting people of all types surrounding him.

"Look at him. He hardly ever shifts his attention away from the game to observe or interact with anyone. His goals in life have consumed him so much that he is living in a bubble, separated from the real world, and therefore incapable of interacting at an emotional level with the world."

This description of Mr Focussed by AJ really threw Alex, as Alex could see that he himself was similar in character to Mr Focussed. In fact, on the rare occasions when Alex played cards with his friends, he knew that he played similar to Mr Focussed. So, Alex struggled to bring himself to agree with how AJ described Mr Focussed, as it was partially an indictment of himself.

However, deep down, Alex begrudgingly recognised that many of the character flaws AJ had depicted in Mr Focused were things that his wife Angela had said to him, in fact screamed at him, over the years.

"Now, on the other hand," continued AJ, "take the last player, Player Four. Look how relaxed he is. He is at ease with himself and life. Let's call him Mr Easy. Look at the constant smile he has on his face. He definitely knows that life is going to throw up all sorts of cards. And the key to it, as you said earlier Alex, is 'to make do as best you can'. So, no point getting overly excited or overly disappointed, with what life deals out to you.

"You see, he has no passion or desire, nor fear for that matter, of whatever comes his way. As a result, he has no anger either. He has, in fact, done something like what Jesus taught us. Namely, he has 'overcome the world' (John 16:33). He is not a prisoner to desire, fear, anger or the passions. He has detached himself from such. Indeed, he is very Buddhist in character.

"He also clearly understands that life needs to be lived 'in the moment'. And so, he is enjoying the people and circumstances around him. He is constantly observing, learning, and, as a result, growing. Moreover, he realises this. And this will stand him well in future rounds; that is, in future lives. He is completely at ease, connecting with the magnificence of the universal creation and so thankful for being alive and savouring life, with all its ups and downs.

"Indeed Alex, watching him reminds me of a verse out of the Hindu Bhagavad Gita. It goes something like this,

'One whose mind remains undisturbed amidst misery, who does not crave for pleasure, and who is free from attachment, fear, and anger, is called a sage of steady wisdom.' (Bhagavad Gita 2-56)"

"You certainly know your Sacred Scriptures AJ," said Alex, "and you're right, Mr Easy is clearly satisfied with life. Look at that permanent grin on his face."

"Yes," responded AJ, "he is the only one who realises there's a world outside the game itself; outside this mundane world of work, consumption and suffering; a separate world that one should acknowledge and understand for one to properly react to what life throws at you. Without that perspective Alex, life can appear meaningless and joyless."

Alex could relate to AJ's last comment. He reckoned he'd drawn some lousy cards in his life; having a wife that couldn't bear children and who constantly yelled and criticized him. And an employer who was profit-centric and had abandoned old fashioned journalism of the kind Alex once treasured. So being satisfied with life and having a constant smile on your face, like Mr Easy, did not come naturally for Alex.

"So, Alex, of all these characters, who do you relate to most?" asked AJ.

And just at this point, thankfully thought Alex, they reached the end of the coffee queue, and their discussion was interrupted by the cafe owner.

"Ciao AJ. How are you, and what can I get for you?" asked Claudio, the owner, in beautiful melodious Italian, as he rested his arms on the raised counter in front of the shop.

CHAPTER 14

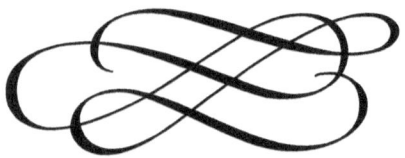

Purpose & Compassion

AJ and Alex ordered and paid for two coffees. They then stepped aside to the edge of the raised counter and stood there waiting for their coffees to arrive. Next to them, a well-dressed husband and wife couple, who had the appearance of being very wealthy, had already received their coffees and stood there chatting to Claudio's wife, Rebecca, who seemed to know them well.

It was impossible for Alex and AJ not to overhear the conversation. The well-to-do couple were telling Rebecca how they had recently found purpose in their life by undertaking a series of projects, involving property design and development for investment properties they had purchased in the country, or sometimes in foreign countries. They would then either sell the property for a handsome return or hold it for their own use when travelling.

They explained to Rebecca that this newfound creative outlet gave their life meaning, and that they very much enjoyed traveling the world to find designs, art works and furniture and fittings they could incorporate into their newly developed properties. It meant they could do things together as a couple; creative things, that according to them, also improved the world. They explained that this was as opposed to spending the rest of their lives simply living off their passive investments and taking exotic holidays, like most of their wealthy friends.

The husband then mentioned that even though they now travel a lot, he had not forgotten his beautiful hometown of Assisi. And that he regularly gave substantial sums of money to several of the local churches and their community efforts.

Rebecca sounded excited by the news of their new project and wished them well with their newfound purpose in life. The couple then wished her and Claudio well, embraced them both and bid them goodbye.

Whilst Claudio kept serving customers, Rebecca went over to greet AJ, who she seemed to know well. AJ then introduced her to Alex, whereupon Alex noted that it was hard not to overhear her conversation with the wealthy couple, and that her friends must be very lucky to have such a privileged lifestyle.

Rebecca nodded enthusiastically, and said, "Yes! How lucky are they, Uh!

"Would it not be a beautiful life to do what they can do with all their money? I wish them the best.

"But you know, Claudio and I know quite a few very rich people, and they are never really happy. They are always looking for what they can do to be more happy.

"And yet, I look at my mother and her sister, my aunt, who live together now. And together, they have not even one percent of what my rich friends have," said Rebecca waiving her hand to emphasise the point, "but they are always happy!

"They have their village friends, their church community, their grandchildren and each other's company. And whenever I visit them, they are always smiling and want for nothing."

"That's because they have found their true purpose," replied AJ. "Their God, their church community, their family and friends, and the love surrounding them, is all they need. And they have a purposeful role and contribution to make to all those around them."

"Yes, AJ," replied Rebecca, "I think you are right.

"You cannot buy happiness, uh?" using her hands to emphasise the point, and then continuing,

"Anyway, the more money you have, the more you spend. The more things you have, the more headaches you make for yourself."

At this point a dishevelled old man with no shoes reached the top of the queue where Claudio was serving. He bent forward closer to Claudio and said something to him, which was inaudible to the rest of them. Claudio then called and motioned to Rebecca, who knew exactly what to do.

She thereupon reached below the counter and grabbed a small paper bag and filled it with a couple of bread rolls, some sliced meat and cheese and went over and handed it to the old man who, nodding his head in approval, acknowledged her and headed on his way. She then returned to talk to AJ and Alex.

"You are most generous," said Alex to Rebecca.

"We try to help people like that if we can," noted Rebecca, "we cannot give big money to the Church, or other things, like my friends you just saw, but we give what we can."

"The important thing Rebecca is to give for the right reason," said AJ.

Both Rebecca and Alex looked pausingly at AJ, as if not quite understanding his point, and so AJ went on to explain it.

"You see, I think you gave something to that poor man because you felt in your heart that it was the right thing to do; the humane and compassionate thing to do. Yes?"

"Yes, of course," replied Rebecca.

"But many people, and maybe your rich friend is one, I'm not sure, give not because they feel compassion or love towards others, but because they think they should do it because it is somehow good for themselves. You know, then they can tell themselves and others that they are generous because they give. It makes them feel good; or maybe that if they do good things, they can buy their way to heaven by giving money, or even their time, to good causes.

"But of course, you cannot buy your way into heaven, just from what you do, or give. God cannot be bought, not with money nor even service.

"Instead, you should give naturally, just like you just did Rebecca. Because you feel inside yourself the love and compassion that you have for humanity. And it is having that natural love and compassion inside you, that will help you find your way to heaven. Not simply the act of giving money or service to others."

"What you say about compassion AJ is very true, and reminds me of a story my father told me that I have never forgotten," said Rebecca.

"He told me a story of what he saw when he was a little boy in his hometown, which made a big impression on him for the rest of his life.

"When he was little, his grandmother gave him money one day to go and get a haircut at the barber shop. Normally, my grandmother would cut his hair, but because they were all going to a wedding, my grandmother wanted him to look very nice, and so sent him to the barbershop this time.

"As he was seated in the shop waiting his turn for a haircut, a poor man came into the shop and asked the owner if he could get a haircut for a discount, because he didn't have much money. The owner sent him away telling him there was no discounts for anyone in his shop, and the owner then immediately joked about the incident with the others in the shop.

"But one of the older men in the shop, who was waiting for a haircut, saw what happened and ran out to talk to the poor man and brought him back into the shop. He then gave the shop owner his own money to pay for the poor man's haircut and then left the shop, but not before telling the owner, very firmly, that one day God will ask him, 'What have you done for others? What compassion have you shown to them? And why should I, meaning God, now have compassion for you, when you have shown none for others?'

"The shop owner then started to cut the man's hair. But as he cut his hair, the shop owner thought about what the older man had said, and when he finished cutting his hair, he did not charge the poor man anything. And he gave him the money that the older generous man had left with him for the haircut.

"That is a good story uh? Even if I stop just there, it is a good story uh? But there's more!" said Rebecca, motioning with her hands and then putting her right hand to her chest over her heart, as if something ominous was coming, "That same night, the shop owner died from a heart attack! Huh! You see!" said Rebecca, raising her hands and then slapping them on her thighs to emphasise the point.

"My father always remembered that story, and I'm sure it made him a more compassionate and generous man. If anyone ever asked him for something, he would always give something. Always!"

"That's a beautiful story," said AJ, "in so many ways."

"Hmmm, yes," echoed Alex.

And on that note, AJ and Alex bid their goodbyes to Rebecca and Claudio and proceeded with the remaining short walk to AJ's house.

CHAPTER 15

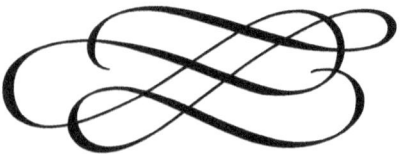

The Divine Sophia

AJ's home from the outside was very modest, unpretentious. AJ opened the front door using a keypad lock alongside the door entrance and ushered Alex inside. Alex wondered inside and was immediately taken by the sense of serenity in the home. He noticed some warm natural light flowing into the living area as he walked into it, but not so much light as to take away a sense of privacy and reclusiveness, which Alex suspected AJ relished.

AJ walked in behind Alex and turned on the lights in the living area, as the natural light alone was not sufficient. Alex could not help noticing how clean and organized everything was in the home. Everything seemed to be in its proper place, and the pictures on the wall, as well as the furnishings, were so well proportionately spaced, giving the impression that AJ must have mathematically measured out exactly where he wanted his furnishings, ornaments and carpet squares, so as to give the home a geometric vibrancy. Moreover, everything looked spotless.

AJ motioned to Alex a lounge, or alternatively, an armchair, that Alex could sit in. But Alex was immediately drawn instead to a picture AJ had on the living room wall and walked over to look at it. He was intensely fixated on it.

It was an enlarged copy of a segment of Michelangelo's painting of the Creation of Adam in the Sistine Chapel. And what particularly caught Alex's attention, especially as AJ had a small spotlight on the ceiling trained directly onto the painting, was the figure of a stunning naked young woman, sitting under the left arm of what was, no doubt, a picture semblance of God. God's other arm was extended, and its index finger pointed at Adam, almost touching Adam's similarly extended arm and index finger pointed at God.

Alex had seen this picture of Adam's creation many times before. He had visited the Sistine Chapel some years back and had also seen the creation picture in many magazines and web related advertisements.

This was an iconic picture. However, Alex like most people who see the picture, had never paid much attention to the figures surrounding the depiction of God. And he was surprised to see a picture of a beautiful looking naked young woman, or even adolescent child, next to God, made conspicuously more alluring by the segmented and enlarged nature of the print, as well as the fact that AJ's ceiling spotlight was directly focused on her.

AJ knew exactly what had attracted Alex's attention, and wandered over alongside him also to face the picture and said, "She's beautiful isn't she?"

"Yes," replied Alex, "she's stunning. I've seen this picture many times before and never noticed her."

"Hardly anyone does," replied AJ. "They focus on the main figures, but that's the magic of Michelangelo. His art has some wonderful surprises."

"Is she meant to be anyone in particular?" asked Alex.

"Some say she was meant to be Eve, Adam's future partner. And others even say she is a young Mary, mother of Jesus, which personally, I find hard to believe that Michelangelo would paint a naked Mary in that way. They also say that the figure next to her, on her left, is the Christ child, baby Jesus," replied AJ.

"Do you have a view on who she might be?" asked Alex.

"Certainly!" said AJ confidently, "and knowing a little about Michelangelo, I have no doubt about it!"

Alex, without saying anything, turned and looked at AJ in an inquisitive way, effectively asking him who she was, without saying a word.

"She is in fact, a depiction, a young depiction no doubt, of the Divine Sophia, or what is commonly known as the Holy Spirit," said AJ.

"And, to complete the picture, the child next to her is, indeed, the Christ Child, baby Jesus."

"The Holy Spirit," said Alex, somewhat puzzled. "How can you be so sure?" Alex naturally asked, not realizing that he had just triggered a passionate chord within AJ to explain something very dear to him.

"Well," said AJ, with a circular hand motion indicating that he was about to cover a lot of ground, "first, we know that Michelangelo had access to a copy of the Bible, even though the Church made it very difficult then for anyone other than priests and clergy to access one. And in the Bible, we see," as he reached out to a nearby bookshelf and picked up a Bible and slowly opened it to a specific reading (Proverbs 8:22 to 31), "that when God made the world, 'Wisdom', which is another name for the Holy Spirit, was with God at the time.

"Look Alex, it reads here," as he pointed to the specific text, "22: I, Wisdom, was with the Lord when he began his work, long before he made anything else. 23 I was created in the very beginning, even before the world began. 24 I was born before there were oceans, or springs overflowing with water, 25 before the hills were there, before the mountains were put in place. 26 God had not made the earth or fields, not even the first

143

dust of the earth. 27 I was there when God put the skies in place, when he stretched the horizon over the oceans, 28 when he made the clouds above and put the deep underground springs in place. 29 I was there when he ordered the sea not to go beyond the borders he had set. I was there when he laid the earth's foundation. 30 I was like a child by his side. I was delighted every day, enjoying his presence all the time, 31 enjoying the whole world, and delighted with all its people.'

"You see," emphasized AJ, " 'I was like a child by his side' " pointing to and emphasising to Alex the precise verse.

Alex continued, "Then of course, we have the well-known verses in Genesis where God makes Man. In there, He says, 'Let us make man,' you see, the word 'us' is used. Meaning, that God was accompanied by someone else at the time. 'Let us make man in our own image, accordingly to our likeness...' (Genesis 1:26.)

"It doesn't tell us who else was present, but it's very clear, is it not, that God is talking to someone?"

"Sounds like it to me," said Alex.

AJ goes on, "And not only this, but He is asking them for their assistance and suggesting that Man be made in 'Our' likeness, not just His.

"How then can theologians and clergy get away with ignoring the actual words of the Scripture? They come up with ridiculous excuses as to why God is talking to himself in the plural. For instance, they say that it is how 'Royalty' talks!

"Ahh! As if God would model himself on how human royals talk! It's not only ridiculous, but

144

actually very dangerous, because it shows that 'Administrators of Faiths' are constantly prepared to ignore Holy Scripture when it suits them.

"Interestingly, the Quran also talks about God being with someone else, in the plural sense, using the word 'WE', in the Islamic creation story. There it says," AJ knowing the verse by heart it seems, "WE created man from sounding clay, from mud moulded into shape." (Surah 15:26).

"Very impressive!" said Alex, referring to AJ's memory of even Quranic verses.

AJ continued, "But of course, Muslim clerics, just like the traditional Christian theologians, explain the use of the word 'We' away. Again, poorly in my view, in order to justify the Islamic dogma that Allah could not possibly have any divine-like accomplices.

"You see, everyone sidesteps the precise words of Holy Scripture when it suits them!

"Anyway, to return to your question, we also know from the Gospel of Saint John, the famous opening passage in John 1, 'In the beginning was the Word', or in the original Greek, the actual word is, 'The Logos'", AJ added, and then continued on, " 'and the Word was with God, and the Word was God. He was with God in the beginning'.

"Of course, here the Greek word Logos is referring to Christ.

"And so we can see from these biblical readings that Holy Scripture, if carefully read, tells us that both The Logos, that is Christ, and Wisdom, namely the

Divine Sophia, were with God at the beginning of creation.

"Michelangelo naturally includes them both. First, the Divine Sophia is painted as the beautiful young woman, who is 'like a child' at God's side. And alongside her, is the depiction of the Christ Child, baby Jesus. Michelangelo even gives Jesus a slight halo effect in the way he gently creates a fold of the umbrella cloak around his head," as AJ points specifically to the top of the head of the Jesus figure. Look also how different these two figures look compared to all the other less impressive angelic figures surrounding God. Do you see the obvious differences?"

"Yes, I do," said Alex.

"Another obvious reason of course," AJ continued, "is that after the Council of Nicaea in 325AD, and certainly in Michelangelo's time, the Christian God is portrayed as a Triune God; namely, Father, Son and Holy Spirit. They are supposedly three different persons but somehow, nonetheless are, of 'One Mind and Substance'. And it is therefore no coincidence that the cloaked backdrop into which Michelangelo places these three figures, looks like the anatomy of a human brain, symbolic naturally of 'One Mind'. He has ingeniously painted the Triune God, although he has allowed, secretly I believe, a question mark about whether, in fact, they are truly of One Mind, which I will come back to later.

"In addition to these reasons, there is also the strong connection to a medieval age hymn called, 'Veni Creator Spiritus', which is a prayer for the invocation of the Holy Spirit, and commences by asking for the Holy Spirit to,"

And here, AJ again, without referring to any written text, reals off from memory the following verse of the Hymn,

"'Come, Holy Ghost, Creator, come
from thy bright heav'nly throne;
come, take possession of our souls,
and make them all thine own.'"

This prayer goes back to the ninth century and is a famous Catholic Gregorian chant hymn, being in fact, the Vespers hymn for the feast of Pentecost. It was well known in the days of Michelangelo.

Then pointing to the right hand of God in the picture, AJ notes that, "if you look carefully at God's right index finger which points to Adam, this is a direct symbolic reference to the actual text of this medieval hymn, wherein the words used elsewhere in the hymn are, 'digitus paternae dexterae', or God's right index finger, which is assimilated to the Holy Spirit."

Without again referring to anything in writing, AJ recites the following relevant verse of the same hymn,

" 'Thou (referring to the Holy Spirit) who art sevenfold in thy grace,

finger of God's right hand; his promise, teaching little ones to speak and understand.'

"So, in other words Alex, effectively, Michelangelo has here," AJ motioning with his hand to the well-known segment of the picture where God's hand almost touches that of Adam's, "depicted The Father as giving Adam, by means of the graceful extension of his right arm and the precise pointing of his right hand's index finger, his faithful love via the invocation of the Holy Spirit; the same Holy Spirit he embraces lovingly under his left arm."

AJ went on to note that there has been recent modern commentary further supporting the notion that the small figure next to the naked woman is, indeed, the Christ child, baby Jesus. This view is supported by the peculiar placement of God's fingers on the child; the same fingers that a priest would use to raise the Eucharist during the Mass. Since Catholic theology holds that the Eucharist is the Body of Christ, this theological understanding would be embodied in this painting.

AJ noted that if this latter interpretation is correct, Michelangelo's Creation of Adam would be intrinsically linked to the future coming of Christ, who comes to reconcile man after the original sin of Adam.

When I asked AJ if he agreed with this view, he said, "Yes, definitely. We have already covered many other reasons why I believe the figure to her left is the Christ Child, and this recent argument is further support.

"So, when you step back and look at everything in context, you see clearly that Michelangelo is saying that first, God has created Mankind via Adam.

"Second, that God did so with both the powers of the Divine Sophia and the Christ by his side, and likely with their assistance.

"Third, that these powers, including some of the Angelic onlookers, by the look on their faces and their disposition, seem to know in advance that Adam will fail God's initial Garden of Eden test and succumb to a Fall from Grace.

"Fourth, that God will send his Son, the Christ, incarnated as Jesus, to be teacher, exemplar and saviour of mankind. And this, to show that Christ, emptied of his Christ powers and being fully human, can withstand the temptations of the Devil, Prince of this World, even to the point of self-sacrifice, in order to do God's Will. And that once this is done, then, and only then, will God commission to Humanity the Holy Spirit the specific task to finish the mission Jesus started; namely, to open the eyes of those blind to the Truth, or as the Veni Creator Spiritus Hymn says, 'to teach the little ones to speak and understand.'"

"Look closely at the expression of the Christ Child," said AJ as he motioned to Alex, inviting him to look closer at the picture. "You can see the look of concern and almost disdain, reflecting that Christ already seems to know that his own intense suffering and self-sacrifice will ultimately be needed to save Mankind, as a result of Adam's creation and subsequent failure to follow God's wishes.

"Look at the angels around the Christ Child. The look of terror in their eyes telegraph to us that they already know what pain and suffering is in store for Christ, his followers, and the world at large.

"Also let me point out something else important here. The expression on the Christ Child's face is *obviously very different to the expression on either, the figure of God, or the Divine Sophia, is it not?"*

"Yes, it is," Alex responded, not knowing where this was going.

AJ continued, "You can see that Michelangelo is therefore suggesting that, even though he painted all three figures in a symbolic shape of a brain or mind inside a cloaked canopy, that the three are not of the same Will or Mind. You can tell this from the different dispositions on each of their faces and their poses. Indeed, Christ looks as if he clearly wishes to avoid a crucifixion if he can, and as though he'd like to run away from what is in store for him. Even the Divine Sophia has her doubts about God's act of creation as she seems somewhat apprehensive; Yes?"

Alex noted, "Yes. She certainly seems apprehensive. And the Christ child looks like he'd prefer to have nothing to do with Adam."

"Precisely!" continued AJ. "And so, who really are these persons if they have a different Will from the Father? The notion of the Trinity requires that the three members of it be of the same Mind; namely, One Will, not Three.

"Moreover, are they truly divine? Or are they portrayed as merely Angels, albeit perhaps special ones? We don't know for sure. But given that for centuries people have been uncertain who these two figures are, Michelangelo perhaps wanted to portray them as no more than Angelic figures. In other words, yes, they are the Divine Sophia and the Christ Child, but they are not divine in the sense that they are gods,

or that they form part of the Triune God; since they are drawn separately from the Father, and in no way look like they are especially divine in nature. In fact, whilst they may be slightly different, they are not substantially different to the Angelic figures around them.

"Or to be blunt, is Michelangelo's actually challenging the Church's Nicaean dogma that God is a Trinity? Why not draw only the three together in the brain cloak, if he wanted to depict a Triune God? Why include in that formation other Angelic creatures? Why not give them more of a godly image if, indeed, he wanted to depict the three as a Godhead? Why make them look like they have a different Will to the Father and each other?

"We cannot discount here the fact that Michelangelo was a Neoplatonist, and so may well have subscribed to the Alexandrian notion, supported by the Church Father Origen and arguably Saint Clement, that there is in fact only one God, The Father, and the other members of the so called 'Trinity' are not part of the 'Godhead'. They are, indeed, subservient to God the Father.

"Ah!" says AJ with a swift waive of his hand in the air, "I continue to marvel at what Michelangelo could be really saying to us here Alex. Would it not be both distastefully ironic, and yet truly marvellous, if above the very Chapel where Popes are elected, Michelangelo has secretly depicted, by the way, with much praise and fanfare from the Catholic clergy for centuries, a scene refuting the Holy Trinity? It would, of course, take a genius to do something like that!

"Finally, it is worth also mentioning, that Michelangelo, later in his life, secretly became a member of a religious group, or 'cult' you could call it. Secret, because the group was looked at disapprovingly by some senior cardinals and other elements of the Church at the time. And this group, comprised of some distinguished citizens including personages such as, Signora Vittoria Colonna, a renown humanist and poetess, and who became one of Michelangelo's closest friends, along with the English Cardinal Reginald Pole who, by only one vote short, was nearly elected the successor to Pope Paul the Third.

"Now, Michelangelo would not have come across this cult group at the time he painted the Sistine Chapel ceiling, since the group is not known to have been formed for some years after the ceiling was finished. That is not to say however, that the ideas the group stood for were not around at the time Michelangelo painted the ceiling. We don't know for sure. But nonetheless, the group's philosophy is instructive perhaps as to what Michelangelo's thinking might have been at the time he painted the ceiling, given that we know for sure that Michelangelo subscribed to the views of this group later in his life.

"This religious cult," AJ continued, still enthralled in his explanation to Alex, "was very sympathetic to the idea in Calvinism that Man is saved not by doing good works, but by Faith alone in God. Supported, of course, by the saving act of Jesus's death and *resurrection. And importantly, for the purposes of our discussion, that Jesus's willingness to do God's Will; namely, to withstand Satan's temptations and to be prepared to die on the cross in total Faithfulness to God unto death, led God to elevate Jesus to such a high status, such that his mission to save Humanity would thereafter be assisted by the immense power of the Holy Spirit, or the Divine Sophia, who would continue on earth, the process that Jesus had started; that is, to Awaken and ultimately, save Humanity.*

"And so, this group believed that the Holy Spirit would gradually assist many, perhaps most, non-believers to be awakened to God's message, find Faith in God, see True reality, and be ultimately saved. All without the need for good works and in contrast to the clear dogma of the Catholic Church at the time. For this reason, the emphasis of this group was on the role of the Holy Spirit, and so they were called the 'Spirituali'."

Without pausing to give Alex a chance to say anything, AJ continued on, "The Church particularly disapproved of them, because if people generally thought that Salvation can be achieved by Faith alone, through the workings of the Holy Spirit, then people would not need the intercession of the Church and its emphasis on the need for good works, including donations to the Church, or indulgences for prayers, or all the other many ways the Church engineered to collect money from its congregations; the very things that resulted in the Lutheran induced Protestant split of the Christian Church!

153

"The fiercest opponent of the Spirituali, Cardinal Carafa, eventually became Pope and cut off Michelangelo's Vatican pension, and did many evil things to suppress the group.

"This Spirituali group, unlike the Protestants, did not wish to break from the main Church, but rather to engender reform from within. But it was targeted and attacked, and its members persecuted by the traditional elements of the clergy, just as today the blessed Pope Francis has to fight the powers within his own Church in order to reform it."

With a sense of excitement and profundity, AJ turned to Alex and with both hands motioning towards the painting, said, "Alex, do you see what we could be looking at right here? This scene, for all the reasons we have mentioned, oozes the outpouring of the Holy Spirit; the Divine Sophia, whose dedication to which the Spirituali were known for.

"You see Alex," said AJ, as he edged slightly closer to Alex and looked him straight in the eye, readying himself to say something impactful, "Michelangelo here," as he again motioned to the picture on the wall, "he is not painting the point where in the Bible God breathes life into Adam to give him Physical Life. No! He is doing more than that! He is depicting God's grant to Humanity of Eternal Life!

"God is saying to Adam, 'I have given you physical life, and I know that Temptation will cause you to Fall away from my love, and as a result you will endure great suffering. But I promise you that my Son Jesus Christ, will be your Eucharistic Saviour. And if you place your Faith in his message of my Love for you, the Holy Spirit will come and guide you to Eternal Life!'

"Alex, this is therefore a scene, not of the Creation of Humanity, but of the Salvation of Humanity! And, moreover, the Church, with all its rules and dogmas and indulgences, and its emphasis on good works, is nowhere to be seen!

"Imagine, therefore Alex, that in this iconic scene, in the very Chapel where Popes are made; in the Vatican's version of the Holy of Holies, above the very heads of all the world's Cardinals in Conclave when they elect a new Pope, Michelangelo has depicted a brilliant testament, repudiating not only the notion of a Triune God, but along with it, also a vindication of Luther's revelation that Man is saved by Faith Alone, through God's Grace given to us by the Holy Spirit! And the Church, is nowhere to be seen! Can you imagine that for a moment Alex!

"Ahh, what genius!" exclaimed AJ, thrusting his arms first upwards into the air and them immediately slapping them down onto his thighs, with a big thud that must have hurt somewhat.

CHAPTER 16

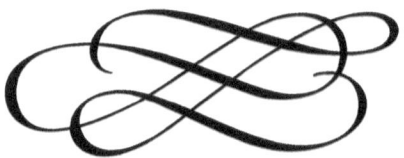

Miracles in an Illusory World

Alex was certainly impressed with AJ's logic and knowledge of the topic. And despite being hesitant about accepting religious notions, the Cafe Dialogue of a few days ago had begun to soften Alex's resistance to such notions.

AJ's explanation of the hidden messages behind Michelangelo's painting were not unbelievable. In fact, they were quite believable to Alex, as he recalled reading some time ago, about Michelangelo's growing antithesis towards the Church hierarchy during the artist's career.

Nonetheless, Alex wanted to push on with the meeting with AJ and eventually get to raise his nightmarish dream. But he had come here on the pretext of wanting to understand AJ's views on miracles, and so Alex posed to AJ the following sensitive question.

Alex:

"AJ, it seems to me that the Church has used the apparent performance of miracles to gain followers from the very start of Christianity, with Jesus, and later his Apostles, having reportedly carried out various miracles. And this led to many people converting to the Faith, having heard of such extraordinary episodes, but not actually witnessing the miracles themselves.

"I know you do not necessarily believe in all Church dogmas, and so I wanted to ask you if you believed in miracles or not?"

AJ smiled, put his arm on Alex's shoulder and motioned him with his other hand to walk a few paces towards the other side of the room, to where another picture was hanging on the wall. Alex obliged.

This picture depicted a scene of a small group of people seated on the floor in a theatre style setting inside a cave, facing the cave wall. Behind them, and not within the view of the seated people, a large fire was burning. In front of the fire, just behind the seated people, a number of other people were parading cutout forms of animals and other objects, so that the effect of the fire's glow was to project a shadow of the cutout objects onto the cave wall which the seated people were facing.

As a result, the seated people were watching a series of shadows projected onto a wall, seemingly unaware of the fact that these images were merely shadows of artificial forms, projected onto the wall by the fire's glow.

Moreover, the seated people were restrained by various chains and bonds of sorts, and so unable to stand, or otherwise move or turn around, to see what was happening behind them.

Behind where the fire was burning, there was a series of steps that led out of the cave to the outside world. Compared to the dark and colourless cave, this outside world looked as though it was an idyllic garden environment, with bright colours and beautiful sunshine.

As both Alex and AJ pondered the painting, AJ asked Alex,

AJ:

"Do you know what this picture is?"

Alex, being familiar with the writings of Plato, responded,

Alex:

"Yes, I do. In my younger days I was interested in philosophy. And of course, Plato being probably the greatest philosopher the world has seen, is well known to me.

"This is a depiction of the famous Allegory of the Cave."

AJ:

"Bravo Alex! And do you remember what it signifies?"

Alex:

"That the world is illusory in nature; that people need to free themselves of the bonds that tie them to falsehood; and that they should seek the true world outside the cave, at least from what I can recall," said Alex, scratching his head pensively.

AJ:

"Exactly, Alex! The world is illusory!

"It is a mere semblance of the true world. And people are unknowingly chained and restrained by attachments to desire for power, pride, wealth, sex and other addictions, which are, in a religious sense, like idols which we worship, and which restrain us from seeing the real world, the world in the light.

"People worship these idols instead of recognizing the true God, who lives outside the illusory cave in the real world; the true God, which Plato called, 'The Good'."

Alex:

"I'm sure this is relevant to my question about miracles," Alex said, smiling at AJ. "But exactly, how is it relevant?"

AJ:

"Well Alex, if the world is truly illusory, then performing a miracle is simply varying, ever so slightly, what is already a pretence or imitation. It is not really changing anything substantive or real into something else that's real. You are simply substituting one imitation for another. It's like having a film with multiple alternatives endings and being able to switch from projecting a version with one ending, to another

version with a different ending, even if the second version's ending is highly unexpected.

"And so Alex, if you have Faith, you may be able to change the ending of any outcome. That's why Jesus once said, 'Truly I tell you, if you have faith as small as a mustard seed, you can say to this mountain, 'Move from here to there,' and it will move. Nothing will be impossible for you'. (Matthew 17:20)

Alex:

"AJ, I can see the force of your argument that miracles are possible if the world we live in is illusory or fictitious. But I'm struggling to accept that we live in a fictitious world. I do recall that Plato thought the world was illusory, but do you think it is?"

AJ:

"Yes, I do. But so have many wise sages and prophets. Some of the great Muslim scholars thought it so too, and with good authority from the Quran."

AJ then reached back into his bookshelf and pulled from it a copy of the Quran. He turned to one of a number of tagged pages.

"For example Alex, here (Surah 3:185) 'Every soul will taste of death. And ye [mankind] will be paid on the Day of Resurrection only that which ye have fairly earned. Whoso [Muslims] is removed from the Fire and is made to enter Paradise, he [as Muslim] indeed is triumphant. The life of this world is but comfort of illusion."

And turning to another marked page, AJ noted,

"And (Surah 57:20) 'Know that the life of this world is only play, and idle talk, and pageantry, and boasting among you, and rivalry in respect of wealth and children; as the likeness of vegetation after rain, whereof the growth is pleasing to the husbandman, but afterward it drieth up and thou seest it turning yellow then it becometh straw. And in the Hereafter there is grievous punishment [infidels and sinners], and (also) forgiveness [for Muslims] from Allah and His good pleasure, whereas the life of the world is but matter of illusion'."

Alex:

"What about the Christian Scriptures AJ? You are Christian. Is there support for an illusory world there, since I've never heard of such a notion in my experience with the Church, when I was young?"

AJ:

"Good question Alex, and the answer is complex. Let me say however, that the Gospels do talk about certain secret teachings of Jesus, but it has remained a mystery as to what those teachings were. I have my own view, but no real authoritative conclusion can be drawn.

"For instance, all four Gospels talk of secret teachings along the following lines,"

As he put down the Quran and picked up the Bible, he turned to a passage he knew precisely where to find, (Matthew 13:10-15)

"10 The disciples came to him and asked, "Why do you speak to the people in parables?" 11 He replied, "Because the knowledge of the secrets of the kingdom of heaven has been given to you, but not to them. 12 Whoever has will be given more, and they will have an abundance. Whoever does not have, even what they have will be taken from them. 13 This is why I speak to them in parables:

"Though seeing, they do not see; though hearing, they do not hear or understand. 14 In them is fulfilled the prophecy of Isaiah: 'You will be ever hearing but never understanding; you will be ever seeing but never perceiving'."

AJ noted that this is evidence suggesting that Jesus had shared secret teachings with the Apostles. AJ noted that similar sayings exist in the other three Gospels (Mark 4:11-12, Luke 8:10 and John 12:40).

AJ explained that he believed Jesus had shared with his apostles that the world was, indeed, illusory, but that it is important for people to think it is real. They will be much more genuine in the way they comport themselves if they believe it is a real-life occurrence as opposed to knowing that life is purely illusory; in which case one could be tempted to disregard or ignore life events altogether.

Alex:

"In the discussions we had in the Cafe the other day, there was a general view that life is a series of training courses, like a school or course aimed at perfecting us. Is that what this illusory world is all about then?"

AJ:

"Precisely, Alex! Think about it for a moment. What is the best way we know how to teach people things? For example, how do we train people in jobs

162

where mistakes could cost them their lives, such as pilots, astronauts, firemen, police forces and soldiers?"

Alex:

"I see where this is going," said Alex reflecting on what AJ had just said.

"The best training is simulated real life training, where people practice roleplay scenarios which are meant to mimic what can happen in real life, like in a flight simulator for example."

AJ:

"Well done, Alex! Simulated practice exercises are what we, as a civilization, have discovered to be the best form of training. Now Alex, imagine that if in addition to say, putting someone in a flight simulator, you were able to make that person think that it was actually a real-life experience! How powerful would that training be!

"That is what an almighty loving Father, wanting to give his children the best education possible, can do.

"He has put us in a flight simulator, but we believe we are really flying!"

Alex fully appreciated the potency of AJ's argument. As a crime reporter, he was familiar with the intense exercise programs police forces put their people through. And he knew that the effectiveness of such training is directly correlated to how realistic the training is modelled on real life situations.

But he was far from convinced about either the illusory nature of the world, or that miracles were just a slight change to the workings of reality, if indeed, they existed at all. AJ then went on to say something that took Alex by surprise.

AJ:

"You see Alex, God wants us to undergo good and evil experiences. This explains the age old, 'problem of Evil', in that, why would a good God allow so much evil to occur in the world. Like the great Greek plays and Italian operas, you need tragedy to arouse the deep human emotions in all of us. It is only in this way that lessons can be etched out in our soul memory. And so, when people suffer and die, this is all but an illusion; all part of an operatic stage play."

Alex was digesting what AJ had just said, but before he could formulate a response, AJ continued.

"It's interesting Alex, to see that Buddhists especially have examined the subject of training oneself in the context of a personalised Life Plan. Moreover, they say much of the planning for our earthly training takes place in an afterlife world, which they refer to as 'Bardo'. They have written about this in a famous text called, 'The Tibetan Book of the Dead'.

"You see Alex, in the spirit world, you are immortal and free from hunger and pain and old age. And so it is hard to learn what it is like to lose a loved one, or to experience ailments, or a loss of wealth or power. So, unlike the earth, it is a relatively sterile learning environment.

"On the other hand, our physical world provides a rich learning environment; especially because of all the complicated interactions, both good and bad of having to experience a variety of family and other personal relationships. This is why suffering, both physical and mental, is such an important and necessary part of our world. It's critical to our learning experience."

Alex:

"I recall reading a little about the Tibetan Book of the Dead some years ago. What was its key point again?"

AJ:

"In short, the Tibetan Buddhists believe that after each life incarnation we, being spiritual entities, review each of our earthly lives and assess, along with some wise spiritual guides, what we did well, and what we did badly. We then agree on a personalized Life Plan for the next incarnation, our next roleplay. And this, effectively becomes our 'Destiny' in the next life."

Alex:

"But if we are destined to lead a certain life, how can we be judged by God for having led a bad life?"

AJ:

"Remember the discussion we had in the Cafe the other day; we always have Freewill to reject or embrace our Destiny. Or indeed, to change it for the better or worse.

"As you heard from the group the other day, our mission is to try to lead a life of continuous improvement. And as we saw from our earlier discussions just a few minutes ago, God has given us the gift of the Holy Spirit to help us do this.

"But we must surrender ourselves to God's mercy by first becoming Awakened to the unseen realm and God's presence; then repent for our shortcomings, ask for forgiveness, and finally, seek his guidance in order to do God's Will. This is typically the path of our Destiny, which we had, before being born, mapped out for ourselves.

"Jesus said, 'Not everyone who says to Me, 'Lord, Lord,' will enter the kingdom of heaven, but only he who does the Will of my Father who is in heaven.' (Matthew 7: 21)"

CHAPTER 17

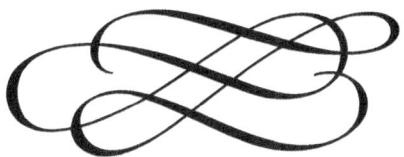

A Galilean Wedding

Alex:

"Okay AJ, assuming for a moment that all this is right, how can you be so sure that if we become Awakened; and Repent and seek Forgiveness; and trust entirely in some Supreme Being by submitting to its Will in order to become 'perfect' or 'Holy' let's say, that it will all be worth it after we die?"

AJ:

"Not only is it worth it after we die Alex, but it allows you to better manage and enjoy Life's present journey.

"How can I be so sure?" reiterated AJ.

"Alex, turn around and look at one last picture," said AJ as he motioned to Alex to a large picture on the main wall above the fireplace.

Alex had seen this picture hundreds of times before. It was a picture of the Last Supper, with Jesus and all his Apostles sitting at a table dining, the night before he was taken prisoner and subsequently crucified.

Alex:

"I definitely know what that picture is," said Alex with a wry smile.

AJ:

"You may know what the picture is, but do you know what it actually means? Many people know this picture, but very few of them know what this event really symbolizes."

Alex:

"I'm all ears AJ," said Alex. "And something tells me I'm about to learn something new."

AJ:

"Alex, to understand the actual event known as the 'Last Supper' in the Biblical accounts, you first need to know how to conduct a Galilean wedding."

Alex:

"A Galilean wedding!" says Alex, showing a great deal of surprise.

AJ:

"Yes. Because what you see depicted in the picture, is only Part One, of a Galilean wedding ceremony."

Alex:

"I knew this would be interesting AJ. Please go on."

AJ:

"First, it is important to realize that Jesus and all his disciples were from Galilee, and so they all understood the local customs, including of course, the marriage custom in that part of the country. The marriage custom itself needs to be properly understood. In Galilee, a wedding was typically arranged by the respective fathers of the bride and groom.

"At the initial stage, during the 'engagement' let's say, the groom's father would typically pay a price, or dowry, to the bride to enable the wedding to proceed. Then, the 'covenant' to wed was sealed by the groom offering a cup of wine to the bride to drink, to signify her acceptance of the marriage covenant. The groom in-turn, then drank from it, and their drinking from the same cup symbolized their commitment to each other.

"The groom would then go and spend about a year or so to build a room onto his father's house to accommodate his new bride, as well as to prepare for the wedding feast to be held in his father's house.

"In the meantime, the bride along with her bridesmaids, would ready themselves for the wedding feast which could come at any time. For example, clothing had to be sorted, and oil lamps had to be prepared and filled in case they were needed to escort the bride and her bridal party to the feast, at any time of the afternoon or evening.

"The hour of the feast was dependent solely on the timing determined by the groom's father; not even his son would know when.

"The approximate one-year hiatus period, during which the bride and groom could not interact physically, also meant that this was a time for the bride to prove her sexual purity; to show her true intention to be ever ready for the wedding feast, and so demonstrate her commitment and eligibility to be wed.

"So, you see Alex, the so-called 'Last Supper', where Jesus and his Apostles drink from the same cup, is symbolic of Jesus entering into a covenant; not only with his Apostles, but with all of us. He was telling us that his Father had agreed to pay the price for the wedding to proceed. That price, of course, was the excruciating torture and death of his very son, Jesus.

"That is what 'God's Will' was for Jesus, if he was willing to accept it. That was his Lifelong Plan, his Destiny. But Jesus always had the Freewill to reject it. And Satan, of course, did his best to dissuade him by trying to tempt him not to proceed.

"After this covenant resulted in the death and resurrection of Jesus and his ascension to heaven, we then had, and it continues to this very day, a hiatus period like that of the bride; to ready, as well as purify, ourselves, so that we can be eligible to be united in heaven with Christ and enter his Father's house.

"In the meantime, we are in Christ's love and care, akin to being engaged to someone, and should look forward to the rapture of being united with him and the Father.

"This is why in the Bible story of the Last Supper, after Jesus drinks from the cup, He says, 'I tell you, I will not drink from this fruit of the vine from now on until that day when I drink it new with you in my Father's kingdom', (Matthew 26:29).

"Of course, we are far from perfect, and so are not likely to be able to do all this preparation and purification on our own. So, as we discussed earlier, God has sent us the Holy Spirit to help Awaken us and to ready us, through various lifetime plans, to make us worthy of reuniting with God.

"The Holy Spirit is in the cave with us, Plato's Cave, as we sit there trying to free ourselves from the chains that bind us to the illusory world we spoke about earlier. She is trying to guide us out of that cave to the true world of Light, but we rarely ask for her help through prayer, and so it is only through suffering and becoming downtrodden, that we finally 'crack' sufficiently enough to let in her light of guidance and grace.

"So Alex, when you ask me, how sure am I that if we do God's Will, will it be worth it in the end? I can tell you that I'm certain of it! Certain of it!

"Why? Because Jesus Christ himself has given us not only his word and covenant in the form of a marriage vow, in the then custom of the day; a custom that every one of his Galilean Apostles ultimately fully understood, but he also gave his life to complete the vow."

"Do God's Will Alex! And he will save you!

"It's a marriage covenant signed in love and blood."

CHAPTER 18

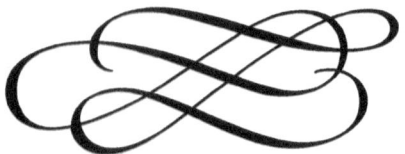

Now It's All Too Personal

AJ had been so generous with his time to Alex and had explained so much to him in such a short time, that Alex felt guilty continuing the pretence that he had come to talk about miracles, when he really wanted to know about his dream and whether it was possible that he may have been reincarnated from a past life.

"AJ, I must confess something to you," Alex said, and he continued.

"You have taken the time to share so many stories with me, but the real reason I wanted to see you today was to get your thoughts on something very specific, if you would oblige me. I wanted your thoughts on the notion of Reincarnation. And more specifically, in relation to what happened to me recently on a trip to the Australian outback, where an Aboriginal elder suggested I had been reincarnated, as well as a very dramatic dream I had a couple of days ago when I arrived in Assisi, and which has me very puzzled."

"Thank you, Alex, for being open with me," replied AJ. "Yes, of course, if I can help you in any way, I will. Please tell me your story."

Alex then proceeded to share with AJ all the background, including his visit to Moree, and Michael's suggestion that he was somehow connected with an historic massacre that happened in the Australian outback years ago in the 1800s; the terrifying Mt Kaputar experience involving screeching black cockatoos that woke him during the fire, and which Michael subsequently suggested were ancestral spirits repaying him for saving two young children during the massacre; the real, or imaginary, sighting of Michael leading him away from the burning mountain. And of course, all the details of the haunting dream Alex had two nights ago that seemed to mirror what Michael had told him about him participating in the Myles Creek massacre.

Alex told AJ that he thought the dream may have been a subconscious fabrication of his imagination based on the story that Michael had told him in Moree, with his subconscious trying to trick him into believing that what Michael had told him was true. But nonetheless, he had never experienced a dream so realistic and intense before and wondered if there was more to it than that.

AJ told him that an intense dream of the kind Alex had could well be an indication of a past life experience. And that it's certainly not uncommon for past life experiences to find their way into our dreams, especially dreams that are unusually intense, and which we somehow intuitively know are meant to convey some insight to us. But equally, AJ confirmed that it is possible that Alex was right in his suspicion that it was his subconscious playing a trick on him.

AJ told Alex there's usually a good way to verify past life tales, and that is by having someone independently "read" the person and attempt to visualize the person's past life window. He told Alex he had learned this technique years ago and had done this on several occasions for people he knew. He asked Alex if he wanted to try it.

By this stage AJ was not surprised by the range of knowledge and skills AJ demonstrated, so Alex readily obliged; after all, what harm could come from a reading he thought.

AJ asked Alex to take off his watch and let him hold it during the reading. Alex handed over his watch and AJ clasped it in his two hands and sat back in his seat with eyes closed. He then went into some form of meditative mode.

After a while, AJ began to speak about what he could see, still with eyes closed and in a meditative state.

He said he could see Alex physically scolding two young Aboriginal children and then letting them run away into a riverbed. That he saw Alex having to explain, in strong terms, to other riders involved in a massacre of Aborigines, how the children got away from him. The other riders were swearing and gestating angrily at him, since by the time Alex had caught up with the others after the children got away, the others had already slaughtered the remaining members of the Aboriginal group. So Alex was now an innocent party compared to all of them. He had no blood on his hands and the others new that therefore Alex was now a potential turncoat witness against them, if ever he was pressured by the police. They were livid with him for this.

He then saw all the riding party, including Alex, dismembering the dead bodies and taking delight at doing so. He could see Alex welding his machete at the dead bodies of young and old; of men and women, cutting off their heads or limbs. He was covered in blood like all the rest of them, but he hadn't actually murdered anyone. They then all washed themselves in the nearby river and drank themselves to a stupor that night. The next morning, they burned the bodies and all the dismembered body parts.

As he heard this, Alex sat emotionless with a look of incredulity. Willing himself to think this is all untrue. He thought to himself, that even if AJ was really seeing all this, there's no reason to believe it was true. AJ himself might be deluded by reason of having heard the dream that Alex shared with him. Alex told himself that, just as he himself was tricked by his subconscious into having a nightmarish dream based on what Michael had told him, so AJ was being subconsciously tricked into seeing all this now, based on what Alex had shared with him. Either that, or AJ was having him on.

But then, AJ ominously continued.

Still with eyes closed and in a meditative state, AJ told Alex that a few days later there was another Aboriginal massacre, perpetrated by the same riding

175

party. He told Alex that he could see Alex sharpening his machete in readiness for participating in this; that he took much pride from its strength and sharpness and its appearance generally.

That the other riders were still angry at Alex for not having participated directly in the earlier slaughter, and Alex promised them he would be heavily involved in this next one.

AJ said he could see Alex and the other riders galloping at pace through the outback and into an Aboriginal station camp. The people in the camp, young and old, were terrified and ran in all directions in fear. The riders on horseback then began chopping down these defenceless men, women and children with swords and machetes and occasional gunfire. AJ said Alex would be revulsed at the sight of the bloodshed if he could see what was in the vision. Again, the men drank themselves silly that evening and burned all the bodies the next day.

AJ said that, sometime after the massacres, he could then see several of the men involved, including Alex, being rounded up in chains by policemen on horseback; and that eventually, they were condemned to death by hanging.

He said he could see Alex being led to the hangman's noose, with his hands tied firmly behind his back. The noose then being placed around Alex's neck, whereupon Alex became enraged and tried to fight off the hangman and untie his hands, but all to no avail.

He saw the hangman step away and then release the swinging floor that Alex stood on, so as to execute the hanging. Just at that moment, Alex managed to free his hands and grabbed at the rope around his neck to try to somehow loosen it. By doing so, he interrupted the normal hanging process of the rope snapping the neck cleanly to give effect to a quick death.

Instead, Alex just prolonged the ordeal. He hung there struggling violently to loosen the rope around his neck. His feet dandling and kicking violently. His neck bleeding from the struggle with the tightening noose, until he slowly succumbed to it and suffocated; his body and feet swinging and convulsing until eventually, he hung there motionless.

At that, AJ paused, gathered himself for a minute, still in meditative pose and then, with Alex's watch still firmly in hand, slowly opened his eyes to look at Alex. Alex sat there, but he was no longer emotionless. He sat with his hands holding his head. His face in a state of silent anguish and despair. His heart pounding with fear and guilt. His face and neck sweating.

Alex knew that what AJ had just told him could no longer be explained by subconscious trickery. There were too many home truths in what was said that AJ could not have possibly known about.

Alex loved his machetes and often enjoyed sharpening them and admiring their appearance. He took one with him just about everywhere he went. AJ could not have known that.

Then there was the birthmark around his neck, which of course, AJ had no knowledge of. This mark was visible only when Alex wore an open neck shirt, which was rare, and which hadn't been the case in his encounters with AJ. Alex's own research into Reincarnation, done after Michael mentioned the black cockatoo story to him when he visited Moree, made it clear that birthmarks can indicate past life trauma, and can be especially indicative of violent deaths such as burnings, shootings or stabbings. His birthmark seemed to marry up with the struggle and injury Alex suffered in AJ's vision, by reason of the struggle with the noose around his neck. The birthmark actually looked like a rope mark across the front of his neck. For that reason, Alex tended to avoid wearing open neck shirts.

And finally, there was Alex's phobia with hangings. No one knew of that. Not even Angela. As a crime reporter he had, of course, witnessed many gruesome death scenes, none of which had ever bothered him, except for hanging scenes. He had reported on a few purported suicides during his career, and he could never understand why a hanging scene had such a nauseating effect on him. He now had his answer.

Suddenly now, the nightmare had become all too personal for Alex. Was he really a murderer of defenceless men, women and children?

AJ could see that Alex was visibly shaken and oozing guilt and despair. He knew it meant that Alex strongly related to the vision. He immediately sought to comfort Alex. AJ told Alex that we, that is, the people we are in this life, are not responsible for what happened in our past lives. We are accountable only for what we do in this life. That whilst past lives can explain our fears, passions and phobias, we are not supposed to remember our past, since it would overwhelm and distract us from living and learning the lessons we were destined for in this life. AJ emphasised to Alex the importance of not becoming dominated by his past. Simply to acknowledge it, but not feel guilty for it.

However, AJ made the point that Alex must have been "guided" to meet AJ, in order to understand that he had a violent past. And this was a means of jolting him into becoming aware of the complexity and wonder of the universe; to make him better understand who he was, and to fully appreciate the grandeur of the universal plan. All this so that Alex may further advance in achieving his present Life Purpose, whatever that may be.

To further placate Alex, AJ even went so far as to suggest to Alex that people we harm in this life, even to the point of murder, do not really "suffer or die", since this life is illusory. Their real self continues to exist in soul and spirit form. They will return one day in a new bodily form. So Alex should not feel guilty about his past life deeds, no matter how horrible they seem.

Alex tried to take all this in, but was still reeling from an unmistakable realisation; a realisation that it is possible that he may well have had a past life, and indeed, a terrible one at that; that Reincarnation was potentially real; and so, by definition, that an afterlife actually exists; and that there may indeed, be some grand cosmic plan, that so far, he had no idea about; in fact, the idea of which, he had constantly denied and ridiculed.

All this went to the heart of who he really was, and what his life was all about. He was really struggling to take it all in. He needed some time alone.

He thanked AJ by giving him a big hug, which was unusual for Alex. He bid AJ goodbye and despondently, made his way back to his hotel, still overawed by the whole experience he'd been through.

As he slowly walked back to the hotel, he remembered having researched the Myall Creek massacre after Harry and Michael raised it with him in Moree. He recalled the research showed that there had been a subsequent raid and massacre, apparently by the same group of riders, of a nearby aboriginal station known as Macintyre's station near Inverell, NSW. And that several people eventually got prosecuted, convicted and hung over the horrific murders.

Upon returning to his hotel, he sat in an armchair in silence, contemplating what he had just experienced. And then silently praying to someone, he wasn't sure who, for forgiveness.

CHAPTER 19

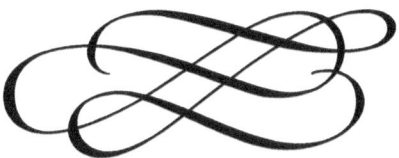

Twilight in the Basilica

The next morning, Alex awoke around midday. He had a restless evening the previous night and only settled into a deep sleep towards the early hours of the morning. His sleeping mind had tried to make sense of the very personal reincarnation vision AJ had given him, but to no avail. Alex was still in a state of partial disbelief of AJ's vision. But deep down, he knew it was too personal to be a total fabrication.

He got up and decided to go to the local cafe for brunch. He took his laptop with him to further research the Myall Creek Station massacres. As he sat in the cafe reading through the case histories of these events, both the bloody and inhuman nature of what had taken place, as well as the then prevailing intransigence of white Australians to have any respect or compassion for the Aboriginal people, disturbed him deeply. He could see the callousness with which Aboriginal people were treated back then.

But it was worse than that. He had an intuition that what he was reading was not new to him. It felt almost second nature to him, since he could easily relate to the racist attitudes of the time, even though he condemned such attitudes now.

He instinctively felt like he knew exactly how the white folk thought about Aborigines back then. They were regarded as primitive, backward, degenerates who should be grateful that the white settlers hadn't simply exterminated all of them. And who would, eventually, all be exterminated anyway, either through diseases introduced by colonisation or other physical means, leading to the gradual extinction of their race. Genocide by stealth. They were regarded as so inferior to white men, that the blending of the black and white races was seen as having a deleterious impact on the future of the settlement, and so should be avoided. And the best way to achieve that, apart from the immediate extinction of the race, would be to prevent aboriginal women giving birth to half castes.

Somehow, he instinctively knew this is how white Australia viewed Aborigines in the 1880's, even if it wasn't in all the research he was looking at. That in itself, made him uneasy.

By the time he had finished his research, it was already close to three in the afternoon. As he opened his satchel to put away his laptop, he saw in it the olive branch Sophia had given him. He picked it up and slowly raised it to his nose and lips and savoured the scent it gave off. He was undoubtedly attracted to Sophia, and after the morbid thoughts of his research on massacres, thinking of her gave him some solace; a sense that the world has intrinsic goodness to offer to counter the obvious evil he had just been reflecting on.

He resolved to go and see her and thank her for arranging the unexpected blessing he received from sister Clemenza at the convent. He also thought he should now ask her what he avoided asking her previously; namely, about the attitude of people toward the Catholic clergy and, in particular, who in the town might have had any grudges to settle with Bishop Degno. But deep down he just wanted to see her again.

He did not want to embarrass her by going to the convent to ask her whereabouts, so he thought he'd walk over to the impoverished part of town, where she did not quite seem to have finished her rounds of checking in on all the lonely people, the first time they'd met.

Sure enough, once he got to the street they had originally met in, an old lady seated in a folding chair in the street was able to tell Alex, upon his asking her, that Sophia had been there only a short time ago and was now on her way to the Franciscan Basilica for afternoon prayers.

Alex then made his way to the Basilica, walking slowly upward along the picturesque pathways of Assisi, marvelling at the beauty of the scenery along the way. The sun was in its late afternoon stage. It poured golden rays over the hills and countryside, including the pathway Alex was on, and it felt warm on his face and body.

As he approached the Basilica's entrance, he noticed the sign on the door indicating that the Basilica was about to close. So, he became anxious that perhaps Sophia had already been and gone.

Upon entering through the door, he saw a monk approaching the door and motioning to his wristwatch, indicating to Alex that the church was about to close. Alex approached the monk and whispered to him that he was here to see Sister Sophia from the Convent. He asked the monk if he knew whether she had already left.

The monk knew Sophia well, as she often came to pray after her mercy rounds of the town's folk. He would typically allow her to stay in the church even after closing, sometimes along with people that had health issues, or were grieving for some reason, and with whom she'd often pray with together. He would close the church doors but would leave one of them unlocked. Sophia knew which one and she would lock it on her way out.

He therefore motioned to Alex to a lone figure kneeling on one of the pews in the church. Alex could see this was Sophia and his heart jumped in joy. Alex thanked the monk, who then promptly exited the church, closing but leaving unlocked the door from which he exited. There was no one else in the entire Basilica other than Alex and Sophia.

Alex slowly and quietly walked alongside the aisle of church pews towards Sophia. It felt surreal that he was alone with her in this vast holy place. As he slowly approached her, he could see that she was kneeling on a pew next to one of the wall frescoes, in solemn prayer or reflection. Even from behind and seeing only the back of her covered headdress and nun's gown, she looked beautiful to him.

Sophia heard someone approaching and opened her eyes and turned her head to look at who it was. Upon recognizing Alex, at first, she looked surprised and looked worriedly back towards the Church door and saw that it was closed. She realised that they were now all alone in the Church. But then her demeanour changed, and she smiled warmly at Alex and motioned to him to sit on the pew alongside where she was kneeling.

"I hope you don't mind my coming to see you here?" said Alex quietly.

"Oh, you came here to see me?" replied Sophia, again somewhat surprised.

"Yes. Is that okay?" replied Alex tentatively.

"Yes. That's ok," responded Sophia, nodding approvingly, and then looking down at the rosary beads in her hands, as if checking in with them that having a man coming to see her was okay with the Lord.

"I will just be a few minutes and then we can talk," said Sophia.

"Sure. Thank you," replied Alex.

As Alex sat there, he could now better see the fresco that Sophia was praying in front of. It was a depiction of two monks, one of which Alex assumed to be St Francis, appearing to exorcise demons out of a country township. Unknown to Alex, this was a famous fresco of the exorcism of demons by Saint Francis that took place in the town of Arezzo.

Still kneeling, Sophia finished her prayers, made the sign of the cross and slowly rose from the pew and sat next to Alex. Alex then motioned towards the fresco of Saint Francis in Arezzo and leaning towards her said,

"Do you think that people, even Saints, can really exorcise demons like that?"

Alex had serious doubts about whether demons actually existed, but he wasn't prepared to raise that with Sophia, as he was sure she believed in them.

Sophia wasn't surprised by Alex's question, but she was disappointed, given that Alex had been at the convent and had seen and heard the various stories of spiritual healing that could take place with deep faith and prayer. She knew instinctively that Alex was on a spiritual journey, even if he didn't know it.

She also felt some connection with Alex that she couldn't fully explain. Perhaps he was some soul mate from a previous life she thought. Catholics were not meant to believe in reincarnation, of course, but Sophia knew better. Or perhaps he was just someone she was meant to befriend and help find his way to God's path. Either way, she knew she was meant to assist him; even to the point where she should share intimate details of her past in order to help him understand the reality of life. She was therefore prepared to disclose to him something very private about herself, that very few people knew about.

She responded as follows,

"Of course, people can cast out demons. The Bible has many stories about demons being cast out. But also, there are many other stories passed down to us, even recent stories, that talk about the exorcism of demons. And this could be done, not just by Jesus, but also by his Apostles and by other faithful men and women, not just Saints.

"Let me share a personal story with you Alex, which I ask if you could keep it just between ourselves, is that's ok?" Sophia asked.

"Of course," said Alex.

Sophia went on,

"I was an only child, and my parents came from a wealthy family. I had happy childhood memories from them, but when I was still young, they both died in a car accident. My uncle then assumed responsibility for me. But when I became a teenager, he started to abuse me, sexually." Sophia paused for a moment pensively, then went on.

"As I grew older, I became addicted to sexual pleasures and became known for this amongst my uncle's friends."

She paused again, and with a melancholy look on her face, then continued.

"Eventually, he regretted what he had made me become, and brought me to the convent under Sister Clemenza. I hated being there, as by then, I had some demon inside me that craved sexual pleasures."

Alex couldn't quite believe what he was hearing. Here was a young novice nun sharing intimate personal secrets with him, and he'd only known her for a few days, even though he felt much closer to her than that. He nodded and showed empathy with her story by his body language.

Sophia continued.

"One day I went into an uncontrollable rage and Sister Clemenza had me brought into her room. After a long night of prayer, and the constant invocation of the name of Jesus Christ our Lord, she somehow excised the demon out of me. I honestly felt the demon leave my body in a rush.

"I immediately ceased my rage and collapsed on to the bed in sister Clemenza's room. I felt a sense of intense tranquillity, like my whole body had been cleansed of some terrible energy. For once in a very long time, I was again in control of myself. That sense of tranquillity stayed with me for some three days. Sister Clemenza let me stay in her room all the while.

"After that, my sexual cravings were gone. I felt liberated and finally able to approach life free of intense sexual desires. I became a new person. And so, when I look at this fresco in front of us Alex, I know exactly what it means.

"I have been fortunate, or maybe unfortunate, depending on how you see it, to have a real-life experience. I can now understand exactly what the Bible and other stories tell us about demons, and how faith and prayer and Jesus, can help to cleanse and heal someone."

"That's an extraordinary story Sophia," said Alex, who was moved by her openness in sharing with him such a personal account, even if he found it somewhat incredulous. In fact, he was so moved by it that he uncontrollably reached out and held her hand to show empathy with her, knowing how trusting she must be of him to share that with him.

They then simultaneously looked down at Alex's hand holding her hand, and without saying anything, they both felt their hearts skip a beat. Suddenly, it became a little harder to breathe. Each knew exactly what the other was feeling at that moment.

Alex then said, "Thanks for sharing that with me, as it is a very personal experience and I feel special that you would share it with me, given we haven't really known each other very long."

Sophia again looked down at Alex's hand holding hers and even though the connection felt wonderful, in fact exquisite, she slowly released her hand from under his and responded as follows.

"Yes, you are right Alex, but I trust you, and something tells me I am meant to help you in your life journey, even if it means sharing my most personal experiences."

"Did that experience then convince you to stay at the convent and become a nun?" asked Alex.

Sophia paused in momentary thought and then responded, "At the time I decided to stay a little longer at the convent to learn what it was like to be a nun and see if that was something I would want. I did not have a strong passion to be a nun then, and the sisters did not pressure me for this.

"As the weeks and months passed, I did a lot of praying and reflection. Did I wish one day to find a lover, get married and have children? Did I want to dedicate my life to some other cause, like helping people in need? Could I devote myself to loving God and spend the rest of my life serving him, doing his will?

Was I even sure what his will or plan was for me? So many big questions to think about."

"Yes," nodded Alex.

"But as the months, and even one year passed, I could see how important the role of the nuns and the convent was. Not just to the local community but also to people who came looking for help from far away; people of all kinds, of all ages. And other people, like me, who were lost to God and suffering, not just physically, but mentally. And every day I learned, from sister Clemenza and the other sisters, how to help them, how to heal them, and I saw the power of God and his Angels and Saints, in doing this.

"Once I came to understand the Power that faith and prayer and love can provide, and that I was learning how to use it to create goodness, I could not abandon that calling in return for a more selfish life just for me."

She paused, and then looking directly at Alex with her piercing blue eyes said , "once I understood the true Power of learning and mastering the connection with God and things Divine; the Power it provides to do good to others and the Power to free yourself from all other distractions of the world, and yet to still be able to experience love; ultimate love; the intense love of God and Humanity, I knew then, that this is what I wanted; that this is what was intended for me. And so then, I decided to stay and become a nun, God willing."

Alex looked into her mesmerising blue eyes, still taken by the intense generosity of heart inherent in her story. He felt real love for her. He wanted to reach out and embrace her. To hold in his arms this incredible human being; this incredibly caring, compassionate and stunningly beautiful person. But he restrained himself from doing so.

Sophia could read Alex's desires at that moment. She knew how much he wanted her, but that he was decent enough to restrain himself, unlike the many men she had previously experienced in her life.

She too, at that moment, felt strong feelings towards Alex. All alone in the immensity of the Basilica, just the two of them connecting in ways Sophia hadn't felt with men before. She knew she was meant to play a pivotal role in Alex's awakening. She also felt sure this somehow involved pouring out her love to help him.

She then had to remind herself that she was a novice nun. One who had decided to devote herself to chastity and the aims of her Order. She knew exactly what to do, and that was to tell Alex that they had to now leave the Church; that she had to return to the convent.

But staring into his alluring dark brown eyes, as if peering into his soul, something overcame her. An all-embracing sense of love, as if she had been doused with a magic love potion. This intense sense of love was aimed at Alex. She felt like hugging him fiercely but restrained herself. She knew instinctively this love energy that befell on her was either, heaven sent, or devilish in nature. She was prepared to wager it was the former, but in that moment, she didn't care. That triggered her to make a momentous, indeed fateful, decision.

She reached out to Alex's hand and clasped it firmly. She then stood up, and led Alex along the church aisle, slowly but determinedly, towards the front altar. Her gaze fixed on the altar and the crucified Christ that hung above it.

Alex, of course, accommodated her. He was in a surreal state by then, having this beautiful angel reaching out and holding his hand and then, leading him down the aisle, all alone in a massive and slowly darkening church, as dusk approached.

As Sophia led him towards the altar at the front of the church, he looked up and saw the late afternoon sun projecting, at a gentle angle, its warm golden rays through the stained-glass windows onto the altar, towards which Sophia was headed. The entire experience was now more surreal than ever. He knew Sophia obviously wanted to show him something important, but he had little idea of what was to follow.

As they approached the altar, Sophia deliberately took Alex around to the back of the altar, then stopped, and positioned herself in between the altar and Alex, with her backside gently touching the altar, while she faced Alex front on. And directly behind Alex, suspended from the ground, was a large cross with the crucified Christ on it, which Sophia could see hovering above Alex's head, as she looked directly at him. Sophia then reached out to hold Alex's other hand and they stood there. She was transfixed between altar and Alex, with each hand holding Alex's hands by her side, and her beautiful eyes gazing piercingly into Alex's.

The sun rays continued to stream through the stained-glass windows, alighting gently on the altar and now warming Alex's back, creating an even more surreal feeling of loving warmth for him.

Alex's heart was now beating furiously, his breathing constricted. He could sense this moment was something he had never before experienced and may never again. Gazing firmly into her unwavering bright blue eyes, he felt an intense feeling of love. But it wasn't confined to Sophia. It was as if he had transcended his body and was now in an all-embracing energy field, which generated a sense of loving bliss all around him.

Sophia then let go of Alex's warm hands. She reached up and gently caressed his face with both her hands. And, still staring into his eyes, she gently leant over towards him, closed her eyes and kissed him on the mouth slowly, dearly and longingly. She then pulled gently away, but stood there still caressing his face, and staring into his eyes with those angelic blue eyes of hers.

Alex knew this was the most exhilarating moment he had ever experienced. He wasn't going to hold himself back now. He put his arms around her slender torso and pulled her back onto himself, reaching out, he kissed her gently but passionately, on the mouth.

The two of them stood there for just a little while, but it seemed to both of them, an eternity. Holding, caressing and kissing each other with their hearts full of love for each other.

Sophia then slowly reached down with her hand and started caressing Alex's penis, from outside his clothing. It didn't take Alex long to react. He hardened up quickly, and her caressing of him felt as heavenly as any moment Alex had ever experienced.

Almost intuitively, he reached down and undid his trousers and allowed Sophia to handle him unclothed and natural. As he continued to kiss her passionately on her mouth and around her neckline, he then reached down with his hands and began to raise her gown, feeling occasionally her soft smooth legs and buttocks in the process. Sophia, all the while, had her eyes closed and was in a semi state of rapture, as she allowed Alex to kiss her passionately, while she simultaneously caressed and fondled his now iron hard penis.

When Alex had raised up all of Sophia's gown up to her buttocks, she voluntarily lent forward away from the altar to allow Alex to lift her folded-up gown above her buttocks and up to her waistline, before again leaning back with her buttocks onto the edge of the altar, now with only her underwear sheltering her buttocks from the marble of the altar, which was itself warm from the afternoon sunlight raining upon it.

As if previously choreographed, Alex then, intuitively, lifted Sophia and placed her buttocks onto the altar, as she simultaneously, separated her legs and allowed Alex to place his hard penis on top of her vulva, still wearing her underwear. Alex then pressed himself upon her, as she embraced him around his neck, and continued to kiss him passionately.

After a while, in this fervent embrace, Alex reached down and gently removed Sophia's underwear, which she gladly facilitated. He then inserted himself into Sophia, who by that stage had become incredibly wet and slippery, and so easily accommodated him.

As Alex gently, but forcibly, imposed himself into her, Sophia began to moan. She then leant back and rested head long against the altar so that rather than looking at Alex, she was looking directly at the figure of Christ on the cross hovering above Alex's head.

Alex gradually increased the force of his penetration of her. He was rock hard. He was not having any of the erection problems he typically had when making love to Angela. He was also in a state of semi-rapture, as he continued to thrust himself into Sophia at a sustained and constant pace.

Sophia's moaning grew louder, and her eyes continued to be fixed on the crucifix, although they would at times roll back, as she closed them from time to time, and simultaneously groaned with her mouth open, indicating her blissful ecstatic state. With every inward thrust from Alex, she would momentarily raise her head from the altar, moaning and groaning in complete rapture. As she continued to do this, she began to mumble in between the groans, something in Italian, indecipherable to Alex. Her eyes, when open, were constantly transfixed on the cross. The words, although inaudible to Alex, and addressed to the figure of Christ on the cross, were, "Lord, you are my

Husband, and I am your Bride. Lord, you are my Husband, and I am your Bride, etc".

Alex knew she was looking over his head and saying something to the cross behind him, but he didn't care. He could see she was in rapture. He could not remember where, but he knew he had seen this scene before. He then recalled that it was the scene in Bernini's statue of St Teresa in Ecstasy, whilst being thrust with Cupid's arrow.

They were both in rapture now. There was no relenting of Alex's desire in his constant and methodical thrusting motion. Nor of Sophia's upward convolutions and accompanying groaning and mumbling at the cross.

Alex, although in rapture himself, could also envision the scene from outside his body; as if he were viewing it from a drone that hovered in front of the altar, facing the crucified Christ, with golden sunlight behind, and all around, the crucifix and altar. And as the drone slowly hovered away from the altar and approached the Basilica's high ceiling at the opposite end of the Church, and Alex's presence became less and less visible, an extraordinary and shocking scene emerged.

It was as if the Christ, on the hovering cross above the altar was, in fact, the person making love to Sophia. Alex was a hardly discernible, almost invisible, instrument of Christ's love making thrusts into Sophia, who was in both audible and physical rapture from the love making.

The whole scene, in the immense solitude of the Basilica, with sunlight streaming through the Basilica's west facing windows, embracing all three protagonists, Sophia, Christ on the hovering Cross, and a barely visible Alex, along with the constant accompanying groans and convolutions of Sophia on the altar, was literally, a depiction from out of this world.

CHAPTER 20

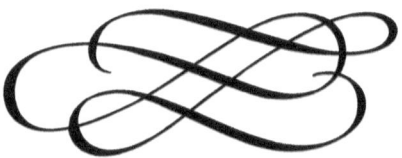

A Jealous Body

The next morning, Alex awoke in his hotel bedroom from a deep sleep. He had been so tired from the incredibly long-winded love making session with Sophia the previous evening, that when he got back to his hotel the night before, he just went straight to bed without dinner. Exhausted, but incredibly relaxed nonetheless, he slept right through the night uninterrupted.

He woke up around eight am and was naturally hungry. He was getting ready to go downstairs and find some breakfast, when his phone rang. It was Junior with the results of the police report findings on Degno's murder. Junior told Alex in a clear and exasperating tone, that the police have basically got, "bugger all!" on any possible suspect. No fingerprints, no DNA, no leave behinds, no clues whatsoever. The police said whoever killed him was meticulous, and obviously professional in leaving behind zero clues.

Apparently, they had interviewed a range of connected people, including Degno's family and associates, Parish leadership, church goers, church sacristan and altar boys; everyone they could think of, and got nothing! No one had given them any concrete leads. Even though there were rumours of him womanising with some of the parishioners, no one had given the police anything. Everyone in the community was tight lipped about anything adverse towards Degno.

Junior said the police seemed puzzled by the professional nature of Degno's murder, especially in circumstances where there is no obvious link to any criminal activities that Degno seems to be involved with. They have also ruled out affairs he might have had with family members of criminal gangs, which might have led to a gang leader ordering a professional hit on him. They are totally stumped.

"That's useless!" Alex replied to Junior.

"What am i supposed to write about? Bloody Bruce will be steaming, as I've been telling him to stop hassling me for anything substantial until the police report comes out. Bloody Hell!" exasperated Alex.

"Surely, they must have something to work with Junior. What do they plan to do now?" Alex barked down the phone to Junior.

"Looks like they're going to back track on all the people they've already interviewed and see if anything else comes of that", replied Junior.

"Bloody Hell!" Alex repeats. "That's a sure sign they have nothing to go on. Keep digging as hard as you can Junior. We need to find something. I'm going to try again and see if I can get anything out of the locals about Degno."

"Ok mate," replied Junior and hung up.

Just as Alex put the phone down, another call came in. When Alex saw the phone contact name that came up, his mood became even more dour. It was Bruce calling.

"G'day Boss," answered Alex.

"Have you got anything useful to tell me?" retorted Bruce.

Alex knew what was coming.

"Apparently, the police report came up with nothing. No leave behinds, clues or suspects. I'm going to have to keep digging for a little while longer," replied Alex, holding his breath.

"You've been there nearly two weeks and so far, given me Jack Shit! What the fuck are you doing! Or more to the point, not doing! You better come up with something significant in the next forty-eight hours Mate, or else I'm going to use your arse for footy practice!

"There's plenty of other Jurnos who'd kill to be in Italy, but you're supposed to be the shit hot crime reporter, and all you've given me so far is a potted history of Assisi, which I can get from a google search! Pull your finger out mate, or you can Fuck Off!"

And before Alex could even respond to that, Bruce adds,

"And another thing. I got lucky last week and won $5 million dollars on the lottery. So I've decided to retire in three months' time and travel the world with my missus and my grandkids. Once I'm out of here mate, I don't give a shit what you do. But in the meantime, I'm not going to be taken for a ride by you or any other joker around here!"

Bruce then abruptly hung up.

"Fuck me dead! Five million dollars! You must be joking!" said Alex talking to himself, as he sat down on the bed to reflect on the call with Bruce.

Bruce had just laid into him about his work, without giving Alex an opportunity to respond. And to top it off, tells Alex he's had a windfall gain, enough to retire on and travel the world. It was the lottery win more than anything else that really hurt Alex. As it began to sink in, Alex struggled to come to grips with how a rude heartless prick like Bruce, can be so fortunate to win the lottery and be set for life, whilst Alex's life is so empty.

In his head, Alex tried to console himself that lots of people are wealthier and better off than him, but it was his body that could not cope with the news. Alex could feel the envy he felt for Bruce radiate through his body, in an away that really surprised him. He could sense the disconnect between what his mind was telling him; namely, not to concern himself with Bruce's fortune and therefore not be jealous of him, versus what his body was feeling, which was intense envy and a sense of gross injustice.

It was rare for Alex to sense such a disconnect between his head thoughts and his body. It was as if there was a sensible higher self in him which was detached from what his body was feeling. And this higher self was not able to control his bodily feelings and mood. Somehow, his body was being influenced by an ego-based dark force.

For the first time he could recall, Alex felt as though the 'true Alex', namely, his higher-self, was observing a lower-order human animal, caught up in base material vices, including pride and envy. And that animal was him.

CHAPTER 21

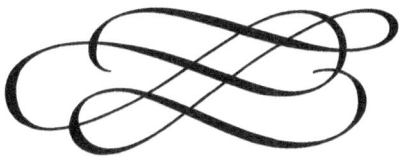

And a Dark Mind

The next day Alex spent the morning talking to town folk, including some of the people Junior had mentioned to him, to see if he could get any information on Degno and any leads on his murder.

He found it to be a fruitless exercise. People either knew nothing of interest, or said they knew nothing. Alex was very frustrated by now and Junior's connections with the local police were also proving fruitless.

After lunch he decided to call Angela. She had been considering coming to Assisi for the anniversary celebrations, but Alex wasn't sure if she'd decided to come as yet, since she had some conflicting commitments which he wasn't sure if she had managed to resolve.

Alex certainly felt guilty about his episode with Sophia, but reconciled himself on the basis that he was not the instigator. He felt sure Sophia would not be telling anyone about what had happened, least of all Angela, even if Angela did come to Assisi and they accidentally met up with each other. He certainly was not going to say anything about it to anyone.

Alex:

"Hi Darling, how are you?"

Angela:

"Oh, hi Darling. I'm a little pooped. I've just walk back into the house from a long protest rally walk."

Alex:

"Really! What was that all about?"

Angela:

"It was a Climate Change rally aimed at getting the local authority to install a Community Battery so that solar power can be stored away during the day. Our local community can then tap into it at night, rather than having everyone installing their own mini battery in their own home."

Alex:

Although not much of a Climate Change advocate, Alex replied, "Well, that's a great idea. Why would you need a protest rally for that? Surely everyone would be in favour of something like that, provided the authority had the funds to finance it. And even then, each household could pay a small levy to help finance it from the savings they'd make from cheaper energy, and not having to buy their own battery."

Angela:

"You'd think so, but there's a noisy group of residents who don't want the community battery to be built in their neighbourhood. And another group thinks the levies proposed by the authority are too high and so they're also against it. These groups seem to

have convinced the authority not to go ahead with the idea. So many of the other residents were out there today rallying in favour of wanting a community battery. So, they're protesting against the authority's decision not to have one."

Alex had seen this hypocritical behaviour before. He always thought these climate change advocates want everything to be environmentally friendly, except when it involves putting a battery or solar farm in their neighbourhood, or asking them to pay more in charges for not using fossil fuels. But he was not about to get into a debate with Angela on that topic now, so he was going to let that conversation go through to the keeper. But just then, as Alex was about to ask Angela about her plans for Assisi, Angela interjected.

Angela:

"Why don't you write something about climate change in your newspaper? It's the most important challenge facing the world right now and endangering the future of the whole human race. Surely, that deserves some coverage in all the things you regularly write about?"

Alex:

"But I'm a crime journalist. My remit doesn't cover things like climate change."

Angela:

"But climate change is a crime! It's the biggest crime facing the world! All these big companies and shareholders are making money from digging up coal, oil and gas and burning it into the atmosphere and choking the planet and everything on it. How can that not be a crime! They are killing everything that walks on the planet! How can you justify writing reams of words on a crime committed on one person, and ignore a massive crime on the whole world?

And before Alex could mutter off a response, Angela went on,

Angela:

"Did you hear what you just said! You're a crime reporter but you can't write about the biggest crime known to mankind that's happening all over the world! Really? What's the point of being a crime reporter if you can't cover that!"

Alex:

Not wanting to have another long-distance argument with Angela, Alex tried to simply play down the situation.

"Well, it's just not my space. There are others who are meant to cover that topic."

Angela:

"Alex what do you stand for? What have you done for this world? What legacy will you leave behind? What drives you! You're supposedly a crime reporter and you don't even give a toss about the biggest crime happening across the whole world! It's somebody's else's spec. Really!

"All you focus on is your job because it makes money and pays the bills. You don't even enjoy it, and you despise the company you work with!

"I look at you and see someone who stands for Zero! Zero! What purpose or passion do you have in life? No compassion for the Planet! No compassion for people's everyday suffering! No interest in spirituality! You have no Purpose or Fire in you at all, Alex! You are dead to the world and frankly such an uninspiring partner to be with."

Despite Alex not wanting a long-distance confrontation, he thought Angela really crossed the line with him now, and his contempt for her constant demeaning of him swelled up into an out-of-character angry rage which he could not control.

Alex:

"Listen! I'm sick and tired of you constantly putting me down! Telling me I'm no good at this or that, and now I'm an uninspiring partner! Well, let me tell you this, you are a constant pain in the arse! Constantly finding something to criticise me about; constantly putting me down; constantly yelling at me for something; I'm sick of it! Sick of it!

"I HAVE got Purpose! It's to be Happy! And that's proving impossible with you because you manage to piss me off with just about every discussion we have.

"You give me no Joy! Just bloody misery! Constant demeaning! Constant belittling! Constant harassment!

"You're apparently the only bloody person around here whose got purpose in life and is doing something worthwhile! Well, I don't give a shit about what you like or do, for that matter. Most of the time I couldn't care less about what you think is important. But guess what's different between you and me? I don't constantly bust your arse over it! I'm not constantly telling you you're wrong and that you should do something different!

"So, stop busting my fucking balls! Stop it! Stop busting my fucking balls!"

Angela, recognising some truth in what Alex said, and knowing she must have cut him deep in order for him to be so uncharacteristically enraged in his response, calmly replied,

"Well, if I don't tell you these important things, who will? And by the way, I've managed to juggle my commitments and will be coming to Assisi by week's end."

And then she calmly hung up the phone.

For Alex, Angela had just completed the already depressing day he had endured. No new Degno leads, his boss on his back; worse still, him of all people to have won lotto, and now a cutting vitriolic argument with Angela that will fester in him for days on end.

He decided he needed to get out for a walk and went on a long reflective one. That evening Alex went to bed still bitter about what Angela had said to him, now even more depressed about the nature of his marriage.

As he lay in his bed with eyes closed, hoping to get to sleep soon and escape from this miserable day, his thoughts wondered to Sophia and the exhilarating time he had with her in the Basilica. He thought how beautiful and gentle a person she was and yet so sexually erotic. His mind contrasted her with Angela, and he recognised that he had little sexual attraction to Angela given her constant demeaning of him. He only got negative vibes from her and yet Sophia was the complete opposite. She was the true Angel rather than his wife, despite Angela's name. If only he could swap Sophia for Angela. Wouldn't it be great if somehow, he and Angela broke up and Sophia left the convent to be with him. That would be amazing. Perhaps Angela's flight to Italy could crash and he'd be rid of Angela and then Sophia could take her place.

At this ever so dark a thought, Alex checked himself, and briefly raised his head from the pillow and shook it vigorously, just like a dog shaking water off its back. And then wondered how such a thought could have entered his mind.

Again, for the second time in the day, he had a sensation of something else other than himself, being inside his head; this time planting vile thoughts of Angela's death in his mind and lust for Sophia.

CHAPTER 22

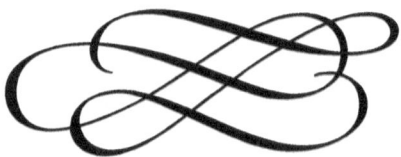

Unforgivable Devastation

Meanwhile, back at the convent, Sophia had endured a twenty-four-hour period of anguish as she wrestled with what she had done to Alex, by using him for her own longing to experience imaginary physical love with Jesus. She knew Alex would not tell anyone of the event, and she prayed and wrestled with whether she should tell Clemenza about it. Eventually, she decided she could not live with herself, especially in the presence of Christ, as the future nun that she hoped to be, without a confession of it. And that confession had to be first and foremost to Clemenza.

She therefore visited Clemenza in her room. Sophia sat opposite Clemenza, both in two chairs facing each other, with a small statue of the crucifixion hanging on the wall, bisecting the two by way of backdrop as they spoke.

Sophia told Clemenza the whole story; about how she and Alex ended up in the Basilica alone; the monk trusting Sophia to lock up the Basilica; her taking Alex's hand and leading him up to the Alter; her undressing herself sufficient for him to make love to her on the alter; her positioning of Alex in such a way as to enable her to imagine that it was Jesus on the cross that was penetrating her; her use of Alex to complete a long desire of love making with the only man she truly loved and wanted to experience love with, Jesus; and the indeterminably long time that the love making took, which seemed to go on forever as she experienced euphoric ecstasy.

She sobbed and wept, as she told all this to Clemenza. She also told Clemenza that from the moment she saw Alex she felt there was a reason why they had met. That she felt that she was meant to help him somehow. She was so comfortable with him, as if she had known him perhaps in an earlier life. That she felt from the outset that their lives would somehow be entangled. But until that moment in the Basilica, she had no intention of using him as she did.

Clemenza, as she listened, began to sink into a shocked and depressing figure. Her hands clasped together and brought up to cover her mouth just below her nose, as if in shock. She could barely believe what she was hearing. Here was her beloved protege telling her she had had consensual sexual intercourse with a virtual stranger, a married man no less, on a church alter; and worse than that, she had instigated it; and performed it in front of Jesus on the cross and pretended it was with Jesus himself! Clemenza knew it was a grotesque, sacrilegious act, of the highest order.

Sophia sobbed uncontrollably by the end of her story, skipping breaths and then pleading repeatedly for forgiveness from Clemenza, as she looked down at Clemenza's feet, unable to look at her face.

Clemenza felt immense shame and repulsion at what she had heard; and yet she unconditionally loved Sophia, and seeing her pain and contrition, she so wanted to reach out and hug and console her, but she resisted doing so. She took a deep breath, calmed herself, and told Sophia what she felt Sophia needed to hear. She could see that Sophia knew she had made a monumental mistake; a sin of the gravest order, and there was little point in scolding her; her contrition was genuine.

In a calm and understanding tone, Clemenza explained to Sophia that when Sophia had first come to the convent, Clemenza saw quickly that the sexual exploits she had been exposed to as a young girl had embedded bad, evil, energies into her; energies over which Sophia had little or no control. That is why Clemenza performed an exorcism of these dark energies from her, as Sophia alone may never have been able to rid herself of them. Clemenza explained that Sophia could, up to that time, plausibly say that she had little control over the decisions she made in her life.

But now Clemenza said that this was no longer the case. What Sophia had done this time could not be blamed on uncontrollable forces. This was her choice; her sin, and her sin alone. She had allowed her sexual desires to be transferred from desires of physically wanting men, to sexual desires for wanting Jesus. And for this Sophia could not simply seek forgiveness. Atonement would be needed to repay all the negative karma created by her action. And that atonement required not only a seeking of forgiveness from Alex, his wife, and God, but pain and suffering of a kind that would be forever embedded in Sophia's learning soul, her soul memory.

Clemenza told Sophia that she could not see how Sophia could ever now become a nun. The atonement needed would include a giving up of her career, a career that Clemenza believed had been part of God's plan. Clemenza always thought that Sophia would be her successor as head nun of the convent after she retired, but this was no longer possible.

Clemenza told her that she had fallen prey to the temptation that Satan puts in both our mind and our body; and that Sophia should have known not to fall for it. That Satan takes great joy in successfully tempting God's most favourite children, but Sophia should have been strong enough to resist this temptation. As a result, Sophia's soul will learn from the anguish and devastation that goes with a failure of such grotesque nature, including a complete and utter loss of reputation, career and all that she longed for, and is currently familiar with.

Sophia heard all this, and her devastation was now total. She sank to the floor crying unchecked. Her tears slowly dripping on the old wooden floorboards. Her cries, although muffled, were gut wrenching for Clemenza.

Clemenza slid off her chair, knelt in front of Sophia, and started to quietly pray for Sophia's consolation. After a while Clemenza rose up, left Sophia there still crying and sobbing, and without saying a word, walked out of the room and went to the Convent Chapel.

When she entered the Chapel, it was dimly lit with an air of tragic solitude about it. She knelt in front of the statue of Our Lady, with a flickering candle burning in front of it. Although Clemenza had knelt and prayed in front of Our Lady's statue many times before, this time she particularly noticed the snake being trampled on underneath the Holy Virgin's foot. In the flickering candlelight, the snake seemed to be smiling gleefully at Sophia's actions.

Clemenza knew full well what a monumental challenge we humans have been set, with evil and devilish temptation to accompany us, often intensifying on those closest to God, to especially sabotage all the good they can bring to the world. She understood the satanic temptation that had been conjured up for Sophia by arranging for her to be alone with Alex, undoubtedly a prior-life soul mate of hers, in the Basilica in late evening, and the monk allowing them to stay, after he had closed the Basilica. The devilish trap had been set to take advantage of the vulnerabilities of both souls, and cunningly, using Sophia's deep love of Christ as part of Satan's seductive snare.

Still in a state of depressing bewilderment, Clemenza nonetheless began praying in earnest.

"Dear Holy Mother, thank you for everything you do to help us; to help all of us in this difficult world. And I know there is so much suffering and pain *happening right now in the world, Dear Holy Mother, that must be anguish for you. Thank you, thank you my Dear Holy Mother for all you do to try and ameliorate all the pain and suffering in world.*

"In amongst all of that, I ask you please, I beg you please, Holy Mother, can you please find room in your heart to help my beloved Sophia; to console her and give her wisdom that she might find purpose and strength from her misery and suffering. Despite her great devotion to the Lord, even she was unable to resist Satan's dastardly temptation.

"Please, Holy Mother, I beg you, please pray for her and intercede for her with our Lord Jesus Christ that her misery and suffering may end quickly. And please, please, Holy Mother, that he may forgive her for what she has done. Sophia is so forgiving of others. I know that in her heart she lives by every word of the Lord's prayer, and she forgives everyone who sins against her. And so, Holy Mother, please, please, ask our Lord to forgive her for what she has done. And to give me a sign of his forgiveness that perhaps even after what she has done, that she may full fill her life's purpose. I beg you dearly, Holy Mother, please, please grant me this wish. Please, please, please, Holy Mother, hear my prayer.

"Hail Mary, full of Grace, the Lord is with thee; blessed art thou among women and blessed is the fruit of thy womb Jesus. Holy Mary, Mother of God, pray for us sinners, now and at the hour of our death."

Clemenza commenced a string of Hail Mary prayers, followed by a string of Our Father prayers, along with a full Rosary recitation; one constantly followed by the other. She prayed, kneeling and without respite, for over an hour.

CHAPTER 23

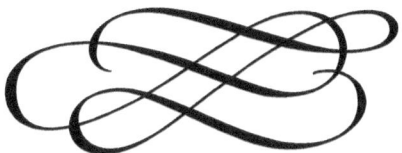

Rocca Maggiore - The Plot Revealed

The following day was only a day away from the start of the Anniversary celebrations, and Assisi was bustling with pilgrims and clergy. Pope Francis was due to arrive in town tomorrow to commence a three-day interfaith conference which would kick-off with a commemorative mass at St Francis Basilica that day.

Alex spent the morning writing up his notes and filing a status report with the office on the state of his case findings so far. After a quick lunch and a walk along the majestic Assisi countryside, thinking about anything other than the case, he again focused his mind back on the murder investigation.

As he was reflecting on all the events so far. He found it incredulous that there were so few leads on such a heinous murder, especially in a small town like Assisi. Some locals must have known something about Degno and why he might have been murdered.

He thought that it was particularly surprising that AJ, being such a devout Catholic and well intertwined in the goings-on of Assisi, could not offer him any useful background insights into Degno. Alex had previously asked AJ about Degno and whether anyone would have a reason to murder him. AJ deflected the conversation by saying that he did not know Degno well at all, and had no idea as to why anyone would want to murder him.

There was also something else about AJ that was concerning Alex. Having been a crime reporter and investigator for over two decades, Alex's intuition was telling him that given Degno's gruesome murder, it was incredibly surprising that the police were unable to find any forensic leads on a possible murderer. This would require an incredibly clinical murderer; one extremely careful not to leave behind any traces of incriminating evidence. Alex reflected on how clean and organized AJ's house was when he entered it to talk to AJ about various matters, including their discussion on reincarnation.

There was therefore something bugging Alex, and more than just a gut feel, about the combination of the fact that AJ offered surprisingly little insight into Degno, as well as the fact that AJ demonstrated all the, "on the spectrum", attributes of a clinically organized mind; perhaps himself capable of conducting such a gruesome murder, without leaving behind any incriminating evidence.

So, Alex decided he would head off now and speak to AJ again by visiting him at his home to see what else he could discern from him about Degno's murder. Alex was not hesitant about visiting AJ even if he thought there was a possibility that AJ himself might be the murderer. Given his extensive career in crime

218

reporting, this would not be the first time in Alex's career that he interviewed an actual murderer prior to him being ultimately arrested and charged. Alex may have had a few shortcomings, but courage was not one of them.

In the meantime, Sophia had a sleepless night after her distressing discussion with Clemenza. The following day, having completed her morning duties, Sophia decided that it was paramount she apologise to Alex and seek his forgiveness for what had happened. And so, after lunch and her first set of afternoon prayers, she set off towards the hotel where Alex was staying, only to be informed when she got there, that he was not there but was seen headed towards the piazza.

Determined as ever to find Alex today, Sophia headed off towards the town to look for him. When she walked past and enquired of the old man whom Alex had spoken to a few days earlier if he had seen Alex, the old man told Sophia that he had seen him walking down the road that, unbeknownst to Sophia, led to AJ's home. So Sophia headed down that road to look for him.

Meanwhile, Alex knew the way to AJ's home well and proceeded down that path, passing the piazza where AJ and Alex had coffee together, before heading a little further down the road towards AJ's home. As he did so, about a hundred meters from his destination, he saw AJ coming out of his home's doorway and acting suspiciously. He was looking around to see if anyone could see him, before turning back to lock the door as he left the house. AJ then walked up the pathway headed towards the Rocca Maggiore, but not before taking another glance backwards to see if anyone was watching him. But Alex was far enough away, and slightly hidden by the curvature of the road, for AJ to not have spotted him.

Again, Alex's intuition kicked in and he thought best not to hasten towards AJ and call out to him, but rather to follow him. He had an inkling that AJ was going somewhere where he did not want to be seen or followed. Hence, Alex carefully followed him so as to avoid being seen.

After a good twenty-minute walk up the hill, it became clear to Alex that AJ was headed towards Rocca Maggiore, which Alex had visited himself out of interest a few days earlier. He continued to follow AJ carefully and at a distance, so as not be seen, but never losing him completely out of his sight.

As AJ proceeded to walk up the pathway to Rocca Maggiore, he could see a figure dressed in priestly clothing at one of the entrances, beckoning him to come up the hill and follow him inside the Rocca. AJ waved his hand at the figure and proceeded on up the pathway. It seemed that AJ was expecting this figure to be there, and that this was the person that AJ was going to clandestinely meet with.

Alex was probably a hundred meters behind AJ, but it was close enough to see the priestly figure beckoning AJ to join him. Accordingly, Alex continued up the hill towards Rocca Maggiore to see who AJ was meeting with.

As AJ entered the doorway where the priestly figure had been beckoning him in, he was immediately set upon by two assailants that were hiding behind the doorway. They quickly grabbed him, taped up his mouth, tied his hands together and searched his body for any weapons. AJ had, in fact, a large dagger hidden underneath his clothing which they removed. They then took him down an intricate pathway and down a cold mould smelling staircase towards the basement of the Rocca. They placed him in a dimly lit stone walled room, still with his hands tied and slammed shut the heavy wooden door to the room and locked it.

The two men who had surprised AJ, also knew that Alex was following him, as they previously saw both AJ and Alex approaching from their lookout position on top of the Rocca. They knew Alex was about to arrive. So they rushed back to the doorway to equally surprise and apprehend Alex on his arrival. Which they did, even though Alex had approached and entered cautiously. They taped and tied him up as they had done to AJ.

They then brought him down the pathway and staircase and into the same stone room cell as AJ was in, and locked them both in it with their hands still tied and mouths taped up. They left them there and retreated back up the mouldy stairwell.

The cell room in which Alex and AJ were locked was down towards the basement of Rocca Maggiore, such that there were no windows. So even if Alex and AJ managed to remove their mouth tape, any screams or cries for help could not be heard outdoors.

Alex and AJ found themselves alone, gagged, tied up and terrified about what was happening. Even though they could not speak, it was obvious that AJ was looking at Alex with shock and anger. He was not only shocked that he himself had been apprehended and held captive, but angry that Alex had obviously covertly followed him there.

Alex, in turn, had a look of terror in his eyes and obviously was wondering what was going on. But even before they had a chance to regain some composure, they heard the terrified muffled screams of a woman echoing at a distance, from the cold and damp stairwell.

Sophia had stumbled into the same trap, as she had followed Alex to Rocca Maggiore. She also had been sighted by the two assailants as she approached the Rocca and on entering it, she was immediately apprehended and gagged, but not before letting out some muffled screams. She was then tied up and dragged down the pathway and staircase, to the locked room where Alex and AJ were being held.

The door to the locked cell room was then yanked open by the assailants, and Alex and AJ were visibly shocked to see Sophia there, mouth gagged and hands tied. She was then thrown onto the cold stone floor of the cell with them. The door was then loudly slammed shut, and the noise reverberated through both the cold stone cell and their frightened bodies.

The three of them, Alex and AJ standing, and Sophia strewn on the floor, all looked at each other in shock, incredulity and silence, except for Sophia's muffled sobbing.

Not long afterwards, the cell door was again yanked open and the two assailants entered. One brandishing a rifle pointed at AJ and the other holding a long sharp dagger. They were followed in by the priestly figure who was, in fact, a cardinal who held a senior position in the Vatican and was known to AJ. His name was Cardinal Bertocchi.

In a cold, almost automated voice, Bertocchi explained to them that it was unfortunate for them, pointing to Alex and Sophia, that they had followed AJ to the Rocca. Unfortunate, because in the next twenty-four hours all three of them would soon be dead. And that AJ had played straight into the trap that had been set for him by the cardinal. The three prisoners looked at each other again with a sense of incredulity, but this time also showing deep fear for their lives.

Bertocchi told them he felt obliged to tell them why they would soon all be dead, since this is now their undeniable fate. He went on to explain that the present pope, Francis, had been a thorn in his side ever since his inauguration as pope. And that Bertocchi had become sick of having to deal with the pope's incessant meddling of the affairs of the Vatican, which other popes in the past had, after a while, chosen to ignore.

Although not disclosed to the three prisoners, Bertocchi was the leader of a group of Vatican cardinals and other operatives, that all benefited personally from nefarious dealings involving Vatican finances, as well as lurid subterranean and sexually

223

explicit behaviours. This group had received a tip-off from a close confidante of the Pope that the Pope intended to undertake a major purge of this group. He intended to expose them and have them all arrested on mass soon after the Franciscan Anniversary celebrations.

The informant also told them that the Pope had intended to resign his position for some time given his health issues, but he wanted to wait to enable him to celebrate his name's sake St. Francis anniversary. And so, the purge would likely take place a week or two after the Anniversary celebrations, and before the Papal renunciation of this position sometime soon after that. As a result, the nefarious conspirators new that they had to put their assassination plan into action now.

Bertocchi recounted to them, that he had been given the task of assassinating Pope Francis. And that he had come up with a brilliant plan to attribute the assassination to AJ. In fact, AJ himself had given Bertocchi such an idea by virtue of AJ having written, almost a year ago now, to the Pope's General Secretary, who was known to AJ, a letter that had come to Bertocchi's attention. The letter listed out, in some detail, a litany of alleged church failures, particularly against women and children, and promising that God would take out his wrath on the Church unless it addressed these allegations, especially those in respect of the treatment of children.

Bertocchi carried a copy of AJ's letter with him, since he had recently been showing it to senior Vatican officials to reinforce the notion that there were crazy loners out in the community that threatened to harm the Pope. And so, he pulled it out of his pocket, carefully unfolded it, and took particular delight in reading the letter to the three prisoners to show what a brilliant assignation plan it had spawned.

"[To the Papal General Secretary

… let me make my position very clear, that unless all of this disgraceful and illegal activity that I have outlined above is made transparent by the Holy See immediately, and is made subject to thorough investigation by the proper authorities, and the people responsible for it are held to account, God's wrath will come down on the Church, including on the Holy Father himself, who is responsible ultimately for all that transpires within the Catholic Church."

Bertocchi, with a wry smile, then noted that if you wanted to write a threatening letter to Pope Francis, you could not have worded it better than this letter written by AJ.

And so, all that was needed now, was that the pope would tomorrow be shot dead by a rifle shot from the roof of Rocca Maggiore. And that soon afterwards, AJ would be found dead on the roof, having shot himself suicidally after having committed such a heinous crime.

Moreover, two innocent people, who had unsuspectingly stumbled across AJ's plan, would also be found dead in Rocca Maggiore, having been slain by the same rifle that shot the Pope.

Bertocchi noted that the Vatican authorities would have no hesitation in quickly concluding that the Pope had been assassinated by a crazed catholic loner, who had threatened to do just that in writing only some months beforehand. And the world would mourn the death of a saintly Pope, along with two innocent bystanders.

Bertocchi then gave orders for the hand ties to be removed and the ungagging of the prisoners' mouths. He knew, without saying it, that there should be no evidence of AJ in particular having been subjected to any bodily markings of restraint. He then turned around and left the cell. The assailants untied and ungagged the prisoners and left them there, locked in a cold windowless room to consider their ill-fated destiny.

A few hours had past, and the afternoon had turned into dusk and then nighttime. Deep in the Rocca, in a cold stony cell lit by a dimly orange coloured ceiling lamp, AJ, Alex and Sophia sat, still in disbelief at their predicament. Sophia sat cross legged on the cold floor, eyes closed and deep in prayer, especially calling on our Lord Jesus Christ and Saint Clare for divine assistance.

Meanwhile, back at the Convent, Clemenza knew something was not right when the other nuns had mentioned that Sophia had missed afternoon prayers and was not back in time for dinner. She had a bad feeling about the situation as this was unlike Sophia. Clemenza alone, also knew what else Sophia had been struggling with of late.

Clemenza went straight into the chapel and knelt before the Lord's crucifix and started praying, petitioning him for her safety and wellbeing.

CHAPTER 24

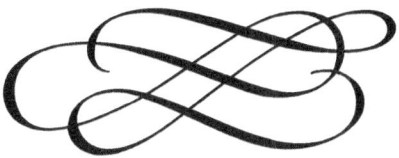

Confessions

Sophia

Back in the basement cell at Rocca Maggiore, the three prisoners were resigned to the terrible reality that, at some point soon, the assassins would open the door and systematically shoot them. Alex also knew that, at least in AJ's case, they would need to kill him as close as possible to the Pope's shooting, but they could come for himself and Sophia anytime soon.

Sophia stopped praying for help, and with a steely determination, stood up from her cross-legged position and told the others that she needed to now confess her sins and seek forgiveness, in readiness for her imminent death. She then knelt in front of both Alex and AJ, who were seated side by side, and started her confession.

"Forgive me Father, for it has been..." she blurted out, whereupon AJ raised his hand and told her to stop, because he was no priest and could not absolve her.

She immediately and determinately responded,

"The Lord will hear what I have to say! And I confess to him and you both, and seek forgiveness from him and from humanity alike!"

Alex and AJ then both understood that this was an important cleansing process for Sophia. So, they agreed to sit and listen, intently and with reverence, to whatever she had to say.

Sophia went on, with bowed head and hands clasped as if in prayer.

She started by giving thanks to the Lord for the life he had given her. Especially, for guiding her to the convent when she was young and lost, and for the love and guidance of sister Clemenza and her fellow sisters there. She asked the Lord to take mercy on her uncle and his friends who abused her as a child, and she sought forgiveness for anything she did, or failed to do, during those times to prevent it.

She then went on to seek forgiveness for the many the times in the Convent when she would masturbate in front of the statute of our Lord, imagining that he was making love to her. She knew it was sinful to do so, but she could not resist the temptation. As she started to sob, and intermittently burst out crying, she said that she wanted to experience sex with someone she actually loved, and she loved our Lord so much, even though she knew it was so wrong to be using him in this way.

And then, to AJ's complete surprise, she then openly confessed and sought forgiveness for seducing Alex to fornicate with her on the altar of the Basilica, under the pretension of the Lord making love to her. As she continued her staccato confession, amidst sobs and tears trickling down her still beautiful face, she looked up directly at Alex and begged forgiveness from him, and from his wife, for what she had done.

Alex, with AJ turning to him still in complete surprise and disdain for what he was hearing, looked at Sophia, his eyes starting to water, and nodded his head and motioned with his eyes that, of course, he forgives her; not that Alex thought it was something he needed to forgive her for, as it had been for him, the most exhilarating moment of his life.

Sophia then went on to thank the Lord for sending, what she knew to be angelic assistance, to save her from killing herself.

Looking puzzled, AJ interjected and asked what she meant by this. To both Alex's and AJ's almost utter disbelief, she then went on to describe to them what had transpired after she had told Clemenza about the fornication in the Basilica.

"....... after Clemenza had left her sprawled on the floor in Clemenza's room, as she went off to pray for Sophia in the chapel, Sophia picked herself up, and making sure no one could see the desperate state she was in, made her way back to her room.

Once there, she lay on the bed, face up, one hand resting on her forehead. Soon afterwards, all the fears seized upon her, '.....She would have to leave the convent as there was no way that a novice nun would be allowed to stay and progress as a nun having done what she had done.....She would find herself cut off from all her friends, all who were connected with the

229

convent and local community…..She had no other means of supporting herself…..She had no other livelihood skills, and having no family, she knew no one she could call on for support……She would be homeless and penniless and still addicted to her sexual fantasies of Christ, along with the eternal guilt of what she'd done both to him and to Alex….etc, etc '

The fears racked and roiled her. She twisted and turned but nothing she thought of had any light or joy, just misery, loneliness and helplessness. Having desecrated Christ on his very own alter, she could not bring herself to ask for his help and forgiveness.

She lay in torment in her room for hours. Her head incapable of finding a way through her dilemma, '…... Shame, Shame, Shame was all she could hear…… "You're a whore and always will be a whore!" she could see her Uncle's friends saying, when they knew she was being cloistered in a convent ……She had let so many people down, especially Clemenza……She would now be forsaken to a lifetime of misery and shame, and worst of all, a disconnection from God for what she had done, including what she had done to Alex's life……She had seduced a married man and led him into a defilement of his marriage vow….. Shame, Shame, Shame! roared the voices in her head….'

As her fears and guilt continued to seize her for hours longer, all of a sudden, she fastened on an eerie solution; one that solved everything and would do so immediately. She would be able to end her misery now.

She rose from the bed, threw a shawl over her head and shoulders, and suspiciously walked out of the convent so as not to be seen by anyone. Once outside, she took the path by the outside convent wall towards the forest. The sun had set hours ago, and nightfall was well advanced, but a full moon provided enough light for Sophia to find her way along the path.

After some twenty minutes of determined walking, she had arrived at her destination. A water well which was little used these days, but which she knew still had deep enough water at the bottom, more than sufficient.

As she approached it, walking on a slight upward incline, a sense of destiny came over her. The well sat atop a small hill, silhouetted against the moonlit sky behind it. The rope and bucket dangling like a hangman's noose. She knew this was where it would all end. It struck her that she had seen this image before, probably in some dream or Dejavu memory. She knew she was meant to be here.

She approached the well eagerly, knowing that all her misery would soon end. She climbed upon the well wall and sat on it facing inside the well, with her legs dangling in its dark foreboding mouth. She composed herself one last time to offer a prayer to the Lord, as embarrassing as that felt, given how she had so shamelessly desecrated him. She closed her eyes and prayed for forgiveness, not only for what she had done, but also for what she was about to do.

Then, just as she was ready to open her eyes and take the plunge, a wolf howled eerily nearby, so close that the howling vibrated through her bones. Her eyes shot open in fear, and there she saw him, only meters from the well. He was white as snow, with deep blue

231

inset eyes. Bigger than any dog or wolf she had ever seen. His fur glistening in the moonlight. He looked majestic. And looking at her, and raising his head, howled once more; again, sending a shudder through her body, as she wrapped the shawl ever closer to herself.

Although racked with fear, Sophia told herself that he was no threat to her, since she was about to plunge herself down the well and he could not prevent that. Indeed, it would hasten it if he approached further. So, she sat there to watch this majestic animal. She thought to herself, it is as if someone wanted her to see one more wondrous thing before she left this world.

But the wolf did not take a threatening stance towards her. Instead, it sat down and laid low on all four legs, its head resting on its two front paws, looking straight at Sophia, disarmed. He then started to whimper gently, as if showing signs of concern about what was to take place. Then, still hunched down on all fours, he gradually inched his way ever closer to the well, not wanting to frighten Sophia, and continuing with his gentle whimpering.

Sophia became emotional at seeing this. She knew now the wolf was not threatening her. She knew that he knew full well what she intended to do and that he was concerned about her. In fact, he was more than concerned about her, he didn't want her to die. She was no longer afraid of the wolf.

Ever gradually, and with his ongoing soft whimpering, the wolf inched his way to the edge of the well wall, right where Sophia was sitting. His beautiful piercing blue eyes focused on her relentlessly. When he finally reached the well, this majestic animal then rose up slowly and put his front paws on the edge of the well, inches away from Sophia. And then laid his head on them, still whimpering ever so softly, with his eyes this time looking straight ahead away from Sophia. It was as if he wanted to sit with her for a while, as she decided whether to take the plunge down the well to end everything.

Sophia then understood this was no ordinary wolf. Her eyes teared up, and she began to sob. She knew this was an angelic sign from above. That it was intended to stop her doing what she had intended. But she also knew she had a choice. And whoever had sent her this majestic animal to comfort her, did not mean to take away her choice. Nonetheless, her intuition told her that miraculous signs like these, should not be ignored.

She slowly reached out with her right hand towards the wolf. His eyes were fixed straight ahead, but he knew she was reaching out to him. Her hand slowly touched his soft furry head, glistening in the moonlight. And she gently stroked it. They sat there together for some time. Sophia stroking the wolf and still contemplating what she would do.

In the end, she chose not to end her life that night. The wolf her spirit guides had sent her, saved her.

Alex

Sophia stood up after her confession, visibly more at ease with the situation they found themselves in and

233

then sat down next to Alex. Alex, like AJ, was still gob-smacked at Sophia's attempted suicide story.

She then turned to him and said emphatically, "Your turn!"

Alex was taken by surprise. The idea of confessing any regrets he had in life, let alone seeking forgiveness, was not something he had ever considered. Yet he could see the benefit that Sophia had felt from the process she had just gone through.

He thought to himself, if they were all about to be murdered, which seemed certain, then there's nothing to lose by discussing his regrets and seeking forgiveness, since if by some chance, there was life after death, it might be important to seek forgiveness and mercy. And if there wasn't, what few secrets he was about to share with Sophia and AJ would not go far in any event. There was also one thing he particularly wanted to get off his chest, regardless of whether there was some superior power listening or not. So, still seated, Alex bent forward and clasped his hands, closed his eyes and commenced.

"I seek forgiveness for my inadequacies as a husband to my wife Angela, who I still love very much, despite the fact we seem to be constantly arguing about things. I obviously lack the skills needed to have nurtured a better relationship with her, and regret that I have not tried harder to develop those skills in order to improve our relationship.

"I particularly regret the terrible thoughts I had recently, regarding wishing she would just die and allow me the freedom to be with another woman".

At this, Sophia gasped and put both her hands to her mouth in shock. She knew what Alex meant by this. She immediately realized the potential enormity of the evil she had unleashed by seducing Alex in the Basilica.

Alex, unfazed by Sophia's reaction, continued.

"I now wish to seek forgiveness for something that I'm not entirely sure I did, but I am more certain of it than not. If, in another life, I have participated in heinous acts of massacres and brutal murders of innocent men, women and children, with all my heart and soul, I seek forgiveness from all who I have harmed, and mercy from anyone who will judge me."

Praying earnestly, Alex strengthened the clasping of his hands and blurted out,

"Forgive me, forgive me, forgive me, for I am so so sorry for whomever I have harmed, or failed to protect."

Sophia looked at Alex totally puzzled by this last confession, as the Alex she had come to know, even in such a short period of time, surely, was not capable of such acts. However, she also knew that he was talking about his actions in a past life; one that he must have come to recall.

None of this, of course, was a surprise to AJ, with whom Alex had shared this recollection. It nonetheless moved AJ to place his hand on Alex's shoulder and comfort him, saying,

"My dear brother, take note that your prayers of forgiveness and mercy will be heard. And if you are truly repentant, the yet unactioned karma of your deeds will be dissolved."

Alex then unclasped his hands and sat upright, with eyes still closed. All three of them sat there in silence for a few moments, allowing the vibrations thrown off by Alex's confession to dissipate.

AJ

Without any prompting from Alex or Sophia, AJ silently slid off his seat and sat cross legged on the floor, facing both Alex and Sophia, with head bowed down to avoid eye contact. His hands individually clenched into fists and each rested on his knees. He closed his eyes and commenced his confession; a confession that would send shudders through both Alex and Sophia.

"Dear brother Alex and sister Sophia, I confess this to you and only to you, my story, the truth.

"In a small town in Veneto, not far from Venice, where I lived before coming to Assisi, there also lived a married woman, who perhaps through destiny, I fell in love with and had a child with her. All this unbeknownst to her husband, who considered the baby girl his own. As she grew, I loved and worshiped that little girl from afar, and hoped one day, that I would be able to meet her and do something useful for her in her life.

"That little child, when she began attending primary school, became the subject of sexual abuse at the hands of the local priest of the town. Years later, as a teenager, that abuse took its toll on her and tragically, she took her own life. I did not know at the time, even after she had died, that she had been abused. Her death shattered my world and of course, all those that loved her, especially her mother.

"Some years later, it emerged that the Catholic Church around the world had been guilty of abusing many young children. Gradually, rumours emerged in the town that the local priest may have been guilty of such heinous deeds. But no one in the town was prepared to make accusations of him and the police were too weak to investigate. I confronted her mother at about this time, and she admitted to me that our little girl had indeed been subjected to abuse. No evidence was ever brought forth regarding her abuser.

"When I served in the Italian military, I served in the commandos and I was well skilled in secret surveillance, sabotage and even assassinations attempts. I made it my passion to investigate this local priest. To my disgust, I found evidence that he had abused various children and may well have abused my beautiful daughter. I knew that taking this evidence to the police would be pointless.

"I decided that I would take justice into my own hands. But before i could move on him, the church had elevated that vile priest to the role of Bishop and moved him to Assisi."

At this, both Sophia's and Alex's jaws dropped.

"At that point, I relocated from where I lived in northern Italy to Assisi, where I would bide my time, and when the time was right, I was determined to revenge my beautiful daughter. To my ongoing disgust, but not surprise, I secretly observed that, even as a Bishop, he was continuing to abuse children, as well as take advantage of some of the local widows of the town.

"When I eventually caught him, isolated and clueless, as he walked through the forest of Assisi, coincidentally, on his way to have sex with a local widow living nearby, I took great delight in seeing him slowly squirm to death. I tied and gagged him, then drove a wooden pylon up and through his backside. I took immense joy from his agonising suffering, his muffled groans, his vile body contortions and bloody convulsions."

At this point, AJ looks up at Alex and Sophia, who are visibly shocked at what they have just heard. Even more frightening, the look on AJ's face, caused Sophia to gasp and cup her hands to her mouth. His face had become devilish, his eyes emitted a red glowing darkness that screamed possession by something evil. This sent shudders through both Alex and Sophia.

AJ then bowed down again, avoiding eye contact and continued what was supposedly a confession, but was, in reality, an affirmation of will, evil will.

"I hereby express no regret or remorse for what I have done. Degno was evil that had to be eradicated from the world. An example also had to be given to all clergy, who had abused their sacred and privileged duty of being Good Shepherds and protectors of children.

"Remember Alex and Sophia, this world is but an illusion, and we should have no regrets in killing what is evil and exterminating it from the face of the Earth."

AJ paused for a moment, then continued.

"I came to the Rocca to talk to Bertocchi. To see if he was truly good, or deceptively evil. Apart from my duty to revenge my daughter's death, I also believe I have been given a mission to protect this unique Pope we currently have. Who personally, has been waging war, virtually single handily, against Church transgressions and devilish evil. And I was prepared to cut Bertocchi's throat, if I had concluded that he was evil. But unfortunately, overtime, my combat skills have waned, and they grabbed me and took away my dagger before I could do anything.

"I sit here so that you can hear the truth; a truth for which I have no regrets."

Alex appreciated then, that evil men can do great evil in the pretence of fighting against it.

CHAPTER 25

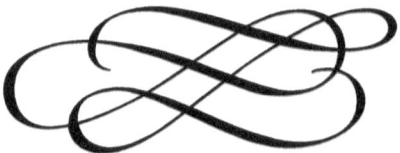

That Stormy Night

After AJ had finished, a few moments of silence passed that seemed like hours, and Alex and Sophia still sat there, stunned and struggling to comprehend what they had just heard, and seen in AJ's facial transfiguration.

Before they could even begin to consider what their reaction to AJ's confession should be, AJ commenced to discuss what would likely happen next. Calling on his commando training, in a monotonous droning voice, he said,

"Our only chance to survive this murderous plot is to make a run for it when they next come for us. (Pause) There are only two assailants plus Bertocchi, versus three of us, since they didn't anticipate you two being here today.

"Moreover, they can't afford to have any signs of physical restraint on my body if they are to frame me. (Pause) They need to leave me alive until just before they assassinate the Pope. (Pause) But you two, they can kill anytime. (Pause) So, they will come for you two first and leave me here for later.

"Our only chance is to rush them once this door opens, otherwise they will come in and isolate me and take you separately. (Pause) As there are three of us and only three of them, we have a fighting chance to upset their plans. (Pause) I will rush out first as they will take care not to shoot or stab me, and I will overwhelm one of them. (Pause) You two take the other. (Pause) Even if Bertocchi is with them, he is unlikely to give us a problem."

Alex looked at AJ, and nodding, said, "Okay," as he knew AJ had summed up the situation as well as anyone could.

Sophia fell to her knees, hands in prayer mode, eyes shut and started praying intensely. She prayed especially to Jesus, and St Clare, to whom she felt a close affinity, and to Saint Francis.

After an hour or so, they could hear the thunder of a huge storm going on outside. The storm was loud enough to be heard even from the basement of the Rocca. AJ knew that a thunderous storm would make it even harder for anyone to hear a rifle shot from the Rocca. So, it provided the perfect backdrop for the shooting to start. He told the others to ready themselves to rush the door when it opened. Alex prepared himself, but Sophia just kept praying, even harder.

Sophia heard the thunder and lightning going on outside and that meant something to her that the others would have been oblivious to. She was a devotee of Saint Clare and had heard of the miraculous feat attributed to the Saint by her having prayed to the Lord to protect the town of Assisi from the ravages of the attacking Moorish Army in the 13th century; whereupon a violent, thunderous storm scattered the invaders from their encampment and resulted in their leaving the town.

As AJ had predicted, the thunder outside provided the perfect sound barrier needed for the assailants to seek to perform their murderous deeds. Suddenly, the cell door bolt was unbolted and the door kicked open, banging loudly as it slammed against the stone wall inside the cell. The assailants wanted to stun the captives, but AJ was prepared for this. He immediately, and fearlessly, leapt from his seat and charged his attackers. Alex knew this was the signal for him to do likewise and he quickly followed AJ out the door.

AJ's thinking that the assailants would avoid using a gun or a knife to restrain him, proved correct. They just stood there, surprised to see AJ and Alex charging at them in pre-emptive self-defence.

However, what AJ hadn't anticipated was that Bertocchi had called for reinforcements. Bertocchi had reasoned that two assailants would have been enough to deal with AJ alone, but once it became clear that there were three captives that needed to be dealt with, he arranged for another two assailants to reinforce the original two.

And so, when AJ and Alex came charging out, in the mist of ongoing thunderous vibrations coming from outside the Rocca, they were faced with four assailants not two, along with Bertocchi, who stood back away from the fray and held a rifle in his gloved hands. No doubt the rifle that would be used to kill, first Alex and Sophia, and then later, AJ and the Pope, with only AJ's fingerprints to be imprinted on it.

The four assailants were too much for AJ and Alex, and they were easily restrained, despite AJ particularly putting up a strong struggle. Sophia walked out of the cell, poised and incredibly serene, given the circumstances of what was occurring. It was as if she knew something her captors didn't.

Bertocchi ordered AJ be put back in the room cell and door locked. He would wait there until closer to the time of the Pope's assassination, so that his time of death would roughly coincide with the Pope's assassination, in a feigned suicide soon after the assassination.

Bertocchi then placed the rifle on the ground at the feet of the leader of the assailants, handed him a pair of white gloves and ordered him to put Alex and Sophia against the wall and shoot them in the head. The other three assailants took then Alex and Sophia and thrust them against the wall, both bouncing off it and falling to the ground.

But just as the lead assailant finished putting on his gloves and started to pick up the rifle, a haunting bone chilling howl of a wolf was heard echoing down the staircase into the basement. Amidst the thunderous ructions coming from the storm outside the Rocca, the proximity of the wolf's howl sent chills through everyone in the basement; so much so, that the leader paused picking up the rifle and stood up in fright and turned to look at the stairway from which the howling was heard.

Before his logical mind kicked back in, so he could reach down again to pick up the rifle, a blackish grey wolf, the size of a German Great Dane, charged down the stairs and leapt straight at him, forcing him backwards onto the ground. Three other massive grey wolves quickly followed down the stairway, each of whom ferociously attacked the other assailants.

Alex knew this was the only chance they had to escape, so he rose to his feet, grabbed Sophia's hand and hauled her out of the basement up the staircase. The assailant leader, who was by far the stronger of the murderous group, managed to free himself momentarily from the lead wolf's attack. He then drew his dagger and chased Alex and Sophia up the staircase, knowing full well that if they got away, he would be destined to be convicted of attempted murder.

Bertocchi stood there stunned witnessing all this. He then tried to run and pick up the rifle, but the lead wolf seemed to know exactly what he was doing, and jumped over where the rifle lay, with eyes glaring and teeth snaring at Bertocchi. That stopped Bertocchi frozen. He was paralyzed in fright as he stared into the eyes of this ferocious beast. He then realized that, for some reason, the wolf was not going to attack him as long as he did not move; so frozen he remained.

The other wolves were ravaging the remaining three assailants, all of whom seemed destined to succumb to the blood thirsty attackers, as the beasts were monstrous and ferociously targeted the throats and back necks of the assailants.

Bertocchi forbade the others from carrying firearms that day, as he wanted zero risk of one of them shooting AJ, and thereby spoiling the lone papal assassin plot. That decision now condemned them all to death. Whilst they carried small daggers, the assailants were no match for the bestial wolves, even if one or two managed to draw their daggers from their sheaths and land some blows onto them.

Outside, the violent storm continued to thunder and blow fierce gale force winds, even uprooting trees around the Rocca.

Alex and Sophia had managed to find their way into the narrow-walled corridor that led away from the Rocca. Sophia knew of this pathway from her previous visits to the Rocca, and guided Alex into it. But the lead assailant was close enough to follow them into it, and he was chasing them down its narrow tunnel, not far behind. They knew he was there, as they could see glimpses of his dagger shining as he ran with it in one hand; the knife reflecting the constant peppering of storm lightning bolts finding their way into the tunnel, and which fortunately provided a flickering lighted pathway through the tunnel down which Alex and Sophia were running.

Alex continued to run ahead of Sophia, pulling her by the hand, and hoping this flickering pathway would somehow soon lead to the outdoors. But they had been running hard for some time and weariness was setting in. Alex could see the assailant making ground on them and he felt Sophia starting to tire and slowdown. The assailant was only a few meters behind them now. The thunderous storm now grew even louder, with a barrage of lightning bolts quickening, almost at the same pace at which the assailant was catching up to them.

Then Sophia tripped and fell to the ground, letting go of Alex's hand in the process. Alex couldn't stop his momentum forward, and by the time he had stopped, he was a good five to ten meters from Sophia. The assailant was making up ground and was now almost upon her from behind.

Alex started to run back to help Sophia. But Sophia, laying helpless on the ground, heard this almighty explosion behind her. The gale force wind had begun to push over a section of the tunnel wall, and the collapse was cascading down and along the tunnel wall to where they were. The collapsing wall then caught up and fell onto the running assailant, instantly killing him. But it kept collapsing passed him and was headed for Sophia. Sophia realized Alex was running straight into its murderous path by coming back to help her. So she leapt up just as Alex ran up to her and pushed him away from the collapsing wall to the opposite side of the tunnel, throwing him clear of the massive brickwork raining down on her.

Alex hit the wall and fell to the ground. Stunned and dazed for a moment, he gathered himself and rose to his feet. The wall has ceased collapsing, but the rain and wind now raged through to where he was standing. Immediately, his attention turned to Sophia.

Amidst the pelting rain, he could see part of her clothing strewn amongst the collapsed brickwork and rushed over to it and started to clear the bricks and rubble on and around her. He was no longer concerned about the assailant chasing them as he could see that he had been consumed by the collapsed wall.

He yelled out to her, "Sophia! Sophia! Sophia!" But she was motionless and not breathing. He then started to give her mouth-to-mouth resuscitation, the rain continuing to fall on them. He tried for what seemed an eternity, but it was to no avail. He knew she was gone. Alex was trained in first aid and resuscitation techniques and had enough experience as a crime reporter to be able to recognise the symptoms of a deceased person. From what he could see and feel, as he reached for a pulse somewhere on her body, Sophia was dead.

In a final act of selfless love, she had pushed Alex away from the collapsing wall to save him, knowing that by doing so, it would over topple her.

Kneeling alongside her, with the rain still pouring down on both, Alex put his head on her chest and wept loudly, with gut-wrenching grief. Alex had never shown such emotion before. After a few moments, he gently reached out and closed those piercing blue eyes of hers, for the last time.

CHAPTER 26

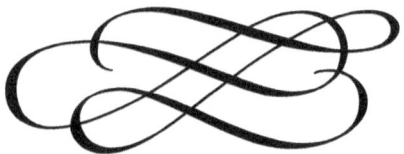

The Convent Chapel

At the convent earlier that evening, after Clemenza had prayed for Sophia's safety, she had been given a premonition that Sophia was in danger, and that it was somehow connected with the Rocca Maggiore.

She quickly summoned a small group of sisters. They piled into the convent minibus and headed straight for the Rocca, despite the pelting rain and howling storm winds.

As they approached the Rocca, thankfully, there was a lull in the storm and the driving rain abated somewhat. On driving up the road towards the Rocca's main entrance, Clemenza noticed the broken wall section of the tunnel passageway where Alex and Sophia were. The broken rock wall was the image she had been given in her premonition. She immediately directed the sister driving the minibus to head straight for the broken section in the wall.

Alex, still kneeling over Sophia's body, gently caressed her face, sobbing and still stunned and incredulous as to what had transpired that day, culminating in the death of this most loving, angelic, selfless creature.

He looked up and through the rain saw a set of car headlights heading his way. He honestly couldn't care less who was in the car, friend or foe. It didn't matter anymore. Sophia was dead. And he wasn't about to leave her.

The convent minibus pulled up close to where Alex was, and Clemenza shot out the door and ran to where she could see Sophia's body. She immediately looked for any signs of life, and when she found nothing, she paused to take a moment to say a prayer over her. She then told the other sisters to take Sophia's body into the minibus and set her up in the convent chapel.

She checked Alex for any signs of injury and motioned to him to get out of the tunnel and to join them in the minibus, which Alex did. He knew it was illegal to remove a body from a crime scene before police had arrived, but he didn't care. He wanted Sophia's body removed from the wet cold rubble as soon as possible.

On the way to the convent, the sisters alerted the police to the scene at the Rocca and told them where AJ had been imprisoned. But they were careful not to give away that they had sequestered Sophia's body.

Once back at the convent, the sisters, still sobbing and crying over Sophia's death, gently took Sophia's body away, cleansed it, robed it and set her up on the altar of the Convent Chapel. Facing upwards, her head on a cushion, they surrounded the alter with burning candles and quickly began praying for her, led by Clemenza.

Alex was offered some dry mendicant clothes in the form of a monk's habit, which he duly changed into. He was then ushered to take a seat on a church pew towards the back of the Chapel. He was exhausted from not having had any sleep, as well as the mental and physical ordeal he had been through at the Rocca. As much as he wanted to stay awake, he found himself laying down flat on the pew, and in a short time, fell asleep.......

Earlier

After Alex and Sophia had run up the basement stairs and escaped from the Rocca, just after the wolves first arrived and began attacking the assailants, the scene back in the Rocca basement turned into something out of a horror movie.

As Bertocchi stood frozen still in fear, transfixed on the snarling beast of a wolf standing over the rifle, the other wolves continued to ferociously maul the remaining assailants. The ongoing sounds of screaming men and growling wolves, filled and echoed through the basement, along with the putrid odour of excrement coming from the mauled assailants.

A couple of the assailants managed to withdraw their daggers from their sheaths and landed a couple of blows on their attackers, but they were no match for the blood thirsty monsters, whose toughened coat-skins readily withstood what few stabs the assailants managed to land.

Bertocchi wondered in fear why he was being spared from attack, and was hoping the snarling wolf would be distracted by the other struggling assailants just enough so that he could pick up the rifle. But it soon became obvious why he had been spared so far.

From down the staircase, slowly walked in the alpha male wolf. A majestic snow-white beast, slightly larger than the other wolves. When he reached the ground step, he slowly turned towards Bertocchi. As if on cue, the snarling wolf guarding the rifle retreated, and eagerly joined the other wolves at mauling what little resistance was left in the bloodied assailants, who were now strewn all over the blood-soaked basement floor; their bodies in contorted poses, with pools of blood streaming from their throats and the back of their necks. The wolves themselves were covered in blood, from their faces and necks right down to their shoulders, some still with growling jaws locked on their prey, waiting for all movement to halt.

The white alpha male wolf then trod carefully over the rifle whilst snarling, teeth gleaming, at Bertocchi. He paused, and then, with one almighty pounce, thrust himself onto Bertocchi, grabbing and crushing his throat in one ferocious joust. He commenced to maul Bertocchi mercilessly; the wolf's snow white main quickly became covered in red blotches of Bertocchi's blood…….

Back at the convent chapel, Alex stirred from his sleep to the sound of a large thunderclap, and a flash of lightning that permeated throughout the chapel. He slowly sat up in the chapel pew, and looked up and saw a scene at the chapel alter, so surreal, that it would remain with him forever.

Sophia still lay there stretched out on the alter, face up in her nun's habit, her hands carefully resting lengthwise along her sides. Scores of candles now adorned the otherwise dark chapel, their flickering light gently illuminating her white face, along with the chapel statues near the altar, of a crucified Christ, a prayerful Saint Clare, and an adoring Saint Francis looking up to the sky with stigmatised hands raised in petition to the Lord.

But it was the sounds that raised the heckles on Alex's neck. The nuns, now some thirty of them in all, gathered in droning prayers. It sounded as if the chapel had become a beehive, with the drone from the prayers reverberating off the stone walls and swirling within the chapel chamber. He could make out one group of nuns praying repeatedly the Our Father. A second group, regurgitating Hail Mary's'. And a third group, repeating some other prayer he could not recognise.

In the background, thunder and lightning raged outside from the storm which had again intensified. With every loud thunderclap, the nuns' prayers briefly got louder in unison, to then temporarily retreat as the thunder subsided. Each repetitive lightning bolt outside illuminated the scene by entering through the chapel windows, momentarily lighting up and emphasising Sophia's starkly cold full-length body on the alter, as well as the crucifix and saintly statues near the alter. It was as though pulsating strobe lights had been turned on inside the chapel.

Alex sat there entranced by this full sensory experience of constant pulsating sights and repetitive sounds; melodious droning, whirling prayers, flickering candle imagery, lightning flashes, thunder claps, and through it all, Clemenza stood next to Sophia, hands gently and slowly touching her head, then her arms, her chest, all parts of her body as she mumbled some sort of repetitive prayer, which Alex could not possibly hear in the cacophony of noise.

He was not sure how long this had been going on for, but he surmised he must have slept for at least twenty minutes or more. He now really wasn't sure what was going on. The prayers and actions of Clemenza and the nuns were not consistent with what he thought should be a peaceful passing of a person's life. Instead, they seemed to be prayers of petition, as if they were asking God to still help Sophia in some way.

As if it were even possible, the storm seemed to be intensifying even more. The lightning and sound of thunderclaps were increasing. To Alex, the whole scene had become unnerving in that, despite being indoors in a stone building, it felt that the force of the storm was so strong now as to be able to blow this edifice to bits if it so desired, not unlike what had happened to the Rocca passageway wall.

Clemenza's droning prayer also seemed to get louder as the storm grew stronger. And as her droning intensified to match the storm, so did the prayerful droning of the other nuns. The chapel had now grown to become, not a peaceful mourning of Sophia's passing, but rather an eerie, if not frightful, experience of increasingly loud droning and intensifying lightning and thunderclaps, so much so, that Alex pulled his clothes closer to himself and raised the hood on his cape over his head, as if anticipating the chapel roof ready to explode away.

At a certain point, with the ever growing crescendo of noise and reverberating lightning, Clemenza's prayer turned into one involving yelling at Sophia, so loudly, that Alex could make out in Italian that she was yelling, indeed commanding, Sophia to, "Get up! Get up! Get up!"

Just when Alex thought that the sensory experience could not become more intense, the noise no louder, the lightning no more riotous, just then, a big bone-chilling howl of a wolf reverberated throughout the chapel, as if it were on the inside, leading all the nuns to put out an almighty gasp in the middle of their loud droning, and then they continued on as if nothing had happened.

This was immediately followed by an almighty thunderclap and accompanying massive lightning bolt that exploded one of the glass-stained chapel windows close to the alter. And somehow, to Alex's and everyone's complete fright, resulted in Sophia's body convulsing upright at the waist, virtually forcing her to sit upright amid the breaking coloured-glass and rain that then showered in over her head from the exploding window pain, close to the alter.

As a result, there was a collective shock that overcame everyone in the chapel, except Clemenza, who jumped up onto the alter and wrapped herself around Sophia's upright body, embracing it and holding it from falling back down. The droning prayers continued.

But what then sent the heckles up everyone's neck and started everyone gasping and crying whilst still praying, was when Sophia slowly raised her arms, which had been dangling by her side, and gently hugged Clemenza around her shoulders, as they both then sat on the alter embracing each other.

Sophia, without moving from her embrace of Clemenza, then turned her gaze toward Alex as he sat at the back of the chapel. She somehow knew exactly where he was sitting. And she stared directly at him, with those piercing blue eyes; the same eyes Alex had closed at least an hour ago when she lay dead in the Rocca ruins.

This was too much, even for a hardened criminal reporter like Alex, and he passed out, slouching back down onto the pew and hitting his head hard on the wooden seat in the process.

CHAPTER 27

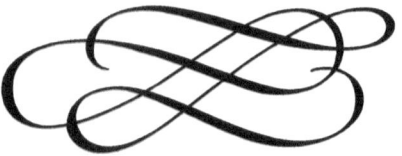

Awakened

Fifteen years later, 2041

Alex:

After that day in the chapel many years ago, my life changed, unrecognisably. The day after falling and knocking myself unconscious in the chapel, the nun assigned to take care of me at the Convent organised for me to meet Sophia in an open convent area.

I remember sitting there waiting for her as she came down the hallway to the open area. I was looking for all the bruises and scratches that were all over her face and arms from the collapsed wall at the Rocca, but there was nothing there. She looked perfect, and beautiful as ever.

She sat down across the table from me and asked me how I was. At that point, I burst into tears, marvelling at how this incredible soul could be concerned about me, instead of me having first asked about her. But that was Sophia, always concerned about others rather than herself.

I was still coming to grips with the absolute miracle that I had witnessed in her resurrection from, what was without any doubt to me, her being clinically dead. Moreover, I could see plainly, and miraculously, that her body showed no signs of the tumultuous injuries she sustained some forty-eight hours earlier.

That was the moment I considered myself to be truly Awake.

Sophia told me I had been Awakened by the Power of the Holy Spirit. I jokingly added, 'and by Wolves and Black Cockatoos.'

From that moment on, I knew there was a spiritual realm; an unseen realm, which was real, incredibly important, and was undoubtedly the underpinning of the religious Faiths, which I had up until that point, rejected outright.

In the years that have gone past since, I have spent much time devoting my journalistic investigative skills towards researching the basis of this unseen realm. And I have come to understand many of the things that both Sophia, AJ, Michael and of course, my wife Angela, had tried to teach me back then.

This realm was not exclusive to a particular religion. It clearly spanned across the key religions, which those goodly souls in that Assisi Cafe, had discussed with me so insightfully years ago (viz. The Cafe Dialogue). But it also covered the Indigenous religions; certainly, the Australian aboriginal myths that Michael believed in (viz. Moree and Mount Kaputar).

Over the last fifteen years, I had also come to realise that the essence of this unseen realm was vested in a series of Universal Laws. These laws included both the notion of Karma, and the Reincarnation of souls into a material world; all for the purpose of advancing the development of those souls, through learning, from both suffering and experiential knowledge, towards an ever more advanced state of perfection.

Sophia was an example of an advanced soul, who despite her advancement, still needed to be in this material world to both, evolve further, and importantly, to help others in their journey of evolution and development; one of which, of course, was me.

The key to Awakening was to have some form of Faith; that is, to believe in these Universal Laws, and consistent with them, that there is a Supreme power who designed them with good intentions at heart; a Good God or Universal Designer. As Sophia had explain to me during my time in Assisi, this requires True Faith in a God, without the need for obvious scientific proof thereof (viz. Sophia).

That day at the convent fifteen years ago, as she sat across the table from me, she told me about her near-death experience; what she had experienced during the time when she was technically dead. Importantly, she shared many insights with me which I have come to better understand in the years that followed.

She even brought a pen and notepad down and handed them to me, so I could take notes of our meeting. She knew it was important to share with me what she had learnt from her spirit guides. I am referring to those notes now as I relay this to you.

She did not go into minute details, but she said she had met with her spirit guides who had told her that it was not her time to leave this material world. She had a key purpose in her ongoing life here, and that was to support Clemenza in running the convent and all the good that comes from it. And eventually, to take over from her as the head nun, which she did some years later.

To assist her in her work, she had also been given insights by her guides as to what was to transpire in the world in the near term. And especially, how important it was for her and the convent, to assist in the process of both Awakening and Healing, both of which would be needed in the years ahead.

She spoke about the world entering a period of Transition, in which the religious Faiths will be challenged and undermined. That over time, they would evolve into more sympathetic and universal Faiths, shedding the man-made dogmas that gave them the appearance of being very different to each other. But this Transition would involve much dislocation and suffering in the meantime.

The connectivity of the Internet would bring both good and bad aspects to this Transition, not dissimilar to the invention of the printing press and the revolution in knowledge that followed from it. It would improve Truth Telling, including, discrediting many man-made dogmas. As an illustration, it will become apparent that the religions based on the Abrahamic

Tradition (i.e., Religions of the Book) namely, Judaism, Christianity and Islam have all been corrupted in many respects.

The Old Testament God (Yahweh), for example, could not possibly have been Jesus's Father that Jesus talks about in the New Testament. In this regard, AJ was absolutely correct when he said that Religious Administrators blatantly disregard what is reputedly Holy Scripture when it suits their agenda. For instance, how often in Christian church services is **2 Samuel 24** read out to the congregation? Answer: never, because it tells of Yahweh's violent displeasure of King David daring to take a census of his men who had attained fighting age. And Yahweh's punishment for this was to slaughter 70,000 Israelites.

Nor is **Deuteronomy 20:16-18** ever read out to congregations, since it recounts Yahweh's order to the Israelites to commit Genocide against Isreal's enemies. It reads, "As for the towns of these peoples that your Lord God is giving you as an inheritance, you must not let anything that breathes to remain alive. You shall annihilate them – the Hittites and the Ammonites, the Canaanites and the Perizzites, the Hivites and the Jebusites – just as the Lord your God has commanded."

Various other examples support this subterfuge. For instance, Yahweh's proclaimed death penalty for those working on the Sabbath (Exodus 35:2) or for pre-marital sexual intercourse (Deuteronomy 22: 13-21) and the requirement for a priest to burn his daughter alive if she became a prostitute (Leviticus 21:9).

Obviously, this Yahweh can not be the Father which Jesus speaks of as his own, the One who sent him to preach Compassion, Forgiveness and "Turning the other cheek" (Matt 5:38-48).

Another example, of corrupted teaching relates to the claim in the Quran that Jesus did not die on the cross and was not resurrected. Growing scientific and historical knowledge of the Shroud of Turin and the Sudarium of Oviedo will assist in this Truth Telling.

Ongoing scientific research, and particularly its dissemination via the Internet, will gradually make clear that Reincarnation is also a fundamental Universal Law.

Moreover, the knowledge revolution fostered by the Internet will also reveal lost ancient civilisations of a sophisticated nature, contrary to the existing historical narratives, and whose inhabitants were progenitors to many of the stories later recounted in the Genesis biblical text, which was copied from much earlier ancient sources.

The revealing and dissemination of these truths in the Internet Age will, at first, create disillusionment amongst the followers of the traditional religious Faiths; Faiths that have been based on centuries of dogmas, which will now be shown to be false. But overtime, this dislocation will give rise to a new "synthesis", leading to a New Age set of religions. The old religions will not entirely collapse, but rather, evolve to accommodate the revelation of these growingly undeniable truths.

Equally, the development of the Internet will give rise to new forms of suffering that had not been experienced in previous epochs. Mental illness will rise. But just as harmful, the Internet will be a new source of "distraction," making it even harder for people to awaken to the unseen realm. Since not only will they be distracted by their existing material world and all its allures and addictive habits, but now the Internet will give them another artificial world (or false god) in which they can lose themselves in and waste their lives becoming further divorced from their spirituality. It can also be a portal for evil.

The expanding world of incessant pharmaceuticals, and increased use of vaccines, will also stifle people's physical ability to truly Awaken. And evil forces can easily operate through these mediums, pretending in many cases to be forces for good.

But with faith, prayer and an allegiance to a true spiritual devotion, evil forces can be held back, even exorcised (viz. Miracles in an Illusory World and Twilight in the Basilica).

There is indeed a good and merciful God, who has the objective of the advancement of our souls to a higher level of perfection, and who has built a set of Universal Laws to achieve that.

Those souls who Awaken to understand this, will better accept the purpose inherent in their own suffering, and that of their loved ones and the world at large. And they'll be better placed to help mitigate it (viz. Purpose). Those who are not Awake, will find the workings of the world hard to understand, and their struggle with it will seem disheartening and futile (viz. The Locals and The Card Men).

Regardless of which religion one follows, the Holy Spirit (viz. The Divine Sophia) is ever present, and is waiting for us to let Her light into our hearts, either voluntarily, or ultimately, through the "cracked walls" caused by our own suffering.

Sophia also told me that the Universe had pre-designed life lessons for us, even before we were born, including determining which families we would be born into. We thereafter create our own ongoing karmic lessons, via our words and our deeds (viz. The Card Men). Only compassion, repentance and forgiveness can help us mitigate these (viz. The Café Dialogue and Confessions).

The Holy Spirit will especially help those who seek guidance and assistance, and Sophia emphasised the importance of prayer in this process (viz. Assisi, The Divine Sophia and The Convent Chapel).

AJ was partly right in saying that the material world is somewhat illusory and not the true realm. But he was vastly wrong in assuming that this material world has no ongoing relevance to us, and that what happens in it is of little importance. Ultimately, this world we live in, or more precisely a hybrid version of it, will become a permanent home for those resurrected souls who will thereafter live in the grace of our already resurrected Lord Jesus Christ.

God has a plan, a clear plan, which may not be understood entirely by us, but we can learn a lot about it by listening to the great religious founders of the past, (viz. The Café dialogue) and particularly, our Saviour Jesus Christ (viz. A Galilean Wedding).

Jesus came to save everybody, including those of other faiths. Overtime, it will become apparent that he himself was a devotee of many of the Faiths that preceded him, including Buddhism and Hinduism, which both practiced Reincarnation. But he was not a devotee of the man-made dogmas that accompanied such Faiths.

It will emerge that he travelled to India and Tibet during his teenage and later years, as already documented in Buddhist scrolls describing the life and teachings of the Buddhist Saint, Saint Issa. And he then returned to Judea in his thirties to start his, ultimately fatal, Judean ministry. How could you hide a child prodigy such as Jesus for almost twenty years, without a mention in any biblical story from the age of twelve to thirty, whilst living in a small country environment like Judea?

Many old myths will also prove to have truths in them, such as the story of the indigenous Spirit Biame, in Australian Indigenous culture, as well as the story of the Seven Sisters, a story also replicated in various myths across the globe. This story will eventually prove to be a euphemism for real events, involving an epic history of Mankind's cosmic engagement with extraterrestrials; a story yet to be fully told.

Sophia, when I asked her what all this means for me, counselled me that I to have a purpose to assist in this Transitional Evolution. When I asked how, she simply said that I have obviously been given various gifts, being all the skills that a good investigative journalist needs, including the ability to research thoroughly and to write and speak clearly and convincingly. And that I should give thought to, and pray for guidance on, how to devote these skills now that I have been Awakened.

She told me that the visions I had be given in dreams regarding Indigenous massacres and wrongdoings, were given to me for a reason. And that I should reflect on them and ask for guidance on the purpose of their revelation to me.

She implored on me the importance of the Power of Prayer to help me in my journey going forward. And she reminded me, as I experienced myself, that we not only learn from our suffering and experiences during the daytime, but also from our dreams at night, where insight and guidance can be received.

She cautioned that evil does exist in the world, and that these evil forces, although eventually doomed to failure, will attempt to cause much havoc and to derail those who are assisting in God's plan of Awakening others, and transitioning the world to a better place (viz. Twilight in the Basilica and Unforgivable Devastation).

She, of course, had been right all along fifteen years ago, when she told me I was on a spiritual journey the first day I met her. I was just too asleep at the time to be able to appreciate it.

CHAPTER 28

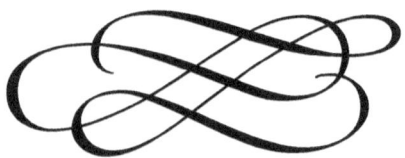

Epilogue and Repentance Day

Back to October 2026

The planned papal mass celebrating St. Francis's 800-year anniversary went ahead without a hitch.

In the days following the event, Alex told Angela everything, including what had happened in the Basilica.

Sophia separately met with Angela and begged her forgiveness. Angela gave it freely, as in the short few days she had been with Alex since arriving in Assisi, she could see Alex was a different man, vastly different. She knew he had undergone a massive transformation, and she also knew that only the power of the Holy Spirit could have done that.

She could also see the light and divine goodness in Sophia and knew she must have been part of God's plan to transform Alex and give him purpose, something he desperately needed.

Alex and Angela went on to have a child in the years ahead; a beautiful girl, which they named Chiara.

AJ survived the harrowing wolf attack, unharmed in the Rocca basement, by being safely locked away in his cell. But he would be tried and found guilty of Degno's brutal murder and sentenced to life imprisonment, never to be released.

Sophia completed her noviciate apprenticeship and was admitted as a fully-fledged sister of the convent. She became Clemenza's protege and would eventually succeed Clemenza as the convent Mother Superior. Neither Clemenza, nor Alex (except for telling Angela), not even AJ, ever told anyone about the incident in the Basilica between Alex and Sophia. Clemenza reasoned that God certainly knew about it, and his healing of Sophia from death evidenced his forgiveness of her, and that was better than any forgiveness the Church authorities could ever give.

Sophia continued the great legacy Clemenza had handed over to her. Her connection with the Lord continued to grow stronger, and she would ultimately become one of the great mystics of her time, and inspire many nuns and lay people during her long career.

With the help of Angela, Alex discovered a philanthropic foundation that was devoted to researching synergies within the key faiths of the world, including Indigenous beliefs. He gave up his job and took a fulltime role with the foundation, using all his research and other journalistic skills to help it. He was particularly active in interviewing people and writing about the synergies between Christianity, Islam, Buddhism and various Australian indigenous beliefs, including of course, Reincarnation.

A few years later, Alex befriended a senior retired Australian politician who coached him into becoming *a local member of Parliament, fighting for the causes he had become personally passionate about; Truth Telling and Treaty Rights for Australian indigenous people, crimes against our Environment, and the importance of Awakening to spiritual meaning and healing, including the Power of Prayer.*

Parliament House
   October 3, 2041
   Australia
   Alex's Parliamentary Repentance Day Treaty Speech - The Light of Compassion overcomes The Darkness of Fear

Having walked down the long corridor, Alex walks into the Parliamentary Chamber, with a steely determination in his eyes, his written speech held tightly in his right hand, and makes his way to his seat. On this auspicious day, Alex is now in the House Chamber and readies himself to give his long-awaited speech.

In the busy Chamber, a member of parliament comes in and takes her seat. She seems unsure of what is on the House Agenda but knows that Alex is about to stand up and propose a Bill dealing with indigenous issues. She looks around to her colleagues and whispers, "What's he going to talk about?"

One colleague turns to her and says, "We've already got more public holidays than you can shake a stick at, and he wants another bloody one!"

Another looks at her and whispers, "He wants a day off for everyone, paid for by employers mind you, so that we can all sit around remembering what a bunch of white fellas did decades ago to blacks long dead; and expecting the government to provide public reparation of it all; and to benefit who? Subsequent generations of blacks who hardly remember their ancestors!"

Another member, overhearing the discussion, turns and says to her, "He also expects us to hand back to them all their sacred sites. For all I know, that might include handing over the bloody Sydney Opera House! And more than that, he wants us to commit to a Treaty with them, including more land rights, just so they can forgive us for something this generation didn't do!"

She responds, "He'll never get the support. He's got Buckley's chance."

Her colleague retorts, "Of course, he'll fail! And he'll be an embarrassment to all of us, as well as all indigenous people, who will never forgive him, or us for that matter, for another bloody botched reconciliation farce!"

Alex stands up, his speaker notes in hand, looks glaringly at everyone in the chamber over the top of his reading glasses, as if he wanted to be able to remember all who were there on the day, and then in a raspy voice, commences his plea.

Alex:

"My dear parliamentary colleagues, we come together today to make history; history that will endure for the ages.

As a child, I was brought up as a Christian. But whether you are Christian, Jew, Muslim, Hindu, Buddhist, Baha'i or a follower of any other major Faith, I've grown to learn that there are two important linchpins to any Faith; they are Compassion and Forgiveness. For instance, it has been said that the four Christian Gospels, can be summarized in just two parables that Jesus gave us; namely, the parable of the Lost Son, dealing with Forgiveness, and the parable of the Good Samaritan, dealing with Compassion.

"Don't tell me he's going to talk about religion for Christ sake!" whispers an MP to one of his colleagues.

Alex continued.

Alex:

"The parable of the Lost Son tells a story of a father and two sons who lived in an idyllic home and farmland setting. One of the sons, euphemistically representative of Mankind, decided to cash in his future inheritance from his father and, in defiance of his father's wishes, moved to the big city to experience its allures and delights. After a time, he realized that the world of materialism and desire was not a fulfilling one. It was superficial and without meaningful purpose. Upon becoming penniless and destitute, having wasted his father's inheritance on city pleasures and the like, he awoke to the reality of the situation, and decided to return home; to seek the forgiveness of his father, and to ask him to be accepted back as a mere servant in his father's household.

His father, having every right to be angry at his son's wastefulness and naivety, did not reject his son.

270

Instead, he rejoiced at his son's return. He not only forgave him completely, but elevated him to the status of a joint heir to his estate, alongside his other children, once again.

In the parable of the Good Samaritan, the story tells of a person who, traveling on foot from one town to another, was set upon by thieves and thugs and left penniless and battered alongside the roadway. He was bypassed by a number of people who tread carefully past him, for reasons fearful of what might happen to them if they stopped to assist him. However, a passerby who was a Samaritan, then regarded as inferior people, saw him and not only stopped to assist him, but took him to a nearby inn and paid the innkeeper sufficient board for a time to enable the man to recover from his ordeal.

Dear colleagues, these parables talk of the quintessential essence of Forgiveness and Compassion. They teach us that these fundamental traits are what separate the Humane from the Barbarous.

Whether you have a religious Faith or not, is it not clear that Forgiveness and Compassion are the characteristics pertaining to a good nation, and absent from a callous one?

The question we face here today, my fellow Australians, is therefore this: do we want Australia to be a good nation, indeed, a great nation; not only for the good of our own people, but as a beacon on the hill for others to emulate? Or do we want it to be a nation driven by fear and callousness; one that represents a *selfish, self-centred people? This is my question to you all here now!*

We celebrate in this country many public holidays; sporting holidays, birthdays of Royalty and Nationhood, religious days, days of remembrance of those fallen in battle. We celebrate these because these are days of significance to us; days that define who we are.

And if we are truly sorry, and genuinely seek forgiveness for the long-drawn-out tragedies that have befallen our Aboriginal brothers and sisters, does this not also need to be recognised?

[One or two muffled "Hear, hear" are heard coming from the floor of the House]

Is this not of such significance to our Nationhood that it also requires public recognition?

[A couple more muffled "Hear, hear" are heard coming from the floor]

Does this still scarred and bleeding wound not require treatment and healing? Does this part of our story as a Nation not also define who we are?

[A few clear and assertive "Hear, hear" are heard coming from the floor]

Surely, we owe this to our indigenous brothers and sisters, and to the memory of their ancestors. Do we not also owe it to our future generations, who will one day look back at us and wonder, in sombre amazement, at our intransigence, even at our callousness, in doing so little?

[A few clear and assertive "Hear, hear" are heard coming from the floor]

I need not cover here in detail all the bloody massacres that took place in the past. I need not cover here all the racist and apartheid behaviour that has taken place. I need not dwell here on all the pain and suffering of children, and even deaths, that flowed from stolen generations. I need not cover here the many deaths in custody, that even continue to this day; the high rates of youth suicide; the poor state of housing, education and health, of even the present generation of indigenous people; and of course, of the damage we've done and continue to do to the land and environment they nurtured for more than 60,000 years before we arrived and claimed it as ours, and then promptly managed to degrade its soil, water, and air, all in the space of a mere 200 years!

You already know enough about these tragedies to know that we have much to seek Forgiveness for; and much Compassion yet to give; not only to our indigenous brothers and sisters, but to Mother Earth itself!

[A few clear and assertive "Hear, hear" are heard coming from the floor]

What I ask of you today is that we set aside one day, every year, wherein we remember the atrocities, Truth Telling, the pain and the suffering, the damage we and our predecessors have done, and take the opportunity on that day, "Repentance Day", as a Nation, to not just say Sorry, but to seek Forgiveness by committing to actions that show Compassion. And, for our indigenous brothers and sisters, should they feel *inclined, to show Forgiveness towards us; something much more difficult than our request of it from them!*

[A few clear and assertive "Hear, hear" are heard coming from the floor]

And what are some of the things that might incline them to do so, we might ask? What should a Treaty with our indigenous brothers and sisters covering these matters provide for?

Well, we could start by returning and honouring their Sacred Sites, rather than despoiling them, or at times even destroying them!

[A few clear and assertive "Hear, hear" are heard coming from the floor]

And, as if we shouldn't be doing this anyway, showing them we care as much about our own country, the land, the sea and the atmosphere, as they once did. Showing them, by ceasing to pollute our own country, that we too hold these gifts as precious. That we too can be stewards and not plunderers!

[A few clear and assertive "Hear, hear" are heard coming from the floor]

Establishing such a Day, to be recognised every year, will be a step of enormous significance as we embark upon an ongoing journey of Truth Telling and Repentance. A journey needed to heal the wounds of the past, and to address the many ongoing problems. And, of course, to elevate the culture of the whole Nation to a new level; to that of a Caring and Compassionate Nation!

[An increasing number of clear and assertive "Hear, hear"]

And of course, we should build a National Memorial of atrocities and massacres; of stolen generations; of deaths in custody; of all things that need the brutal Truth to be told! So that no one can say that the Truth was swept beneath the carpet! So that no one can say that a 60,000 year plus people almost went silently in the night, and no one remembers how!

[An increasing number of clear and assertive "Hear, Hear"]

But there are some naysayers among us who say we should not bother with such a proposal! That to do so would be admitting to heinous wrongdoings that this generation did not commit! That it would expose this and future generations to reparations for the actions of earlier generations! That it will create a sense of National guilt, which would only lead to a never-ending cycle of indigenous dependency on Government! That to commit to these things, including showing compassion towards our unique and now precarious environment, would be an unacceptable drain on the economy and the public purse!

In other words, that to seek Forgiveness and show Compassion to our fellow Australians and the living planet we abide in, will give rise to such adverse consequences as to imperil the Nation! And which should therefore be avoided at all costs!

Well, I say to those people who say this; and indeed, I say it to you all! that this is the politics of Fear! Of Fear and Trepidation!

[Quite a few loud and assertive "Hear, hear" are heard]

It is the use of the Devil's greatest asset; Fear and Trepidation, to scurry us away from the path of Light and Love.

[A few louder and more assertive "Hear, hear" are heard]

No Great Nation, or Great Person for that matter, is dictated to by Fear and Trepidation!

Great People and Great Nations overcome their fears!

[An increasingly louder and assertive number of "Hear, hear" are heard]

Let me recall to you the tale of Darcy Brown, a decorated soldier in the Australian light horse in World War One, who when confronted by heavy and relentless enemy fire, and retreating at pace from the enemy under his commander's orders, saw his mate hit by shrapnel and fall to the ground. He stopped retreating! He turned back, into enemy fire, and scurried to his mate to assist him away to safety, in total disregard for his own safety.

I ask you dear colleagues, do you think that Darcy Brown, if he were here with us today, do you think he would be fearful of what the naysayers say?

[Several clear and assertive "No"s ring out]

Out of Compassion for his mate, he put his own life at enormous risk in the face of terror. Do you think he would be fearful of saying Sorry; of Repenting, and of seeking Forgiveness from our Indigenous brethren?

[Several louder and more assertive "No, No"]

I ask you, what do you think!?

[An increasing number of clear and assertive "No, No, No!"]

And what about David Camallari, a decorated firefighter, who in the torrid Black Friday bushfires found himself at a hellish scene of a distraught mother, standing in front of a burning house, with hell raging all around her, and screaming for someone to rescue her young child still inside.

Did David Camallari allow himself to be driven by Fear and Trepidation?

[A growing number of clear and assertive "No, No, No"]

Did he sit back and decide that the possible adverse repercussions to him of entering into that inferno should be avoided at all costs?

[A louder number of clear and assertive "No, No, No"]

I ask you, did he?

[A increasing number of louder and assertive "No, No, No"]

No! He did not!

He acted with the same compunction that Darcy Brown did, with Compassion and Courage!

Was he reckless and unafraid of the situation? No! Of course he was afraid. But his Love of Life, his Compassion for the mother and her child, and the Courage this mustered up in him, overcame his Fear!

[A growing and loudening number of clear and assertive "Hear, hear"]

And what of Jamila Adejia, one of many resolute nurses who in the early days of the COVID 19 pandemic, in that lethal second wave in Melbourne, Victoria, was at the forefront of the fateful wave of hospitalisations, well before any vaccinations were available. Jamila, who with a young family, and her husband, and her aging mother, all living together at home, took an enormous risk, every day I should emphasise, every day, by going to work and treating infected COVID 19 patients in hospital.

Did she sit back and decide that assisting infectious patients carried adverse consequences that should be avoided at all costs?

[Several very loud and assertive "No, No, No"]

I ask you, did she?

[An increasing number of loud and assertive "No, No, No"]

No! She did not!

Was she reckless and therefore unafraid? No! Of course she was afraid; not only for herself but for her whole family, every day she went to work! But her Compassion and Courage overcame her Fears!

And so, my fellow Australians, we know very well from our own history that, The Light of Compassion overcomes the Darkness of Fear!

I ask you therefore my fellow Australians, do we want a Nation that Darcy Brown and David Camallari and Jamila Adejia ought to be proud of?

[A very large number of loud and assertive "Yes, Yes, Yes"]

I ask you, do we?

[An increasingly large number of loudening and assertive "Yes, Yes, Yes"]

Do we want a Nation that our Fallen-in-Battle men and women will say, "It was worth fighting for!"?

[An ever more increasingly large number of loud and assertive "Yes, Yes,Yes" to the point where virtually the entire floor of the House was joining in]

Do we?

[An increasing crescendo of loud and assertive "Yes, Yes, Yes"]

Do we want a Nation that our firefighters, our police forces and all men and women of duty who have lost their lives in sacrifice, would say, "For this country, my sacrifice was worth it!"?

[A larger crescendo of loud, clear and assertive "Yes, Yes, Yes"]

Do we?

[An ever increasing crescendo of loud, clear and assertive "Yes, Yes, Yes"]

Do we want a Nation that our nurses and doctors and health workers who, in times of need, have put themselves and their family's safety at peril for our sake, will say, "Yes, for this Nation, I would do it again and again!"?

["Yes, Yes, Yes" rang out loud, assertive and resounding across the whole chamber of the House]

And what about our future generations I ask you! What do we want them to say? What do you want your children, your grandchildren, your great grandchildren, and their descendants to say about us *when they look back and contemplate what we did or didn't do?*

Don't we want them to say, "Thank God our forebears finally acknowledged the Truth; and had the gumption to do something about it!"?

["Yes, Yes" rang out loud, assertive and resounding across the chamber of the House]

Don't we want them to say, "Thank God they had the guts to protect our Environment when they did, in the face of avid corporate greed and self-interest!"?

[An ever louder crescendo of clear and assertive "Yes, Yes, Yes" rang out again to the point where the entire floor of the House was now joining in]

My word we do! My word we do!

Then let us not allow Fear and Trepidation to overcome our Mission!

["Hear, hear" rang out loud, assertive and resounding across the chamber of the House]

Let us act with the same Compassion and Guts shown to us by Darcy Brown, David Camallari, Jamila Adejia, and all our courageous men and women who have made this great Nation what it is today, and say "Yes!" to Repentance Day, and "Yes!" to this Treaty, here in front of us today!

[Loud cries of "Yes, Yes, Yes" rang out, from not only the floor of the House, but also the onlooking Galleries]

Let us say "Yes!" to a Day of Remembrance, and Reconciliation, and Forgiveness, and Compassion; to a Day of Courage to Truth! Say "Yes!" to Repentance Day! "Yes!" to Treaty!

[Large and loud cries of "Yes, Yes, Yes" again rang out from not only the floor of the House but also the Galleries]

My fellow countrymen and women, let us show the Courage this great Nation deserves from us. Please stand with me now on this Day of History. Will you stand and join me!?

[Large and loud cries of "Yes, Yes, Yes" again rang out from not only the floor of the House but also the Galleries]

I say, will you stand and join me!?

[Virtually everyone in both the Chamber and the Galleries rose to their feet crying out even louder "Yes, Yes, Yes" repeatedly and thrusting their hands in the air and then clapping and cheering loudly]

Alex looks up into the Gallery and pumps his fist at the cheering onlookers who include Angela, with her hands cupped to her face and crying of joy, their daughter Chiara next to her. Alongside them is Michael with his now adult autistic son by his side. (Clemenza and Sophia had managed to help his son). Michael has a big smile on his face and gives Alex a big thumbs up.

Outside, over Parliament House, in the pink dusk just before sunset, fly two yellowtail black cockatoos, screeching out their familiar cries.

End

AFTERWORD

CHIARA
December 2041, Italy

Some weeks after his Repentance Day speech in Parliament, Alex and Chiara went on a three-week father and daughter trip to Italy. Chiara was now 14 years of age and Alex wanted to spend some time with her in Italy, especially in Assisi. He also thought that spending at least one White Xmas in the northern hemisphere, and in Italy especially, would be a wonderful experience for Chiara. But there was one thing he particularly wanted to do, and that was to visit AJ in prison and take Chiara with him. Angela had been reluctant about this idea. But she eventually approved of it as she had come to understand Alex's motivation, once he fully explained it all to her.

AJ had been sentenced to life in prison without parole, particularly due to the gruesome and premeditated nature of Degno's murder, along with the apparent lack of remorse demonstrated during AJ's sentencing hearing. The prison was located three to four hours train ride from Rome central station, Roma Termini, followed by a short cab ride after that.

Alex loved being in Rome, his favourite city second to Assisi. As Alex and Chiara, hand in hand, made their way to the entrance of Roma Termini, a busker outside the station was playing Italian songs on his accordion. Alex paused, closed his eyes, and just stood there, taking in the music. Chiara stopped, and still holding his hand, stood there watching him. After a minute or so, he opened his eyes, looked at Chiara and smiled, whereupon she said, "What are you doing Dad?"

Alex replied, "I don't think I ever told you the story about the violinist playing outside Sydney Central Train Station, have I?"

"No, you haven't," replied, Chiara, and knowing her dad well, she knew it would soon be coming her way.

"Would you like to hear it," said Alex, hopefully.

Pausing for a moment, and appreciating how important this whole trip was for Alex, and especially knowing that he wanted it to be a bonding trip, Chiara said, "OK, sure."

The Sydney Central Station Busker
Alex:
"There was once a busker playing a violin outside of Sydney's central railway station. For a whole day, he played some of the best music he knew. Since he played during both the morning and evening rush period, his music was heard by thousands of people who walked by. Yet only a few people stopped to listen to him throughout the entire day; perhaps thirty or so, and he collected just a few dollars.

"The passersby who walked straight past him without paying him any attention, were too busy, immersed in their daily work or social preoccupations,

often reading or talking on their phones, as they walked by. Many of those who stopped to listen to him on the other hand, were jobless, or often in financial or health difficulties and relished a pause from their preoccupied thoughts. They were not distracted by their daily preoccupations. In fact, they wanted a break from their daily concerns.

"Yet, unbeknown to all those passersby, the busker was a great violinist, who had only a few days ago played at the Sydney Opera house to a sold-out crowd. The violin he was playing looked a little old, but was, in fact, a Stradivarius violin, worth a lot of money. He played some of the most renown and beautiful music ever written.

"He could have come out and proclaimed to all the passersby who he really was, as well as the nature of his great music and the unique instrument with which he played it. Had he done so, no doubt many people would have stopped to listen to him. They would have stopped not because the music "sang to them", and they related to it, but rather because of his obvious fame. However, he did not want to attract those types. He just wanted to see who really loved the music, and to attract those who innately had a deep love for it and placed that love ahead of their work and social preoccupations. In other words, he wanted to attract those who, by their very nature, were in tune with the music and loved it for what it was, not for the fame and fortune of the player, or his instrument.

"God is very much like the Sydney Central Station busker. His message is constantly playing for whoever stops to listen to it. And it is played for lovers of the music, not for lovers of fame and pomp. He plays it without advertising himself, and he relies on the innate faith of the listener for establishing an allegiance to him and his message. In his busking plate, he asks not for money, but for faith and allegiance. In return, he will play you his incredibly beautiful and life satisfying music.

"Unfortunately, he has found that those preoccupied with daily work, social and other preoccupations in life, have little interest in his message. It seems that it's only those who are divorced from life's treadmill of wealth, ego, social and other concerns that seem to hear the beauty of the music best. It's life's 'down and outers' that get it best and are therefore best placed to give their allegiance to him.

"As the Bible tells us, (Luke 14:21) as well as the Gospel of Thomas, (Saying 64) it's the 'down and outers' who accept God's invitation to his feast, rather than those invitees who are preoccupied with fame and making money. And so, in the end, it is much easier to see why, Jesus said, (Matthew 19:30, 20:16) the 'first' in this world will be last, and the 'last' will be first.

"God's message about Life's Purpose, is there for all to see. If we pause to listen to it, we will find it mesmerizing, sublime, pervasive and all satisfying. But we must make the effort to stop and listen. To take time to seek it. For, as it is said so often, those who seek shall find; listen and you shall hear."

And with that, Alex paused and smiled at Chiara.

"Thanks Dad, I like that story," responded Chiara, with a smile, which melted Alex's heart.

When Alex and Chiara finally arrived at the Prison, they were ushered into a visitor's room by a female prison guard, wherein a solid glass barrier, reaching almost to the ceiling, divided them from the opposite side of the room. A male prison guard stood on the opposite side, next to a doorway. They were the only visitors in the room and the female prison guard stayed with them on their side of the room.

Soon afterwords, the door on the other side of the room opened and a male prison guard ushered AJ into the room and motioned for him to sit in a chair at a table that faced towards the glass panel. Equally, Alex and Chiara, then sat at a table on their side of the room, facing AJ and abutting the glass panel. Microphones were embedded into the glass panel so that people on each side of it could easily hear each other. AJ had aged considerably since Alex had last seen him years ago. Even so, his eyes still had that sparkle of insightfulness and worldly knowledge.

They exchanged pleasantries and spoke about some of the personalities they had both encountered in Assisi fifteen years ago, including, of course, Sophia.

Alex told AJ that he had been looking forward to seeing him again, and that he continued to feel eternally grateful to him for the many insights, as well as the mentoring, that AJ had given Alex during his short stay in Assisi all those years ago. AJ was visibly taken by this sentiment from Alex and told Alex how pleased he was to hear that.

AJ then turned to Chiara and asked her whether she had ever heard of an inherently good person, motioning with his head towards Alex, thanking a convicted murderer of a heinous premeditated crime, for acting as his mentor. Chiara, surprised by the question, paused, and replied in the negative.

AJ went on to tell Chiara that that is because her father was a unique individual, who has the wherewithal to understand that even criminals are capable of worthy deeds and should be given some degree of respect and compassion. Chiara nodded approvingly.

Whilst not showing it, Alex was delighted to see this exchange between AJ and Chiara, since the key reason for having brought Chiara to meet AJ, and indeed, the reason Angela also ultimately supported him taking Chiara to see AJ, was that he wanted Chiara to see for herself that criminals in prisons, including those who commit heinous crimes, can have worthy souls, and have something to offer all of us.

And then, in typical AJ fashion thought Alex reflecting on all the stories AJ had shared with Alex fifteen years ago, AJ initiated another story telling lesson, but this time for Chiara.

He said to her, "You've come to Italy at Christmas time, but I wonder if you know the true story of Christmas; a story I learnt many years ago, and whether you'd like to hear it?"

Chiara said, "Of course, I'd be happy to hear it."

AJ was very glad that Chiara wanted to hear the story. In his time in prison, very few people had come to visit him, and so he rarely got an opportunity to talk to someone outside of the prison, let alone tell them stories of a kind that many years ago he was so fond of telling.

AJ laid back in his chair, with his hands on the table clasped together, and then in a way that reminded Alex of the stories AJ had told him years ago, proceeded to enlighten Chiara on such an important topic as the Incarnation of Christ.

AJ:

"Well, there was a family who lived in upstate, where Xmas time is typically cold and snowing. The mother was Christian and would attend midnight Xmas mass every year with her teenage daughters. The father was a practicing Muslim, and even though he respected the Christian faith, like all Muslims, he couldn't countenance the idea that anyone other than God the Father (or Allah, as Muslims call him) could be divine or godly in nature. So, he could never understand how Christians made such a fuss about Jesus being an 'incarnated god', sent to save humanity. He thought it was all nonsense.

"One Christmas Eve, his wife and daughters left to attend midnight mass at the church, down the road not far from their home. It was a bitterly cold evening. As usual, he stayed at home that evening and attended to the magnificent open wood fire that warmed up the entire living area of the home.

"Then, from his window, he noticed a solitary native bird that must have got separated from the rest of its flock, all of whom had already taken off to fly to warmer weather south for the winter.

"He knew that there was little or no food or shelter for the poor bird in the cold of winter, and that sometime soon, the bird would die from exposure.

"He felt such compassion for the little bird, that he was trying to figure out how he could rescue it and bring it into his own home and provide it food and shelter for the winter.

"He knew if he tried to lure it in, or capture it, the bird would likely fly away in the process. Even throwing out some food to it would not prevent the bird from dying from exposure to the cold.

"And even if he, by some miracle, did manage to snare or capture it against its will and bring it inside, he would have to confine it in a cage, which he didn't want to do against its will, since the little bird would want to be back in the wild and would, without doubt, take every opportunity to escape back to the outdoors again. He gave it a great deal of thought and concluded he could not realistically do anything to help the little bird.

"Imaginatively though, he wished he could talk to the bird and tell it that, if only it would come into his home, he'd take care of it and give it lots of love and save it from certain death.

"It dawned on him that the only way he could do that without scaring it away, would be if he could turn himself into a little bird and go and talk to it, and explain to it that if it was prepared to walk away from everything outside and come into his home, it would be saved.

"Just as this thought occurred to him, the nearby Church bells began to ring out the Christmas service.

"At this point, the man dropped to his knees in sudden appreciation of the message he had just received, and with deep devotion, thanked the Lord for having given us an incarnate saviour."

AJ looked at Alex, and said quietly to him, "The power of Parables," to which Alex nodded approvingly.

The conversation between the three of them continued for a little longer, and just as time was about to run out, Alex mentioned that Chiara was part of the school choir. At this, AJ perked up attentively, and asked the prison guard if he could write something on a notepad that was sitting on the desk in front of him and have it passed on to Alex and Chiara. The guard said yes, provided he could review it first.

Alex, then jotted down a series of short verses, handed it to the prison guard who read the verses and approved them to be handed over to Alex and Chiara, which they duly were.

AJ then explain to Alex and Chiara that this was a short hymn that he composed, as an ode to the Holy Spirit, and which he wanted to share with them. And that it could be sung to the melody of 'Amazing Grace'.

Upon receiving the note, Chiara opened it and read it aloud, as follows, to the tune of 'Amazing Grace'.

"An Ode to the Divine Sophia"

Forgive me Lord and cleanse my soul, that I may return to thee

For your Word and your Grace have awakened me, and now, I can truly be

Divine Sophia, guide me back home, to where boundless love awaits

That I may arise in the All once more, even stronger than before

Lord, your Word and your Grace have set me free, and now, I long to be with thee."

Chiara thought it was beautiful and became visibly emotional. Once she finished the verses, she folded up the note and held it to her bosom with both hands. She then looked at AJ with her misty eyes, and said, "Thank you, thank you."

The prison guard looked at the clock hanging on the wall and then opened the door. It was time to leave. Alex and AJ looked at each other and both nodded approvingly. They then both rose from their chairs, but instead of turning to leave, Alex moved to the side of the table and approached the glass wall dividing the room and put both his hands up onto the glass, palms open.

AJ took the cue and moved over to the glass wall towards Alex and did the same, placing his hands palms open onto Alex's hands, on the glass in between. Then both men stood there for a moment silently, looking into each other's eyes. Alex then slowly put his forehead onto the glass wall and AJ followed suit. They stood there, hands and foreheads touching in silence, knowing they'd never see each other again. Tears started to form and drip from both men's eyes.

Chiara watched and became emotionally affected by this obvious sign of love between them. She knew then that her dad truly felt a great deal of gratitude to AJ for having helped him awaken all those years ago.

She never forgot this moment. It made a lasting impression on her. In the years ahead, including after Alex had passed away, she would go onto become a great advocate for the rights of prisoners.

That prison visit, especially that one act of silent love, recognition and appreciation by Alex, had changed her life, and given her great purpose to serve others.

FIN